PROLOGUE

Naomi Miller stood beside the buggy, the corner of the front wheel inches from her side. Eugene Mast's fingers were wrapped around hers. She looked up at him, the shadows from the moonlight hiding his blue eyes, leaving only the sides of his face visible.

"Do you really have to go?" Naomi whispered.

"*Yah*," Eugene said. "It's something I need to do. But I'll be back before you know it, and things will be like they always were."

"Nine months is an awfully long time."

"*Yah*, but *Da Hah* will be with us. He will help us bear the pain of absence. And we are promised, you know."

"But what will Bishop Enos say about this? We are both members of the church." Naomi's hands shifted in his. "What if there is trouble?"

Eugene laughed. "I don't think there will be trouble. Bishop Enos knows I have no plans to forsake the church."

"Even though you are running off to Iowa to teach at a Mennonite church school? It's a terribly long way from Indiana."

Eugene leaned forward, kissing her cheek. "I will write often, and that will help with the loneliness."

Naomi pulled away. "Will you miss me? Perhaps a little?"

Eugene laughed again, causing his horse to turn his head to look at him. "I will miss you terribly, Naomi. I just believe this has to be done. If I don't take the chance now, I'll always look back and wonder."

She sighed. "But it's so dangerous out there. And the Mennonites can put all kinds of ideas in your head. Then you'll never come back."

He shook his head. "Please, Naomi, don't make this harder than it is. I'll come back. I promise." He glanced at the envelope she had given him earlier. "Thank you for the card. I'm going to save it to open when I get to Iowa."

"Okay. I think you'd better go," she said. "I can't stand this much longer."

"I'm not much at goodbyes anyway," he said. "I will always love you, Naomi. Goodbye…for now."

"Goodbye," she said, stepping back as Eugene climbed into the buggy. He slapped the reins against his horse's back, waving once on the turn-around in the lane, his hand a brief movement from the dark interior. Watching the buggy lights move down the road and fade out of sight, Naomi stared long into the darkness. She then turned to walk back toward the house, pausing to look over her shoulder once more.

Jerry and Tina Eicher

My Dearest, Naomi

Jerry & Tina Eicher

HARVEST HOUSE PUBLISHERS
EUGENE, OREGON

All Scripture quotations are from the King James Version of the Bible.

This is a work of fiction. Names, characters, places, and incidents are products of the author's imagination or are used fictitiously. Any resemblance to actual persons, living or dead, or to events or locales, is entirely coincidental.

All poetry in this book, except the one by Frances R. Havergal, was written by Jerry Eicher, © 2012.

Cover by Garborg Design Works, Savage, Minnesota

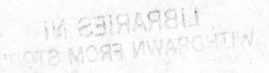

MY DEAREST NAOMI
Copyright © 2012 by Jerry S. Eicher and Tina Eicher
Published by Harvest House Publishers
Eugene, Oregon 97402
www.harvesthousepublishers.com

Library of Congress Cataloging-in-Publication Data
   Eicher, Jerry S.
   My dearest Naomi / Jerry S. Eicher.
      p. cm.
   ISBN 978-0-7369-3942-3 (pbk.)
   ISBN 978-0-7369-4246-1 (eBook)
   1. Amish—Fiction. I. Title. II. Eicher, Tina.
   PS3605.I34M9 2012
   813'.6—dc23

2011044606

Printed in the United States of America

12 13 14 15 16 17 18 19 20 / LB-SK / 10 9 8 7 6 5 4 3 2 1

AUGUST

My dearest Naomi,

Greetings from Iowa. This finds me installed in the upstairs bedroom of my new home. The time was a little past eleven o'clock the last I looked. We pulled into the driveway of this little farm around nine, but I couldn't see much in the darkness. We were met at the front porch by Lonnie and Luella Hershberger, the older Mennonite couple I'm staying with. The school board members who brought me out said their goodbyes and drove off in their van. I was shown around the house by Lonnie and Luella. After the tour, we ended up in the living room talking.

They seem like very nice people even though I've only just met them. Their house is a white bungalow with everything inside neatly arranged and in order. The kitchen is by the front door, with the living room in the back. I'm in the front bedroom, upstairs, overlooking the lawn. They said I could see the schoolhouse from my bedroom window, but it's dark right now.

I feel strange and a little frightened to be out here alone. I'm missing you, of course, and the community. This awful sensation is wrapped around me, as if all the familiar props are knocked out from under me. In the meantime, I have to act as if everything is okay and be full of smiles. I can imagine right now you're saying "I told you so," but then maybe not, being the nice person you are.

I can't thank you enough for the card you gave me before I left. It means so much to me. If I didn't have your love to fall back on, I don't think I could stand it right now. I know part of my problem is that I'm just so dead tired I could fall off the chair. The trip was long and more tiresome than I expected.

I suppose I'd better be off to bed. I won't even start unpacking tonight.

The suitcase is still open on the floor with only the things taken out that I need immediately. And that's good enough for now.

Tuesday morning...

Good morning. I awoke to Luella hollering up the stairs. We had decided last night she would be my alarm clock since I didn't bring one along. There is an electric alarm clock sitting on the desk, but I told Luella I didn't know how to run one. And I sure wasn't going to take the time to figure it out last night. She laughed and said hollering would be the Amish method anyway, and that it should make me feel right at home.

I smiled and said *yah*, but I didn't mention that any reminder of home causes more pain than comfort right now.

I came downstairs to a breakfast of eggs and bacon, which I ate quickly. Then I stepped outside for a look around. The weather is nice, and I can indeed see the schoolhouse down the road. It's a large, white, wooden structure with tall windows on the side. There's a bell tower on top, placed toward the front. There's a single tree in the yard.

Back upstairs, I started to unpack until I saw your second card. That brought a halt to the unpacking for a while. Who would have thought being away from you would be this hard?

As of now, the plans are that I will take the rest of the week to settle in at the schoolhouse. They only have a half-day scheduled for school on the first day, Friday. Then no school on Monday, since it's Labor Day. Beats me how I'm supposed to keep myself occupied all that time with so little work to do.

The chairman of the school board told me the teacher who taught last year will be at the schoolhouse today by 10:00. She will give me details on the lesson plans and other pointers she might have on how to do things around here. I've been told it shouldn't be that different from the year I taught at our Amish school, but I shall see.

While I think to mention it, I forgot to give you the other dove from my farewell cake at our families' going-away supper. Somewhere in all the goodbyes it slipped my mind. I have the one, and you were supposed to get its mate. My sisters have it now and are supposed to pass it on to you. Hopefully we can match them up when the school year is over.

Luella said the mailman goes past at quarter till nine, so I'd better get this letter out. Here's my address and a little rhyme. I know it's not much, but it lets you know how much I'm missing you.

When the new moon hangs in the starry sky
I think of love, of ours, of you and I.

With all my heart,
Eugene

My dearest Naomi,

"He that dwelleth in the secret place of the most High shall abide under the shadow of the Almighty…he shall give his angels charge over thee, to keep thee in all thy ways." Psalm 91 is close to my heart at the moment. I grew to love that passage the year I taught school back there at home. One morning Eli Byler, my co-teacher, read the chapter for devotions. All the children sat listening intently at their desks that morning, and I could imagine in a small way the care God must have for us all.

Tonight finds me even lonelier than last night. I'm sitting here wondering what you're doing right now. At the moment, even the thought of home is enough to bring a dampness to my eyes that shouldn't be there. I'd better think of something else. I never imagined I would get homesick so soon. It's not like I've never been away from home. Here in Iowa I don't know a single soul—and that's a first for me.

The countryside here is different too. It sort of rolls along—not so flat as at home and there are fewer trees than I'm used to. Lonnie tells me that in the wintertime, when the fields are bare, I'll be able to see for miles.

I've been asking Lonnie and Luella lots of questions. The answers have surprised me. For one thing, the church here doesn't have many worldly things. I always thought Mennonite churches were fairly liberal, but this one has rules prohibiting cameras and recording devices. Still, it wouldn't surprise me if some members had them. I doubt if human nature changes, whether you're Amish or Mennonite. There also are no radios or televisions, they said. The men have CB radios, judging from the antennas on the few trucks I've seen, but that's it.

The differences in our practices are greater. They wear multicolored clothing, drive cars, have electricity in the house, and speak only English. It will take some getting used to.

I spent most of the day at the school going over the books and familiarizing myself with the children's names. The first day of school will be my first opportunity to match faces with names, and I'm looking forward to that. One thing for sure, I'm going to be a lot busier with schoolwork than I was the year I taught back home. Here they have all eight grades. All grades have students this year except the second. And there's only one teacher—me! Seventeen pupils in seven grades should keep things interesting, but I'll manage it…somehow.

By the way, I wrote last night that school would start on Friday. Well, I managed to get the date changed today. I'll have school all day Thursday and Friday and have the usual Monday off for Labor Day. I can imagine the kids aren't too happy about that, but I want to get started as soon as possible. Now that I'm here and ready, there's no reason to delay even one day.

The inside of the schoolhouse is large. It's one room and has a high ceiling of suspended tile. I hollered inside—when I was alone, of course—to test the acoustics. It's not all that great compared to the Amish schoolhouses at home, which have drywall everywhere. I expect this will affect the children's singing at morning devotions, but we'll have to make do. I think singing with the proper surround sound adds so much.

I went out for a ten-minute run this evening since I haven't worked a lick's worth of manual labor these last two days—well, three days now. I have to get some exercise.

I think of you often.

With love,

Eugene

SEPTEMBER

Wednesday evening, September 1

My dearest Naomi,

Greetings of love.

"They that wait upon the LORD shall renew their strength; they shall mount up with wings as eagles; they shall run, and not be weary; and they shall walk, and not faint" (Isaiah 40:31).

Well, I think I'm feeling a bit more at home finally. Maybe once I get more familiar with things, my feeling of loneliness will decrease. I hope so anyway because something has to be done. I stepped on the scales, and I've lost five pounds since I left home a few days ago. I don't know where the pounds went, but the chairs feel a bit harder when I sit down. And it's not like I have much to lose.

I went back to the schoolhouse again today. I had this feeling of being penned up while I was there. I couldn't figure out why until I noticed the iron drapes or blinds they had hanging over all of the windows. Each one covered an entire window with their solid strips. I tried to tilt them open first, which helped a little, but I still wasn't satisfied. So I pulled them up all the way and latched them into place. Right away I felt the greatest improvement. Now I can see out. They will stay up permanently if I have anything to say about the matter.

This evening the young folks had a softball game at the schoolhouse. That's not my favorite sport, but I heard they might also play volleyball afterward, so hope lay on the horizon. The softball game started at 6:30, with the meal served at 6:00. Since I didn't have anything to do at Lonnie and Luella's, I walked down at 5:30, arriving before anyone else.

The softball game went until dark, and then the volleyball net came out. They played by the light of the electric yard light. It sure beats lanterns on the buggies for light, but there wasn't quite the same feel of home.

13

That may have been a good thing for me right now. I don't need a lot of reminders of what I'm missing. We played two games. The first round our side got skunked, and the next game we beat them twenty-one to five, so it was their turn to get skunked.

None of the men wear beards. I did see a mustache, which was a little strange. But then I don't know that much about Mennonites. The girls are dressed differently, both in dress design and color.

Afterward, I walked home in the moonlight—the moon was almost full. That brought back a lot of memories, and I longed to have you with me. But wishing does no good for a parting that cannot be changed.

I still haven't received a letter from you, but perhaps you've written one and it's on its way here. I hope so.

With all my love,

Eugene

Jerry and Tina Eicher

Dear Eugene,

Hi! I am home from babysitting and still shaky from running around the house trying to get all the work done before the regular chores. We had another cow go dry this week, and I don't think Dad plans to replace her. I believe he may be thinking of eventually giving up milking altogether, with the prices the way they are. But with Don getting older, he probably won't. Boys need things to do, and there aren't many factory jobs around here.

Mom, of course, teased me when I arrived home. "Are you bored? Because if you are, we have something for you. A treasure hunt. Rosanna and Betsy have been working hard hiding your 'treasure.'"

The little teases. I knew it was a letter from you and let out a shriek. Mom and brother Larry, who happened to be around at the time, got a good laugh out of that. I raced around following the clues. When I finally found it (in the bread box), I took it outside and sat by the hay wagon to read it at once.

It was so good to hear from you!

I've had a lonesome time from Sunday evening till now. I kept hoping to somehow hear from you—as if that were possible before you wrote. I've been waiting anxiously, figuring you hadn't had time yet. Still, when there was no letter yesterday, I went up to my room and cried. Big cry baby, I know, but you have my heart. Don't ever forget that.

This morning I got really sensible and figured the letter surely would arrive today. And it did! You can't imagine how much happier I'll be tonight now that I've heard from you.

Each night when I go to bed, I lie there wondering how you're doing, what you're feeling, and if you're as lonesome as I am. Last night I wondered about the home you're in, but after reading your letter, I now know the answers to that.

I want to know everything, Eugene. How the people are, what the scenery is like, what the schoolhouse is like, and about your pupils once you start teaching. But most of all about you.

I'm joining the other young folks tonight in cleaning the schoolhouse. This will be my first time attending the young folks' gatherings without you since we have been going steady. I'm not at all sure I would go except that I'll probably be more lonely just staying home.

I'm sure I wouldn't go if it weren't for your letter. It cheered me up, and I feel like I have energy again. But I should go now. Dad will have the buggy hitched for me, and I don't like being late. I will write more later.

After 11:00…

Here I am, back from the youth gathering. I felt like crying all evening, often catching myself glancing around, thinking I heard your voice rumbling amongst the boys' but knowing in the back of my mind it couldn't be. Would you please hurry back? It was hard to see other couples talking together as we all cleaned the schoolhouse since I know what I'm missing.

Tomorrow night the young folks are supposed to husk corn if it doesn't rain. I don't know if I'll go or not. Anna Hochstetler told Mom I'm not supposed to quit attending the young folks' gatherings because they need me. It made me feel better, but I don't understand how they need me. I mostly go to keep occupied so I won't get quite so lonely.

I'd like to write something cheerful and make you happy, but I don't quite know what it could be. Maybe we can think on the future when we can be together again. When I think of that time, it seems a long way off so I get quite impatient. As you know, I'm not especially blessed with patience—not in some things anyway. Sometimes I imagine how it will be in our future. How wonderful when that day will finally arrive.

Usually when I'm looking forward to something, I have this awful fear of being disappointed. Sometimes I have been, and other times I'm nicely surprised. But since my future involves you, I don't know how I can ever be disappointed.

Wednesday…

I brought home two books of poetry from the lady I work for. They contained all different kinds of poems, with one that really expressed the feelings I have about us. Well, it would be even better if you were here, but this is the best I can do for now. So here it is…

From My Heart…

May our friendship uplift us and draw us together,
May it continue transparent though trials we weather.

Jerry and Tina Eicher

May our love be as strong and as pure as the snow,
May it grow in the sun and deepen in woe.
May our joy in each other never dim or decrease,
May it climb into ecstasy and decline into peace.
May our hope be as bright as the sun in its shine,
May the shadows remind us of the light that's behind.
May our love ever deepen and sweet'n the way,
May it ever grow dearer with more wonder each day.

—T.T. Wells

Well, it is past 11:00, and I should get some sleep. The rest of the children are in bed. Mom and Dad spent the evening at the Burkholders, and I can just now hear the buggy drive in. They must have had a good time to have stayed so late.

I'm thinking I'd better finish this letter tonight as I go to work tomorrow and I might not have time.

Write me everything, please. It all interests me. I even wonder how everyone looks, not that I expect you to describe everyone, but try.

With all my love,
Naomi

P.S. Eugene, would you cut this stamp off the envelope and send it back for Betsy? She is collecting stamps, and she doesn't have this one. Thanks.

My dearest Naomi,

"In the world ye shall have tribulation: but be of good cheer; I have overcome the world" (John 16:33).

Whee…and so ends my first day of school, which went fairly well, all things considered. Those first graders are something else. You have to keep them occupied every minute or they start squirming in their seats.

I purposely didn't plan too heavy a schedule for the first day, as the year I taught in the Amish school I'd started in too fast. But today I ran out of things to do before the day was over. The school here has an extra hour of schooltime, for which I will need to make adjustments.

Everything is strange and different, and the adaptations keep hitting me in the face. First there was meeting Lonnie and Luella that first night, followed by seeing the countryside when it got daylight, visiting the schoolhouse, getting to know the young folks, and now watching all the children sitting there looking at me expectantly. It did bring back a lot of memories from my previous year of teaching though.

Here are the big events of my first day…

I called two girls down for whispering, and saw at once that their faces looked funny. I asked them, "Were you whispering?"

They said, "No."

So I said, "Okay, then." Didn't know what else to do with them. They looked so innocent…and yet I know they were whispering.

One of the first graders stuck up his hand and asked me something I couldn't understand. I had him repeat it three times and still couldn't understand him, so I simply said, "Okay."

He then got up and shoved his desk over beside his sister's desk. So that was what he was asking.

A first grader said he had to blow his nose and didn't have a handkerchief. I gave him mine.

Well, they are a lively bunch and pretty well behaved, so I shouldn't have any problems in that area. Wish me well and the best of success. I think I need it.

My love is always yours,

Eugene

Hello, dearest Eugene,

Greetings in our Savior and Comforter's dear name.

We had a great time at the youth cornhusking last night. I actually broke through my loneliness for you and enjoyed myself. Don just turned sixteen yesterday, so he got to go along. It helps having company on the long drives to and from the gatherings, even if it's my brother.

Don is helping Dad with the hay making today. I suppose Mom and I have to go out after chores and help them unload a wagon or two. When I got home from babysitting, I noticed they were letting things stack up. I'm still very tired from last night, but so it goes. Before long I'll be like an old mare with a limp and a bent back.

I squealed tonight again at the sight of your welcomed letter. I sat down and read it right away. I'm so glad to hear you're well occupied with school. I can imagine it helps pass the time better. I thought, "Oh, if only I could be there to help you." But that, of course, isn't possible.

How is the weather? Ours has been kind of cool the last couple of days, but it was warmer this morning for a change.

Your sister Mary told me tonight that one of your chinchillas had more babies. I want to look at them Sunday, a day I'm afraid is going to be pretty hard without you. Especially since church is right there at your place.

Mary also told me that some of them want to go out to see you sometime soon. She said I could go along. I can hardly wait.

You are in my thoughts,
Your Naomi

My dearest Naomi,

Christian greetings of love.

I hope it doesn't bother you that I write so often, but I have to do something to relieve my homesickness. Maybe later on I will get used to things around here and won't have to write to you constantly.

I received a letter from my folks Friday evening, which helped some, giving me a few minutes of profitable time reading the letter in the living room. Luella glanced in while I was reading, so I gave it to her afterward. Don't worry, I don't give her your letters. Lonnie and Luella are very interested in any news from our community and act like they want to make friends with our folks if they get the chance. They have a soft spot in their hearts for Amish people.

All of which doesn't help me much at the moment, as I sit around in my loneliness. Every once in a while I think it's gone, but then it's back again. Especially when I sit here remembering it's Saturday evening, and I can't look forward to seeing you tomorrow. Sort of breaks my heart.

This loneliness makes me wonder why I ever came out here in the first place, which doesn't help either. I hope you know how much I miss you and how much it hurts. I try to keep my mind off of home as much as I can, but it doesn't always work. Especially like this evening, when I have too much time to think, so the memories of our good times together come rushing in.

I sit back on the couch here and remember your cozy room upstairs, your living room with the old woodstove, the hand-written Scriptures on the wall, the couch where we sat and talked, and talked, and talked.

There seems to be so much security one draws from familiar places, and yet here they are all gone, as are you. Well, you aren't really gone. I guess it just feels so.

Memories, memories, and more memories.

Sunday afternoon…

I missed you at church this morning. The service was nothing like the Amish church service at home. There was not a buggy in sight, just cars and more cars filling the parking lot. They have a large congregation here, which is surprising. As far apart as the places are, and as open as the fields are, there doesn't seem to be that many people around, let alone Mennonites.

The church house is huge, but the minister wasn't as interesting as some of our Amish ministers are, but maybe I'm just not used to them yet. I did miss our slow German singing. English singing on Sunday morning is something I will have to get used to. There's no one around here who even knows the German language, let alone our German tunes.

Lonnie and Luella told me the sad tale of their daughter last night. What provoked the story was my mentioning how lonesome I am, so I guess Luella thought I should know that other people also have problems.

Their only daughter ran away with an *Englisha* man when she was only nineteen. Luella said a bunch of younger local Mennonite boys had been interested in her, and one even drove down from Michigan, but the daughter kept turning everyone down. For the longest time they couldn't figure out why, until she told them she was interested in the *Englisha* neighbor boy, whose sister she was good friends with.

So for the next year or so, with much ruckus involved, they tried to keep her away from the neighbor boy, but she would sneak out anyway. When they put the daughter under further restrictions, the boy set a ladder up against the side of the house, under the daughter's upstairs bedroom window. I guess he was going to have her climb down. They caught him in the act and ordered him off the place, but it didn't do any good. They finally gave up, and the daughter ran off, marrying the boy in a quick ceremony in front of a judge.

It's hard to imagine all of this happening so many years ago in this house, and some of it in the room next to mine. I haven't dared look in, as the door is shut all the time. It would have to give one chills to stand at the very window where an *Englisha* boy had his ladder extended, trying to extract a young nineteen-year-old girl from her parents' home.

Yesterday, we drove down to the Amish auction at Fairfield. There is a large Amish settlement there, but I doubt if I will have much contact with them because of the distance involved. The auction had a lot of nice things to sell, but everything was going sky-high in my opinion. Probably because nobody seemed to care how much they paid for the items. All of the proceeds go to the Mennonite Central Committee, which is the Mennonite's mission arm. One of the quilts sold for over 800 dollars.

I had a surprise when we arrived in Fairfield. Lonnie and Luella had

Jerry and Tina Eicher

been talking on the way down about their good friends who lived there, a couple by the name of Ben and Mary Miller, and how they wanted us to meet them while in town. When we arrived, they introduced me. We soon figured out that Ben is a cousin to my grandmother on my father's side. After that juicy bit of knowledge, they really started talking.

In local news, I kept hearing about Stan Miller. He is the youth leader here, and a good one they say. He's married and leads the youth group when they have Bible study every week. From what Lonnie and Luella say, some of the people in church aren't too pleased with what he teaches, including themselves. But I was still looking forward to meeting the man. And this morning I was introduced to him. He's extremely self-confident but soft spoken. I think I will like him.

Well, I'd better eat supper so I can be at the singing on time. It starts at six o'clock. Everyone was glad to hear that I enjoy singing, and they're expecting to really have a good singing tonight. I'm afraid they might be expecting too much out of me. As you know, my voice isn't the greatest.

Monday evening…

We aren't having school today because of Labor Day, so this morning I painted garage doors for Lonnie. They had company in for dinner—some older people who talked about their bygone days. I didn't know any of them, but it was kind of interesting.

The singing was lousy on Sunday evening, and I'm not sure why, as they sing many of the same English songs we do after our German singing on Sunday nights. Maybe our Amish young people come from good singing families, I don't know, but I don't blame them for only having one singing a month. Things went a little better halfway through when a couple of the young people sang three songs by themselves. That must be where the good singers were hiding.

There was a young folks hot dog roast planned for this evening, since it's Labor Day, but we got rain most of the day so they called it off. Instead, they had a gathering in one of the homes, where we played board games till nine o'clock. One of the young boys picked me up and dropped me off afterward. It's nasty not having your own transportation, even if it's only a buggy and a horse.

One of the girls tonight said that the next time I write to you, I am supposed to tell you "Hi" for them. They said they're all excited to meet you. I'd told them my family and you have a trip planned out here.

Keep me informed on all the news at home—the weddings and such. And if you get tired of so many letters, you'll just have to say so.

So long,

Eugene

My dearest Eugene,

Good morning! You are probably still in dreamland as it's 3:30 in the morning here. I'm brightly awake, wrapped in a blanket, and sitting in front of my dresser. Before I lit the kerosene lamp, I looked outside. It's bright moonlight again. It reminded me of what you had written in your letter about bringing back memories—precious ones.

I went to bed at 10:30 last night, but I had slept most of the day yesterday, so maybe I'm finally slept out. I had stayed indoors all day with some kind of flu. It must have been a one-day affair because a good day's rest seems to have knocked it out. I got up Saturday morning sniffling and blowing my nose, but with the sleep I've been getting things became progressively better as the day went along. Now at 3:30 a.m. it's nothing but an irritation. I think I should be able to go to church without any problem.

I plan to wear my new light-blue dress today. I was going to wear it last Sunday but got too *grivlich* and late to finish. It's not the nicest light-blue you ever saw. In fact, my sister Rosanna called it a light-blue denim when she caught a glimpse last week. I'm not going to pay her any mind, as she's back in her royal critical mode. It must be a phase she's going through, although a lot of it gets done in teasing. Larry teases me until I'm ready to pull my hair out.

Well, I don't know what else to write, so I'll catch a quick nap before the others get up. I'll write some more after the singing.

Sunday evening...

Here I am again, sitting alone upstairs and wishing you were here. Both your dad and mom spoke with me today, but they didn't have any more news from you than I did, which made me feel good. That's probably selfish of me, but I like it that you are writing me plenty of letters.

Today I was standing with the girls after getting the first batch of people to the tables. Rebecca Helmuth was standing beside me with everyone talking around us. She leaned over and whispered, "I'll take you to the table at Richard and Joan's wedding."

I laughed and said, "Sure, why not." So I might have a partner when the notorious time comes to pair up for the evening singing—and not one who you can be jealous of.

We had to sit in for a members' meeting after church today. It was about the new James Yoder family who just moved into the community. Apparently he has some former beliefs in eternal security. Dad thinks he must have picked up Calvinistic doctrines somewhere by reading *Englisha* literature. This all came about because someone heard James say that he feels he had no more to do with his spiritual birth than he had with his physical birth. Bishop Enos said they want to make things plainer to people so that everyone understands how James feels and what he believes. They had him stand up and explain. Mom claims James said quite plainly before that he doesn't believe in Calvinism anymore, but that he used to. Dad said he was glad to finally hear the situation fully explained, and perhaps this will be the end of the matter. As you know, it's been roiling the community for some time now. Bishop Enos also said they'll vote to take James and his wife, Millie, in as a proving member at precommunion church, which is in two weeks. If that vote passes, Millie would at least be able to finish her six months of probation and be accepted as a full member.

Don and I drove to the singing, and I had the most awful time of it. Maybe it's because it hasn't been that long since you left, but the singings are the hardest part of Sunday for me. I long so much to be with you, I can almost taste it. I thought today would be hard, but I guess I didn't think it'd be this hard.

Well, even if I feel empty and sad, I still have my physical exercises to do, so I'd better get them done. Goodnight...and how I love you.

Monday evening...

Hello! Hello! I finished clearing the table and washing the dishes. Mom and Dad are downstairs relaxing as this evening winds itself down. I'm enclosing an article written for teachers. I don't normally read things for teachers, but Mom does and she mentioned that you might like to read this. I think you'll like it. It covers the methods teachers can use to illustrate problems on the blackboard, instead of relying only on verbal instructions. It also contains the things to avoid as a teacher. Not that I would know, but these sounded good.

1. Don't think of your task as being an ordinary easy one, but rather as both weighty and filled with opportunity.

2. Don't make rules you can't personally enforce. Especially don't use threats to try to enforce them.

3. Don't talk about your pupils' faults, either in front of them or behind their back. It has a way of leaking out.

4. Don't speak in anger, regardless of how big the temptation is.

5. Don't compare your pupils with each other or let one know you like him better than the others.

6. Don't argue with your pupils. Discussions are fine, but if they find out you are insecure on your principles, disrespect will follow.

7. Don't make rash judgments about any situation without first finding out all the facts. This takes time and effort, but is worth every minute.

8. Don't try to explain lessons to the pupils you haven't learned yourself. You can't teach what you don't know.

9. Don't be afraid to admit you are wrong. It builds respect in your pupils' hearts.

Aren't those good? I think so.

Ada and Norman are our neighbors. Their five children go to school, and they joined up with Betsy and Larry to walk up to the schoolhouse today for their first half day. They have two teachers as usual, with Kathryn taking the first, second, fifth, and sixth graders, and Aaron taking the third, fourth, seventh, and eighth graders. It seems to me it'd be kind of a mess that way, but I guess they thought they'd each have about the same number of pupils.

Mom and I were at home today. I know I didn't accomplish much, other than help work on an antique quilt Mom is fixing for someone. I think the flu from Saturday is still hanging around.

Well, I think it's about time I ended this lengthy letter. Your eyes are probably tired and cross-eyed with all the scribbles and everything.

With all my love,
Naomi

My dearest Naomi,

Greetings of love.

"Let not your heart be troubled: ye believe in God, believe also in me. In my Father's house are many mansions: if it were not so, I would have told you. I go to prepare a place for you" (John 14:1). The minister here quoted the whole chapter of John 14 by heart on Sunday. I thought that was a nice touch.

I could hardly wait to come home from school today, hoping for a letter, but nothing arrived. So that means I have to wait, but I suppose I can manage it.

I think my brain cleared out a little over the weekend because it functions much better at school now. But then, perhaps it is finding a routine that helps. Regardless, I could think better, was able to explain the lessons better to the children, and still could keep track of everything going on—or that was supposed to be going on. With seven grades it does keep me on my toes.

I don't care for the third- through fifth-grade arithmetic books. I noticed this last week when they showed them to me. The words used to explain the lessons are very difficult. The students almost need to carry dictionaries. So I guess we'll teach vocabulary lessons along with arithmetic lessons.

Wednesday evening…

A blessed letter from you finally arrived! I knew Lonnie and Luella were gone all day, so right after the children left school at 3:30, I came down to check the mailbox. After sitting on the front porch to read your letter, I walked back to the schoolhouse and worked until five o'clock. I had to do the chores since Lonnie and Luella won't be back until late, so I didn't work till six, which is my usual time to leave the school.

I'm starting to feel more at home, which is good. It helps the lonesome feelings considerably. Luella was telling me last night about someone from around here whose young wife came here from Florida. Even though they already have children, she still gets awfully homesick, which she hides from her husband. At least that's what I was told. She waits to cry until he's not around. I think the story was meant to comfort me, but it left feelings of despair instead. Like, "You'll never get over your homesickness." Which may be true, but I'd rather not think about that now.

The young folks are having a ball game at the schoolhouse tonight, so even if I'm not too fond of softball, I shall trot myself down there.

Take care of yourself. And I pray that God will protect and keep you in His care.

I love you,
Eugene

Hi, dearest Eugene,

This finds me just back from a long, early morning drive into Worthington with Mom and with half a bag of jelly beans in my stomach. Is it any wonder I have headaches!

Today I have to leave for my housecleaning job at one o'clock, and it's noon now so I'd better write fast.

Dad is away working with Harvey someplace south of here for the day. Harvey wanted help building a small pole barn. I would think Dad has plenty of work on the farm to keep him busy, but you know how it goes. Harvey and he will trade the favor somewhere, I'm sure.

Don is working on the silo-filling crew as usual this year. He told me they have several weeks to go yet, and they should be at our place before too long. Rosanna has our wash out on the line. Betsy and Larry are in school. With our trip into town, I didn't get to see Ada's children walk with them on their way to school. They are such a cute sight.

When we arrived back from Worthington, I unhitched the horse while Mom unloaded the groceries. I'm not sure what Mom is doing right now—something down in the basement. The weather is gorgeous this morning, breezy and cool. I could even see my breath at six o'clock before we started for town.

Harvey's Julia sent me a "thinking of you" card last week, which meant a lot to me. She is one of the most thoughtful girls I know, and I have often wished I could be more like her.

As you can see, I don't really know what to write about. Everything is boring and the same as usual. Please keep telling me what happens in school, as it interests me immensely. I had to laugh at the story of the first grader moving his desk over by his sister's and the handkerchief story. I imagine that was kind of gross.

Mom has to go over to Wayne Helmuth's place tonight to help organize things for the wedding for Richard and Joan. Joan's mom, Katie, said she can't be two places at once. It looks like a lot of people are using the Helmuth place for weddings this year, but it's understandable with their large house and equally large pole barn next door.

Don now says he might take someone to the table at the evening hymn singing, if he's not the only boy his age to do so. I told him to do it anyway, but no, he said he won't. I think he's being stubborn, and when the time comes, he'll give in and take some girl to the table for the thrill of it, if nothing else. I suppose the Mennonites don't have the practice of pairing up all the young people for the hymn singing on a wedding night. You remember how the pressure is. Which gives me another reason for wanting to be out there right now.

Well, I should at least get this room in order before I go to work, so more writing in a little bit.

At my cleaning job…

I retrieved the mail before I went to work, and there was this beautiful card in the mailbox. Oh, thank you so much, and that was a wonderful little poem in the first letter. It means more to me than I can say.

I'm sitting here at the Bachs, finished with the cleaning of the house, but Mrs. Bach is still not back from the health spa in Salem, so I have to wait for another hour. That is, if she keeps to her usual schedule. It's five o'clock now, and John, her husband, is sitting in the recliner drinking Pepsi. I don't know if I ever told you, but John can hardly get around anymore. He's not in a wheelchair yet, but close to it. And Mrs. Bach wants someone with him all the time.

Every time I come he asks, "How's your boyfriend?" He asks all kinds of questions about you—and the same ones over and over, as he's quite forgetful. I was sitting here a bit ago, staring into space, and he said, "That's all right, go ahead and write it down." He loves to tease. Today he asked me how many times I've said "I love you" in this letter. I didn't answer, so he said, "The whole page, huh?"

Maybe you have an idea how my Wednesdays go. By the way, I *do* love you.

Last night one of Mom's *Englisha* friends, Elena Marshall, was here. She talked to me secretly. She wants to bake a cake for Mom and Dad's anniversary on the fifteenth. It's their twentieth, and I was glad because I'd been thinking we should do something.

Well, I have to go. I'll write all about the wedding. Until then, take care of yourself.

Wednesday evening…

"Rejoicing in hope; patient in tribulation; continuing instant in prayer" (Romans 12:12).

I was going to wait until tomorrow night after the wedding to write to you, but I was sitting here lonesome for you so I decided I'd write some tonight. I don't feel very cheerful about going to Richard and Joan's wedding. If only you could be here, it would make all the difference. So much for being "patient in tribulation."

How is school going? If you have time or want to sometime, send me the pupils' names and the grades they are in. Please describe each one and his or her traits. That is, if you know them well enough. I think this would be very interesting.

The weather was warmer here today, eighty-two degrees and beautiful. If it's this nice tomorrow, Richard and Joan will have a perfect day for their wedding. They must have made some changes in the plans because the ceremony will now be at Joan's place. And after that everyone will walk down to the Helmuth home for dinner. The evening hymn sing will also be at the Helmuths. Mom has to be at the Helmuth place tomorrow morning at eight. She will stay all day because she's one of the cooks.

My aunt Hannah, who lives in northern Indiana, wrote today and shared more bad news about her daughter, Jessica, who is in *rumspringa*. I'm so glad our group of young people around here aren't into wild stuff. Jessica goes to town and sits at a bar about every evening. Every time I think about her it makes me sad. We'll have to pray really hard for her. I just finished writing her a letter, as I've felt for a while now that I should. Maybe I should have done it sooner.

Thursday afternoon...

I arrived home from the wedding, and I'm here alone. It's only 3:15, but I couldn't stand it any longer. For one thing, I wanted to see if I had received a letter from you. I also have a splitting headache. It may have come from seeing all those couples together. By the way—there was a letter, and no, I will never get tired of your letters. You can write as often as you want.

Now about the wedding. Joan wore light blue, and the two witness girls a little darker blue. The witness couples were Robert and Beth on Richard's side and Joan's cousin Ella and her boyfriend on her side.

The table waiter girls wore dark blue, and they were seated in this order:

Ryan, a cousin to Richard and Marie
Carl and Bernice

James and Mary (your sis)
Alan and Melissa
Ben and Elva
Steve and Lydia
Lyle and Heidi
Edward and Wilma from Mio
Adam and Brenda

Bishop Enos married Richard and Joan, with a visiting minister having the first part. Everett Gingerich read the Scripture, and Bishop Enos had the main sermon, of course. It was a good one, and not too long. They were all done by noon, which, as you know, is always an accomplishment for Amish weddings.

The weather was warm and muggy, and not nearly as nice as yesterday. I got to sit between Rhoda and Rebecca to eat dinner. I really enjoy those two. The food was excellent. We had ham and potatoes together in one dish, chicken done with an awesome sauce, salad, and fruit. Then, of course, the usual assortment of pies and date pudding. I didn't have supper last night or breakfast this morning, so that's probably the real reason for my headache. But don't blame me or laugh at me. Weddings are special occasions for everyone, even when you aren't the one being married.

Rhoda is a jewel of a girl. If anyone could have made me laugh today, it was her. The two of us, along with Adam and Brenda, were talking about being nervous on our first dates and being ill at ease if we had partners we hardly knew. Rhoda said that if we just say something about being ill at ease it sometimes breaks the ice. She said once when she and Delbert were having a date she was fiddling with her fingers. Delbert asked, "Are you nervous?" She had to laugh and admit it was true.

A lot of people asked about you today and sympathized with me since you're so far away. Rhoda said she and Delbert weren't together for months at a time. I hadn't known much about their courtship, but I guess it would have had to be conducted at long distance since he comes from Holmes County. So we aren't the only ones who go through this, but it still doesn't make it any easier. Also Rhoda said she thinks it's good for a couple to be apart for a while, that it makes them appreciate the other so much more. I think maybe she is right—but still…

I'm going to help clean up at the Helmuths' tomorrow, but for now there is the singing to live through. I hope you're not jealous if I'm taken to the table by someone, as you know how it goes. Those matchmakers don't take no for an answer.

Tell the youth girls in Iowa "Hi" for me. I would love to meet them, but I hope they don't expect too much, as they may well be disappointed. Also tell Lonnie and Luella thanks for taking care of you and that I send my greetings.

Take good care of yourself, Eugene.

I love you,
Your Naomi

My dearest Naomi,

I finished rereading all the letters I've received from you so far—four of them. I'm left with sorrow wrapped around my heart. Not because of the letters, but because I miss you. I've hit my first real low, and I'm not sure why. Maybe because I knew Richard and Joan's wedding was this week. What fun that would have been. I wrote you a letter last night, but it sounded too depressed so I'm not mailing it.

I simply love the poem you sent—"From My Heart." You have good taste when it comes to poetry. Well, you have good taste in a lot of things, and you are beautiful. Have I told you that recently? I don't think so. It would be awesome to spend time with you this weekend. Your presence would soothe me. Your soft-brown eyes with love shining out of them would be out of this world.

I have feared since arriving here that by leaving you our love will be put to a great test. One that could prove too hard for it. Maybe I have hurt you too much already? I hope not. The young people out here aren't helping me much. I hear things like "She'll be finding somebody else soon, Eugene. It's not safe to leave a girl alone for long." They may be teasing, but it still hurts. One of the older boys even told me, "You'll find someone you like better out here. Believe me, it always goes that way."

Well, I have no intention of doing any such thing. Nor do I believe it possible to find a better girl than you. I expect you could find someone better, which is the scary part.

In the meantime, I'll continue writing and hoping this time away from each other will pass quickly. *Yah,* I know—like nine months can be over before too long. I do tend to be a dreamer. Speaking of dreaming, here is a poem I wrote for you. Perhaps it was knowing the wedding was today or simply the memory of your beautiful eyes, but here it is.

Wrapped in Love

To tell the love I have for you,
I'd take the morning's sparkling dew
And pull the sunrise from the sky
And on the grass its colors dye.

I'd sprinkle it with roses red
And pull the lilies from their bed.
A cardinal's song I'd tie around
With spring, and air, and copper sound.

I'd use a rainbow for a bow,
And give all this so you would know
That in this world on land or sea,
How precious is your heart to me.

As always,

Eugene

Jerry and Tina Eicher

Dearest Eugene,

Hi! I wonder what you're doing right now. It's 7:30 on a Saturday night, and chores and supper are over. I finished cleaning up after the day's work, and I'm settled in my room for the evening. Dad said we should all try to get a good night's sleep after all the ruckus from the wedding. He wants us to be fresh for Sunday services. I'm sure that's wise, but I don't feel very tired yet.

I came home yesterday from helping at the Helmuths' place a little before 11:00 a.m., and I still had an hour before I had to leave for work, so I took a short nap. Mrs. Bach pulled into the driveway to pick me up. She had a funeral of a friend in Scottsburg to attend, and she wanted me to stay with John.

John asked how you are again. I told him fine, and he asked, "Any sweet letters coming back yet?"

I laughed and said, "Lots of them."

I didn't have anything to do other than care for John, so I cleaned the house and read *Time* magazine until Mrs. Bach came home.

Larry just stuck his head into my room and said, "Writing Eugene again?" and then gave a loud groan.

I looked at him and said, "I'm going to write him about how silly you look."

He had a fit, but I'm going to anyway. He got himself stung by a bumblebee at the wedding. Right above the lip. And oh my, you should see him. His upper lip is so big it hangs over the lower one, and one eye is swollen shut. He didn't even eat supper last night at the hymn singing because everyone was having a fit over how he looked. Dad was afraid he might be allergic to bee stings, but Larry is okay. He still sounds the same, teasing and all.

And now for confession time. I know you won't be jealous, right? Because there was nothing to this really. You know how these things go at weddings. We girls were sitting on the beds upstairs Thursday afternoon when Robert and Peter came by with their tablets, matching up the couples for the evening hymn singing.

"Poor Naomi," Robert said. "She has no one for tonight since Eugene is gone."

"And keep it that way," I snapped, feeling very grouchy at his big, wide smile.

"You know we can't do that," he protested.

"Of course you can," I said. "At least put me on the bottom of the list. There will be plenty of girls. There always are."

"A nice girl like you shouldn't be sitting the evening out alone," he said, writing my name down. I knew I was a cooked goose. Sure enough, they paired me up with some visiting boy from Holmes County—David Yoder, who is a cousin or some relation to Richard.

He wasn't too bad, I guess. At least he didn't slobber or chew with his mouth open. I'm just kidding, of course, but I did find out more about Holmes County than I really wanted to know. Mostly about the tourist traffic and how hard it is for the locals to get around during certain times of the day. So there, I've told you, and that's the end of it. It should have been you who was by my side. But it couldn't be helped, I suppose.

A couple of people mentioned how much Julia and Martin hit it off Thursday night. Martin took her to the table, so that was the local buzz. I hope they do turn into a real couple. Both of them are nice people.

By the way, about the lady who doesn't tell her husband how home-sick she is but does tell others. I don't approve of that at all. Even if she does keep it from her husband, she shouldn't go telling other people what she doesn't tell him.

Well, I'd better get going.

Sunday afternoon…

I have to leave soon for chores, and then there is the hymn singing at Nathan's tonight. I don't feel like going, but I suppose it will cheer me up. I will gird up my strength and attend. Don is riding with me because he doesn't have a steady girl yet—and shouldn't have one either, as young as he is.

Oh, I forgot to write yesterday in the midst of carrying on about my own woes that Don took the youngest of Harvey's girls, Diane, to the table. He must have pulled something with one of the matchmakers. He's sweet on her, I think, but they don't always pay a whole lot of attention to such things on wedding nights. Maybe Don bribed one of them with a piece of gum. Now that's funny. More than likely he had a conversation with one of the matchmakers early on out in the barn and got his place secured.

If you have ever wondered how we girls deal with the matchmakers on wedding nights, we simply take the first boy they offer to us. So I hope you never read too much into such things. It keeps it simple for us girls, and we can continue living at peace with each other.

I'm sitting on a lawn chair, and the sun is hanging low in the sky. The *Englisha* neighbors across the road, the Thermans, have visitors, and it looks like everyone at the Normans' is at home.

Your mom said today at church that we could all come over to your place afterward, but Dad didn't want to go. So we have ended up back here for the afternoon. After dinner I said, "If everyone gets out of the kitchen, I'll do the dishes alone." Did the girls ever whoop!

Larry wanted something to do after I was done, so I walked down to the bridge with him—the one with the memories—taking my shoes off and splashing around in the water. It wasn't much fun without you there, so we came back home fairly quickly.

Afterward, we all settled in the front yard, enjoying the warm afternoon. I got our colt, Laddie, out of the barnyard. Mom, Larry, Rosanna, and Betsy were on lawn chairs, while I sat on the grass holding Laddie with a strap. We all ate popcorn. Laddie tries to bite sometimes, but usually he just sniffs me. So the sniffing started on my back, and I did nothing until he calmly took a nip. I yelled "Ouch!" even though it hardly hurt. Larry went into hysterics, laughing so hard he practically fell off the lawn chair. I guess it was pretty funny from his point of view.

Did you hear that Wayne Helmuth is planning on building a *dawdy haus* on their side of the road, back behind the current buildings? Word has it they still want to start on the work this fall. It sounds to me like Robert and Beth are going to marry next spring. It's hard to tell sometimes, but I know that Wayne won't continue farming with only three girls left, and they aren't always at home. He would likely still help Robert on the farm, but let him manage everything. How much of this is truth and how much just rumors is hard to tell.

Anna and Mary Yoder told my sister Betsy that they think you and I are engaged and will marry next year. How is that for a guess?!

Well, it is time to chore, and I don't know anymore news so I will stop scribbling. I hope I don't cry at the hymn singing tonight. You are always in my thoughts and prayers.

Yours always,

Naomi

My dearest Naomi,

We are ready to leave for church in half an hour. Starting time around here is ten o'clock, but Lonnie and Luella have to leave early on account of Lonnie being the janitor. Luella reads her Bible during the waiting time. I sit in the empty church house, staring off into space, while Lonnie opens the shades and makes sure the temperature is set properly. I think I'll take up a Scripture memorization program or something to pass the time until people begin arriving. Sundays have lost their spark for me because I can't look forward to seeing you. I often question why I ever came out here in the first place, but it's really too late for such thoughts.

The school year is settling in, and I do enjoy teaching my students, which was my reason for coming. If I keep their needs as my goal, it gives me purpose and determination to go on. Especially right now when I miss you so much.

Sunday afternoon…

Hello there. I'm sitting out on the lawn under a tree at the picnic table. We arrived home from church earlier than usual. No one invited us for dinner, so when we finished eating here at the house it was only one o'clock.

I told Lonnie and Luella that I'd be scared raising a family in a church with the worldliness they have amongst the young people here, and to my surprise Lonnie and Luella agreed with me. Things are also not going well with the church leadership. Everyone seems to be expecting a split this fall, but maybe not until next year, after a new minister has been ordained. My interest lies primarily in what impact this will have on the school. Who would have thought I'd walk into a situation like this when I agreed to teach? Lonnie and Luella are very sympathetic to my concerns and have assured me that things will work out with the school one way or the other. I hope so.

It's not even near Christmas, but for some reason I've been remembering the Christmas dinner that year at the Burkholders. I hope you remember it too. I forget why both of our families were invited, but we sang afterward. I remember how I tried to get closer to you by moving a foot or so down on the bench so I could hear you sing. I had never heard you sing before, and you sang so softly I couldn't hear very well above the rest of the group. Even then I loved the sound of your voice. I still do even as I miss hearing it.

Ha! I remember too that back in those days you wouldn't have batted an eye at me. I had to use subterfuge to find out more about you. I don't think you ever knew some of the things I did to gather information. Someday maybe I'll tell you!

Talking about singing, Lonnie and Luella just left to sing for someone. They wanted me to go along, but I told them I had to finish this letter.

Luella asked, "Is it that important?"

And I said, "Yes, especially since I'm going out with you tonight and won't have time to finish it later."

We're going down to Luella's brother's place. Saul Ulrich has three girls: Janie, Amanda, and Nancy, and one boy, Duane, who's a couple years younger than I am.

Yesterday, I helped Lonnie paint. He wants to give most of his barns a fresh coat of red paint before the weather gets too cold. If you come to visit, you'll see how the farms are laid out. They are very far apart, but the places are kept neat, and the big barns are all fixed up.

On Tuesday evening of next week the young folks are planning a "progress supper." Since I've never heard of such a thing, we will have to see how it goes. Luella is supposed to have corn. I guess you go from place to place, getting one item at each house. I would think the food would be cold by the time you arrived to the end of the line, but perhaps that's part of the fun.

Then on Wednesday night there is a young folks' softball ball game at the schoolhouse again.

At school I'm working hard with the upper graders on their grammar. I spent quite some time with the sixth graders on the difference between transitive and intransitive verbs. It took a little clearing of my own mind, as last year I thought I had it figured out, but it has apparently slipped away. It does get a little complicated, as a transitive verb is a verb that requires both a direct subject and one or more objects. An intransitive verb does not have objects.

Do you remember that I wrote you about Stan, the youth leader? Well, he is one of the friendliest, most outgoing persons I've ever met. After church he came over and talked with me. He said they'd been praying for me. He wished me God's blessings. He said he and his wife want me over for Sunday lunch sometime, and I thanked him for the invitation. That would be a nice break to the routine.

I hope you have a great Sunday afternoon and evening.

With all my love,

Eugene

Jerry and Tina Eicher

Dearest Eugene,

"Let the words of my mouth, and the meditation of my heart, be acceptable in thy sight, O Lord, my strength and my redeemer" (Psalm 19:14).

Hello! How are you getting along? I'm not doing too badly. I'm pretty tired tonight though. Today I "fall cleaned" my room, and you should see it. The frame of my bed was falling apart and I wanted something different, so I have the springs and the mattress on the floor.

I also moved the bed over to where the couch used to be and moved the cedar chest to where my bed was. The chest of drawers I put beneath the clock again. I'm sure glad I could still find a place for the cedar chest after I was done with my whirlwind moving urges.

It's so warm around here. I feel like I'm melting just sitting inside the house. It was 88 degrees, and that was in the shade. Also I suppose I'm warm from doing those dreadful exercises. But they are good for me—or so I convince myself. These are from the instruction sheet the chiropractor gave me last month when Mom took me for my headaches. But I never got to them until this week.

There was a time I thought exercises were going to be fun, but now it's just the same old thing over and over again. I guess I could add some new ones and stop some of the boring ones. Maybe I will. I think my real problem is that I don't like to do them because I know I have to so I'll stay healthy.

Well, I had better get to bed. If my letters are boring, it's because it's very boring around here without you.

Tuesday...

Here I am again, and it's Tuesday evening. It's still warm even though it just rained. The Colombos—another of my cleaning jobs—had the air conditioning on today. I get very aggravated at their 18-year-old son. His mom gave him a list of things to do while she was gone for a couple of hours and what did he do? He sat in front of the TV the whole time! Maybe he did one thing on the list, but that was it.

When she got back and asked about it, he had excuses for everything. I thought they were quite lame because I had been there the whole time and saw what he did, well, rather what he didn't do. We never talk to each other unless he feels he absolutely has to say something. Then he says the words in a tone that makes me feel like he doesn't think I have the right to even look at his face. He goes away to college at the end of this month. Yippee!

How is school? I hope still good. Betsy and Larry are jumping right into the routine again and seem happy about it. By the way, yesterday I drove into Worthington to get furniture polish for my room. I saw the Bryans are still not finished with their garage. Maybe they're remodeling the house too. Remember, that was the last job your dad's crew worked on before you left.

Another of Mom's *Englisha* friends, Della, was here tonight to give me something for my hope chest and to cheer me up. She knows how lonely I get without you. She gave me a set of three glass dishes—one small and two larger. They're beautiful and made of clear glass—almost crystal-like.

I'm reading a sample religious magazine we received in the mail. It's called the *Fundamentalist Journal.* I was a little surprised Dad allowed it in the house. While it's still here, I'm busy reading it. Everything I've read so far, I've agreed with. The magazine says a fundamentalist is someone who believes the Bible is inspired by the Holy Spirit and readily accepts Jesus' virgin birth, sinless life, victorious death, literal resurrection, ascension into heaven, and His second coming. That sounds like Amish beliefs would fit in there somewhere.

My thoughts often go your way. I wish you were here.

Love you,
Naomi

My dearest Naomi,

I was so glad to get a letter from you again today. I don't think I'm ever going to get over my lonesomeness for you. It gets worse instead of better, and if you look forward to getting my letters as much as I do yours, well, I'm going to write as often as I can.

Tonight it was two weeks since I arrived. It seems more like two years, and I wonder if you're going to look and act the same when I see you again.

I worked tonight at the school until eight o'clock, after coming home for supper at six and then walking back there again. The reason for the late hours is that the Bible course they use doesn't have a teacher's edition, so I have to work everything out ahead of time.

I have to keep on my toes with the daytime schedule of classes, rushing to get through most days. I'm tempted to cut corners whenever the opportunity arises. One such chance has been with the reading classes. It takes so long for each class to read the story during class time. Yet the first and third graders absolutely have to read everything out loud since they need the practice. In the other grades it isn't as important, I figure, so I've been allowing them to read the story at their desks. We only check the answers to the comprehension questions in class.

The sixth graders are struggling with subjects and predicates, so we practice and practice, which takes time. Today we started on commas and semicolons, and tomorrow it will be dependent and independent clauses. Then we'll cover simple, compound, and complex sentences.

So it goes, but it's gratifying work. I don't think I've ever had a job I've loved as much as teaching. It's just a shame it doesn't pay more so I could make a career out of it.

By the way, I'm eating more now and slowly gaining weight.

I miss you,
Eugene

My dearest Naomi,

"For God is my record, how greatly I long after you" (Philippians 1:8). I know I'm misusing the Scripture in that verse, but it says what I feel, so there. We've had warm, warm weather around here the past few days. My hair and face were soaking wet from playing with the children during the noon hour. I've been outside with them almost every day, going inside the schoolhouse ten minutes before bell time so I can calm down enough to read the after-lunch story. It's fun joining in their games, and the children love it. Maybe I'm still a little kid at heart.

I came home from school at 4:30 today so I could get ready for the progress supper. That's where you ride from place to place, getting one food item at each stop. Whoever came up with such a wild idea, I don't know. I'll have to see what everyone else does, but I think I'm going to eat my food items hot when they are given to us.

Ah, here is my ride, so I'd better go.

Later…

Here I am again at ten o'clock, just home from the progress supper thing. I'm going to rush since I need my sleep if I plan to teach school tomorrow without yawning all the time.

They used a tractor and wagon piled with hay bales to take us from place to place. The stops were far apart, so we had a lot of time to visit. Everyone had a paper plate, fork, knife, spoon, and napkin. We stopped at each place and lined up outside the front door. Then we filed through the kitchen to get our one food item.

Someone must have been really bored to come up with this game. We were given mashed potatoes first. A mile down the road we got the gravy. Lonnie and Luella were the third stop with their corn. Like I expected, everyone ate their portions on the ride to the next place. Which was fine with me, and it did make for a fun time. The boys hollered, and the girls screeched out their frustrations.

The whole list was potatoes, gravy, corn, bread, meat, salad, boiled carrots, and more vegetables. The dessert was an ice cream mix of some kind. This tastes worse than you might imagine. If you don't believe me, try eating gravy or boiled carrots by themselves! At the last place, we played a game called Crows and Cranes. Two lines of people, standing boy–girl–boy–girl, face each other. One side is designated as "crows" and the other as "cranes." Then the "caller," in our case the lady of the house, hollers crows or cranes. The corresponding side chases the other, tagging them by touching until everyone is caught. The chases were timed to see which side could catch the other the quickest.

Afterward, I ran a footrace against two of the boys, coming in second. That was as good as I could do, and I'm still wobbly, as you can probably tell by my shaky handwriting.

They are a different group of young people than what we are used to. One of the girls had enough nerve to snap my suspenders! What a tease.

I love you,
Eugene

My dearest Naomi,

This finds me home from the volleyball game at the schoolhouse. They play softball until it gets too dark to see well, and then they play volleyball by the electric lights for another hour or so. Our side wasn't having too much success, but I was giving it all I had. I'm worn out as a result, but we did win one game.

The weather has cooled and presented us with a foggy morning. Things cleared around noontime. I'm not sure why, but we practiced the tornado drill at the school for the first time today. Some of the first graders didn't have a clue what to do, so we'll have to practice this more. Not that I expect a tornado to show up, but I was told by the school board that emergency drills are mandated by state law. Apparently state officials can show up at any time and ask for a demonstration, and the school board doesn't want to be embarrassed.

During the practice someone rings a bell. When we hear it, everyone stands and then runs, row by row, at top speed, to the basement. It does add a little excitement to the school day. Especially on a nice, sunny day when no one can see the slightest chance of a tornado bearing down.

I'm trying to start a nature collection for the children. I'm planning on bringing in mice, doves, and possibly sparrows. This morning when I walked to the schoolhouse, there was a big spider with a web on the front door. I thought, "Here's a good start." Catching the spider, I placed it, still alive, in a jar on my desk, which probably wasn't the smartest thing to do.

Nobody noticed it until we stood to sing for devotions. One of the boys hollered out, asking for the flyswatter to kill it. It was making its escape and was headed down the side of the jar. I told the boy no because we want to keep the spider alive to observe it.

I guess the idea of not killing a spider is pretty foreign to them. When the spider moved again, some of the girls giggled and others let out yelps.

I tried to do our devotions next, but that spider in the jar had their attention. I told them of my nature collection plans, and now they are all excited. They had all kinds of suggestions on what to bring.

At recess everyone stayed inside at first to look at the spider in the jar. It was so still, we thought it might be dead after all. A heart attack from the kids' reactions? Eventually I poked it with a ruler, and there it went skittering back up the side of the jar, trying to escape again. I wished I had cotton in my ears to muffle the screams.

At noontime I went outside and brought in a small stick to put in the jar for the spider to sit on. But it didn't want the stick. It wanted out of that jar.

This evening after the ball game I went in and the critter was gone. So there will be more excitement tomorrow when it turns up—likely during class or in the middle of devotions.

The eighth-grade class had nouns, adjectives, adverbs, conjunctions, prepositions, and interjections for their English class today. They thought the lesson was going to be terrible, but after I explained it they didn't think it was that bad after all.

On an unrelated subject, Luella had picked up a recipe for marshmallow cream in Fairfield the first Saturday I was here, figuring I could tell her how to make Amish peanut butter. This evening she had the marshmallow cream ready, and I did one better then telling—I prepared a batch myself. It tasted fair, if I do say so. You know, made by a man's hand and all.

Thursday evening…

I received a letter from my sister Heidi today. So Lydia Gingerich is having a date on Sunday, which will of course have happened by the time you receive this letter. I had told them at home that Lydia and Daniel would make a good match. Not that I am trying to find a match for Lydia, but she needs a phlegmatic man. From what Heidi says, it sounds as if it's going to be hard on her to lose the close friendship she has with Lydia if she marries. Not that anyone knows with this being the first date, but Heidi seems to think it's a fairly sure thing.

I'm alone this evening since Lonnie and Luella have gone somewhere to get apples. It's seven o'clock already, and they still aren't back. Luella left shortcake and strawberries for me, so supper was no problem. Afterward, I found a handful of cookies, apples, and orange juice to enjoy while sitting down to read the local paper. I didn't find any interesting reading. I'd be more interested in *Time* magazine or *U.S. News & World Report*.

I did their chores tonight, as I'm caught up with my schoolwork for a change. The chores only amount to feeding the cat and dog and gathering eggs.

Sometime I want to give you a list of the children's names and their grade levels, but I haven't found the time so far.

The spider turned up this afternoon on one of the stools. He must have been hiding under it. I caught him and took him outside. I figured there wasn't much use putting him back in the jar. He'd just get out again, and next time he might pick a different place to set up shop—like one of the girls' desks.

Today the children brought in crickets, butterflies, woolly worms, and a peacock feather. I'm going down with Duane tonight after dark to Lonnie's barn on their other farm. We plan to catch sparrows and pigeons. We might keep a few of the pigeons to grill later. That used to be quite an outing in my growing-up years, trips over to my friend's house where we grilled pigeons over an old farm barrel. I hope to make them like that again, only I don't have a barrel. Luella is sure the grill will be better. She also said my Amish peanut butter tastes good.

Friday morning…

We caught nine pigeons and four sparrows last night. We kept four of the pigeons for ourselves and two for the school project. The rest we turned loose because there were only three of us to eat the pigeons. The school-project pigeons are white with speckles. I have them together in one cage. The four sparrows are in another cage.

With love,

Eugene

My dearest Eugene,

This has been a rather exciting evening. Don went out after supper to hunt squirrels and found a garbage bag full of green plants. He said he found the bag under the bridge close to East 117 and thought the plants strange looking. So Don brought the bag in for Dad to look at. Dad opened the bag and said, "It sure looks like marijuana."

Mom and I looked the subject up in our encyclopedias and confirmed Dad's opinion. So he went down to the phone shack and called an *Englisha* friend he knows who has connections with the police. The friend called the chief inspector of the county. The man showed up within twenty minutes, and it sure didn't take him long to decide. He opened the bag, looked in, and said, "Yep, that's marijuana."

The inspector took the bag with him. He said it appears to him that someone who didn't know much about marijuana found the plants and thought this was a good way to get rid of them. The reason for this opinion was because they had placed the plants in a plastic bag. He said that keeps the moisture in, and that isn't the way marijuana is dried for sale. He also said marijuana doesn't grow wild around here, so someone must have purposely planted it. So much for quiet country living.

What I most enjoyed this evening, though, was reading your letter, especially since this is the first one this week. I think I've read it four times already. You said you had written a letter but decided not to send it because it sounded too depressed. You should have sent it anyway. I want to know how you feel, good or bad. I was sorry to hear that you're depressed, and I hope and pray that by the time this letter reaches you, you're feeling much better.

I was very happy that you liked the poem! I was afraid maybe you wouldn't because I know I'm not the best judge of poetry. But to me that particular one stood out from all the rest in the book, so I decided you just might like it.

You said people out there don't have much confidence that you will stay true to me. I miss you greatly, but I know you didn't go to Iowa to get away from me, so I'm not worried. I have complete trust that you will stay true to me. And there is nothing in the world that will keep me from being true to you. I mean that with all my heart, and I hope you don't doubt it. The thought has crossed my mind, supposing you meet some girl. It wasn't that I was doubting you, it's just that I'm sure there are a lot of girls nicer than me who would be better for you than I am. I often don't feel worthy of you.

Mom said she doesn't care a whit how often I write you, as long as it's not every day. So I'll say again, please write as often as you want to. I welcome every letter from you with joy!

It's really cool tonight and supposed to frost. "Already!" I exclaimed at the supper table when Dad shared the weather forecast. So I moved my plants in off the roof after dinner. It's really clear outside. Wow! I guess it isn't evening anymore, it's 12:40.

Oh, another thing, I ordered a "string art" kit through the mail, as I wanted something to do in my spare time. So "Miss stingy" spent some of her money. The kit is of a horse head, and I think I'm going to like doing it.

Yesterday was Mom and Dad's anniversary and also Dad's birthday. Last Wednesday Elena Marshall told me she'd decorate a cake for them, and she brought it over last night. It was very nice, but not as nice as your going-away cake was. That was a beautiful cake, which wasn't very fitting for such a sad occasion.

You wrote about the Christmas dinner at Burkholders'—how I wouldn't have batted an eye at you. When I read that I burst out laughing. If you had known me better, you would have realized that I did care for you even then. That's why I ignored you most of the time. I was and still am sometimes a little perverse.

Back then I wasn't at all sure anything would work out between us, and you had dated you-know-who for a while. Before I'd leave for a young folks gathering, I'd resolve not to look at you. I told myself I didn't care for anyone, especially you. But then I'd see you at the gatherings, and all my resolve would fly out the window. I'd get so mad at myself and try all over again the next time. You were and still are irresistible to me. I'm also a bit of a pessimist, and I always figured for you to have feelings for me would be too good to be true.

Your letter warmed my heart. Thank you for the beautiful poem. I wish I could look into your eyes and tell you that I love you…and see the love in your eyes for me. Sometimes I wonder why I didn't tell you more often how much you mean to me while you were here. But I guess I know why. Always when I want to express my deepest feelings, I get all tongue-tied or I'm afraid it'll sound dumb. Yet I never think it sounds dumb when you say sweet things. I get so mad at myself sometimes! Maybe I'll carry a pencil and paper along, and when I feel like expressing myself I'll hand you a note. Now wouldn't that be silly?

Well, it's now one o'clock. Maybe I should stay up all night, but I'm very sleepy, and it's very chilly with my window wide open. Ah, what glories to curl up under the covers on a brisk night with a clear open view right into the starry heavens. Mom says I have no one to blame but myself when I wake up in the middle of the night with my teeth chattering, but it's still worth the experience.

Lots and lots of love,
Naomi

My dearest Naomi,

I'm awfully lonesome tonight and just finished reading, and rereading, your last letters. Especially the one with the wedding news. I don't know about someone taking you to the table. You're scaring me a little. I hope that nasty character from Holmes County wasn't too handsome. Maybe he can take his buggy out in the middle of all that tourist traffic and lose a wheel or something. I know you weren't to blame, so I'll calm down now and control myself.

I can picture how your room is situated after the furniture moving. Is this a girl thing or something—moving things around compulsively? I'd leave things where they are forever. It's more comfortable that way. And doesn't it feel different to sleep on the floor? But perhaps there is some attraction to it that I don't get.

Oh, weekends! I fairly wail from my miserable times and from the sorrows that afflict my soul. Time drags like the stars in their courses. I search for hope that each moment might be better than the last, only to find myself again brokenhearted, lonely, and longing to see your face. But I guess I'd better stop my wailing and fill you in on the news.

I was up to the schoolhouse last night, and all the sparrows were dead. News which fits my current feelings, but I will say no more. So we caught five new sparrows late last night. Maybe this time they will eat. The ones who died had not. I turned the two doves loose because the cages were too small for them so I pitied them.

Here is a list of the schoolchildren.

First Grade

Dawn—average size, chubby, and quiet

Brandon—blond, very confident, and smartest of the class. Will likely be a broad-shouldered giant when he grows up

Laverne—He's a wheezy, frail, sickly boy who has asthma and allergies. He can't stand to be around dust, not even to work on the blackboard

Anthony—looks almost identical to Mark, one of the other first graders, even though he isn't related. Has a thin, short, wispy sort of body frame

Mark—often scared and crying, and then acts extra big to make up for it

Note: One first grader who had planned to attend didn't come this year. The parents thought she wasn't mature enough

Second Grade
No pupils

Third Grade
Lacie—a pretty, bright-eyed, little, round-faced girl

Norman—black-haired, always jolly, full of boundless energy. A brother to Dakota and Dawn

Larry—a jolly fellow who reminds me of a turtle, slow to get in gear, slow to think, and slow to everything. A brother to Anthony, but he doesn't look like it. Maybe they swapped the babies at the hospital by accident

Fourth Grade
Lester—blond-haired, walks straight as a stick, and a brother to Velma and Laverne

Sharon—small, petite, and rolls her eyes like a sophisticated lady

Fifth Grade
Dora—stout girl, very cheerful, and would make some Amish boy a perfect farmer's wife. She's a sister to Lacie

Dakota—short, quiet, smart, and a sister to Norman and Dawn

Lydia—a happy girl, always talking, and has a very bright outlook on life

Sixth Grade

Dennis—short, chubby, happy, and a brother to Crystal

Jackie—a very good-natured, black-haired girl. She has an incurable eye disease, which they expect will blind her someday. Sister to Jared and Mark

Seventh Grade

Velma—thin, active girl, who runs like a deer on the playground. Smart as a whip, and a sister to Lester and Laverne

Jared—dreamy sort of chap who would rather be anywhere but in school most of the time. A brother to Jackie and Mark

Eighth Grade

Dena—a laughing, dark-skinned girl, but given to moods

Crystal—bold, adventurous, and will likely take life by storm. A sister to Dennis. She also has a brother in the young folks group

Note—Both the sixth and seventh graders act sweet on each other, so I guess they start them young out here. In two of the couples who date among the young folks here, the girls are only fifteen

I miss you greatly,

Eugene

Dearest Eugene,

Greetings of love.

You said in one of your nice letters that you wonder if I'm going to look and act the same when you see me again. I suppose I will—at least I hope I will—and if not, perhaps it will be for the better. Let's keep our courage up. Life can bring strange things to our doorstep.

It sounds like you're really busy in school and having an interesting time studying commas and semicolons. I loved English in school, but I may have forgotten some of it. Still, it shouldn't take much to refresh those things.

It's a chilly evening here, and as you can see I didn't get anything written yesterday. This was the first Sunday since you left that I felt so relaxed. I don't think it was you though. I mean because you weren't here, but maybe because I'm getting used to the routine without you. Life does keep going on, no matter what.

I helped clear off the boys' table after church, with them still sitting there, and didn't get nervous once, even when they teased me about you being gone. One of them dared bring up that Holmes County boy, and I gave him a good glare. Of course, that made them laugh all the more. Well, they will get over it. They know good and well how things stand between you and me.

Congratulations on the peanut butter making. There aren't many boys who would dare tackle something like that.

I enjoyed hearing about your nature project and the other things at school.

Sister Betsy said your sister Mary told her they have only received one letter from you so far. Betsy said I should write you and tell you to write them too, that it isn't fair, and I guess it isn't. If you want to write them more and me less, that's okay because they miss you a lot.

We're having the usual *ordnungs* church next Sunday, where we get our minds refreshed by Bishop Enos going over the rules of the church. But I suppose it's necessary. And then communion in two weeks from that Sunday. Both districts are joining together for communion Sunday. I guess we are still small enough in numbers that they can fit the whole community into Wayne Helmuth's big house. At least they can for one day.

I can't think of anything more to write because, as I've told you, life gets so boring around here sometimes.

With all my love,
Naomi

Jerry and Tina Eicher

My dearest Naomi,

One of your wonderful letters arrived today, bringing with it cheer and good humor. It was the one you penned on the Thursday night you didn't get to bed until Friday morning. That's sounds funny! You were up with the night owls? *Yah.* But you really should be getting your sleep, dear one.

The sparrows I installed on Saturday evening at the school are doing fine, flitting and jumping around. They eat during schooltime, scattering seeds all over their pens.

Surprise, surprise! Jared brought a mouse to school this morning, a furry little thing that peeked out from under a blanket. He came complete with a cage Jared had made himself. How about that?

Jared admitted, rather sheepishly, that their cat had caught the mouse and was playing with it in the yard. I guess the whole family rushed to the rescue, only to place the poor thing in prison here at school. Talk about a mouse's hopes raised and dashed again.

The rest of the school has finally fallen into a boring routine, which is good I guess. The students sit at their desks, hard at work, as I rush about as quietly as I can conducting classes.

While I think of it, let me pass on this piece of church news. That is, if you are into this type of thing. I love this sort of history.

The church here belongs to a small group of what are called "The Sleeping Preachers" churches. They are the remnant of a Mennonite revival from the late 1870s when, in reaction to a rapid liberal drift, a few preachers developed an unusual method of delivering sermons called "spirit preaching." They would appear to fall asleep in the early evening, rising a few hours later in a trance to preach on the themes of repentance, spiritual renewal, and a return to simpler lifestyles.

This explains some of the unexpected characteristics of this Mennonite church. Because I'm interested in such things, Lonnie gave me some of the Sleeping Preachers sermons to read. I can't say I was very impressed, but they contain some good things. It explains why so many in this church are opposed to cameras and Sunday school. Both things were preached against strongly by the spirit preachers.

On other matters, I enjoyed the singing on Sunday evening, which was at another church. It reminded me of home, although that certainly didn't help my loneliness. There were around 450 people in attendance, and they started the evening with the whole group singing for fifteen minutes. After that, their Bible class of young people sang, followed by a choir of sixty men and women. To finish things off, the audience sang a few more songs. Most of the songs I didn't know, but all the singing was without musical instruments. The church belongs to the Apostolic churches.

Tuesday evening…

I just arrived home from school, and I am feeling somewhat better tonight, so maybe my depression of the past few days has run its course. Your last letter helped a lot. And that's just a bunch of baloney that there are nicer girls in the world than you. I certainly haven't seen such a girl yet—and know I never will. I always think that if God made anything better than you, He must have made it in heaven. And about not feeling worthy of me, I thought I was the one who felt that way.

When I arrived home, Luella was gone…and who knows where to. There was no note lying around, so I suppose she'll be back before too long.

Loretta, a school board member's wife, was at the schoolhouse this afternoon. We got to talking, and she said she has a confession to make. When she first heard they were hiring a male teacher, she said, "Oh no! Now the schoolhouse will look so bare." But I think she found out there are boys who also know how to decorate. I wish you could see the inside of the building. I feel more comfortable now that I had the children draw lots of pictures, cut them out, and hang them from the ceiling and paste them in the windows. It cheers the soul in this drab land of theirs, so barren of green trees.

The eighth graders didn't seem to know the first thing about percentages and decimals when we tackled the subjects today. Maybe they forgot them over the summer. Or it might be the arithmetic books they used last year weren't very clear. They have new ones this year.

I pray often that God will keep you, guarding and preserving our love until we meet again.

With all my heart,

Eugene

My dearest Eugene,

"Peace I leave with you, my peace I give unto you: not as the world giveth, give I unto you. Let not your heart be troubled, neither let it be afraid" (John 14:27).

Greetings of love. This finds me very sleepy and tired at only 6:45 p.m. I have supper ready and waiting. Mom and Dad should be in from chores before too long. I'm keeping the younger children away from the food right now, waving my hands about the kitchen table as if the children were flies. Little flies with two feet, I guess.

The threshing crew arrived early this morning, and they have been at it hard and heavy all day. The last of the men left not ten minutes ago. Thankfully, I didn't have to make supper for them because the large dinner at noon was enough work. But then I shouldn't complain. They do so much and so quickly. It would take Dad weeks working alone. By the way, Dad sends Don to help on the crew and gets his share in that way. Dad did help out here today, but it would be too much for him to do it day in and day out. Especially with the way the threshing crew works.

Your sister Mary said yesterday they took your sister Sharon to the doctor. She had a temperature of 104 degrees, and they couldn't get it down. The doctor said she has a kidney infection and gave her pills. Mary thought that would take care of things, but Sharon was still in bed the last I heard.

I hung new curtains in my room last week. Mom ordered them through the Sears catalog. They're light blue and very pretty, but a little fancy. Mom is afraid they're too fine. I guess I'll take them down if anyone complains.

Well, here come Mom and Dad in from the barn. They look tired, and I'm hungry enough myself to eat a horse.

Wednesday…

Here I am again on a nice quiet evening. I didn't have to work today, so I washed clothes. I finally got my poinsettias planted in pots again and up in my room. If I can get red flowers or bracts by Christmas, I'll be very happy.

Dad and Don aren't back from Wayne Helmuth's place yet. Dad was helping fill silo there today. I think he's working too hard, but he doesn't listen to me. I filled in for their chores, and now I have supper ready. The hardest thing was throwing down thirty shovels of silage. But it was still loose on top, not like it gets toward the bottom of the silo. There it's so tight I have to pick it loose with the pitchfork first.

I have to work for Mrs. Bach tomorrow afternoon and the afternoons of Saturday and Monday. Plans are for me to stay with John and their new dog, Buddy. I hope Mrs. Bach gives me some work so I won't get bored.

I received a letter from you today—the one with all the pupils' names and descriptions. That was very interesting. Now if you write me incidents from school, include their names. If I don't remember, I'll check back on who they are.

Your family hatched up the idea to invite Harvey and his family and themselves over to our place Friday evening and Mom agreed. The excuse is there were birthdays in September. It's mainly about supper for the old folks and playing volleyball for the young folks. I think the evening will seem empty without you.

Love and prayers,
Naomi

My dearest Naomi,

I had a big disappointment when I arrived home from school and there was no letter from you. Usually they come every two days. Today though, my hopes were dashed. I'm so lonesome for you, I wonder at times if I can endure it.

It's late already, and I'm just home from the volleyball game. The game cheered me a bit. Add to that, the sky was crystal clear for the walk home from the schoolhouse with a bright moon hanging low in the sky.

Since I've wanted to find old pieces of wood for the school nature display, Lonnie told me he has another farm with a woods on it about a twenty-minute drive from here. So tonight before the volleyball game, Lonnie and Luella took me there. What a lonesome feeling came over me at the sight of the countryside down there. It looks almost like home with the gravel roads, little creek, and woods. We even crossed a one-lane bridge.

In order to find my pieces, I climbed out of the truck to walk around in the woods for thirty minutes or so. I could have sat down and stayed all night. I'm not sure why, but it felt so good to be in the woods again. I did go down by the stream and sit for a few minutes, enjoying the flood of memories it brought.

Beside the stream I found what I was looking for—a small stump and two pieces of oddly shaped wood. I also gathered a bunch of acorns. Lonnie and Luella dropped me off at the schoolhouse so I could set the things up right away. Now I can sit at my desk after school is out and see a little bit of home and think of so many memories of you.

As always I look forward to your letters. Here is another poem.

The Words of Love

Your words are magic as can be.
They cross the world from you to me.
They bridge the distance I can't sail.
They heal my heart and tell their tale.

Oh, speak the words I long to hear,
Of love, and home, and hearts so dear.
Hush your howls, you heartless foes.
My love she comes, with words she shows.

Her hand, her heart, her gathered hush,
How does she still this worldly rush?
She reaches far o'er hill and plain,
To speak to me her words again.

With all my heart,
Eugene

Jerry and Tina Eicher

Dearest Eugene,

Hi!

Betsy, Rosanna, Don, and I have just finished playing volleyball. We used a piece of twine to represent the net. Don wanted to practice for tomorrow night when Harvey and your family come. We were playing pretty well when Don's friend Lester came by with his cart and horse. His horse shied from the ball flying around, so we stopped. It was time to quit anyway. I was out of breath and my hands were shaking, so I must have really gotten into the game.

Your mom told me last Sunday how lonesome she was for you. She asked if I had any news. I told her about your nature project, peanut butter making, and that you sent the pupils' names with their descriptions. I said I would let her read that letter tomorrow night, but I think it'd do her a lot of good if you'd write her a fat, newsy letter.

You'd be surprised how interested people are about everything. Rebecca Troyer told Betsy that if she were dating a teacher, she'd want the fellow to write and describe all the pupils. When Betsy told Rebecca you already had, Rebecca asked, "Oh, can I read it sometime?" So now the list is making its way around the girls who are Betsy's age.

I counted your letters today, and there are eleven. It seems like you have been away a lot longer than you actually have. Your mom said the same thing. When I said something in Rosanna and Betsy's presence about it, they had a good roar and little sympathy.

Dad said this morning we should surprise you and plan a trip out to visit. I said, "Well, go with me and his parents! We're planning a trip."

He asked when, and I said, "Around Thanksgiving maybe."

I doubt if they'll make it, but it's the thought that counts. And, of course, everyone else wants to go too, especially Betsy. She wants to visit your school with her bucket of curiosity!

Don also wants to come. Anytime someone goes where he hasn't been, he says he wants to go along. That boy likes to travel to as many different places as he can, but I think everyone is lonesome for you.

Dad finished filling silo today. I think that's the job all Amish farmers like the least, as it's sticky, hard, hot work.

Laddie, the colt, is growing like a beanstalk. I didn't know I could get so attached to an animal, but I figured if I ever did it would be with a horse.

I miss your horse, Frosty, too. Partly because she is linked to you, but also I liked Frosty the first time I saw her run. That was before I even knew she was your horse. I'd stand at the living room window where church was being held and watch this gorgeous horse coming down the road, lifting her feet high into the air. I wondered what it would be like to ride behind her. When one of the girls told me it was your horse, it was even more special. And by the way, I didn't start going with you just so I could ride behind your horse. Don't be getting any wrong ideas!

Friday evening, 10:30...

Harvey and his family and your parents have left after a very wonderful evening. Adam, Harvey's oldest boy, brought his girlfriend, Brenda, along. Anna had her sister Lydia Mae visiting at their house, so she also came.

Your family came at 6:30, and even though it had been a dreary, misty day, your brothers still set up the volleyball net and wanted to play. So we started. Harvey and his family arrived around 7:00, and we played until suppertime at 7:30. We ate, washed the dishes quickly, and then played again by the light of lanterns.

I don't know how many games we played, but on one round one team would win by a large margin, and the next round the other team would do the same thing. It was back and forth, with only one or two games even close. We did more laughing than anything. Your brother, Jared, plus Don, Betsy, and Adam were the clowns. Sometimes I'd be laughing, and the thought of you would cross my mind so it wouldn't be as funny anymore.

This evening I was sitting in the kitchen when I was reading your letter the first time. I laughed out loud at one part, and my was mom curious about what was so funny.

Also, can you give me more details about the "sleeping preachers"?

I finished rereading your letter again. It cheered me even more the second time. This sure has been a great day.

Well, it's 11:15, so goodnight.

I love you,
Naomi

My dearest Naomi,

This is Friday evening, and three weeks of school are now behind me. Not much time compared to what I have to go yet, but at least that's a start.

I'm invited out for supper tonight at one of the school board members' homes. Lonnie and Luella are also going. I like being kept occupied evenings with such things. Last night one of the young folk boys took me to a car show just to have something to do. Not that I'm interested in buying a car. They served free coffee and donuts, which were good. Most of the cars were antiques and quite valuable, I was told. They didn't look all that well made, with wire for wheels and flimsy tops.

Afterward, we stopped at a sale barn where they have an auction every two weeks, and will have one this Saturday evening. I hope to attend. Not to buy because I really don't need anything. Auctions are much more interesting than sitting around the house.

I'm sending you a copy of my schedule at school. Anything that involves reading, like the lower grades' reading class, social studies, and science is where the bulk of my time goes. The first grade has classes for writing and spelling, and everything has to be read to them since they can't read yet. Spelling takes two classes for them because they can't absorb all the instructions in one sitting.

Arithmetic and English quizzes have to be typed up. Arithmetic quizzes come out of the books, but I choose my own questions. English quizzes are also from the books, but the questions are supplied.

A lot of the extra work goes into the Bible lessons, which lack answer books. I have to come up with the answers, which I hope are all correct. If it weren't too much trouble, I'd ask the school board members to double-check them.

The school has an extra hour of school compared to where I taught before. The school day starts at 8:30 and goes until 3:30. I'm trying to get the school board to start thirty minutes later because I have a hard time keeping the children occupied that long. I have no problem being occupied, however. So I'll see what the board decides. What might swing things in my favor is they already switch to a 9:00 starting time when winter arrives. Hopefully my idea will carry.

I learned something new the other day at school. One of the children, Lacie, claimed that "stolon" is a word. I said it wasn't. She declared up and down her mom said it was. So off we went to the dictionary, and the child was correct. Poor teacher.

Saturday evening…

This finds me alone in the house again, and it's impossible to describe the lonely feelings I have. You would have to go through this yourself to understand. I received another of your welcome letters today, and it's always so heartwarming to hear that you still care for me. I have a problem at times believing anyone could love me, including God. I am constantly questioning my worth and coming up far short. I could never be good enough for God, or you, or anyone else. But I am trying hard to believe the fact that God cares for me even with all my faults. Maybe someday I'll have my faith strengthened and be strong enough to fully understand and absorb His love.

I will close this letter. If I've said too much, your wastebasket is always handy.

With all my love,

Eugene

My dearest Naomi,

This finds me happier than I have been since I came out here. The reason lies in the fact that I've just been told I will get to see you over the weekend. Oh, glorious thought! Lonnie and Luella didn't say anything to me about these plans until yesterday evening. They want to come out for a visit because they are anxious to see my home community. They thought a good time to do so would be over our communion, which is this weekend. Yippee…I shall see you soon! It's a good thing you mentioned when communion was going to be or I would never have known.

Last night was a school board meeting. It went really well. Since it was my first one, I was a little nervous, but there was nothing to it. For one thing, they don't have school meetings like the Amish do, where all the parents come, sit around, and take turns talking in public about their concerns. Here only the three board members attend on the first Monday evening of each month. Then twice a year there is a meeting where all the parents can come, bringing in food and playing games. During the course of the evening, each set of parents then has a chance to talk privately with the teacher.

Luella found a poem about a teacher, which she read to me the other evening, and Lonnie and I had a good laugh. The story was told to her about a teacher called Miss Blodgit who was going to spank one of her pupils. She had him stand up in front of her desk and had her stick all ready. Before Miss Blodgit started, she told the boy that if he would write a poem she wouldn't spank him. So the student quickly rattled this poem off:

> Here I stand
> Before Miss Blodgit.
> She's going to hit me,
> And I'm going to dodge it.
> —Anonymous

Janie and Amanda wanted in on the fun when Luella told them the story, so they tried to come up with a poem for me. I ended up helping them out, and this is what we came up with. Everyone got a big roar out of it.

Here I stand
Before Eugene, wary.
He's going to spank me,
And it's awful scary.

With love,
Eugene

My dearest Eugene,

Greetings of love!

I had a headache this morning, and I'm feeling like the flu is creeping up on me. Add to that, we are fasting this morning for communion next Sunday. I fixed breakfast for the younger ones, and I'm quite hungry.

I worked at Mrs. Bach's in the afternoon, and this time John went with her. That left me there alone except for the dog. Dad had been there this morning to do repairs and repaint the roof on their house. I don't think he finished painting, but the roof doesn't leak anymore, he said.

This evening Dad went somewhere to look at two horses—workhorses I think, so he must have next spring's work on his mind already. He isn't back yet, and it's 9:00. We had supper finished at 7:00. I washed the dishes and then walked down to Ada's to play Ping-Pong with Lester and Don. It was fun.

Thursday and Friday I have to work in Salem on my babysitting jobs, as usual. I hope those two days will go zooming fast, but I doubt it.

Well, since I can't find any more news to write I will sign off.

> I wish I could see you
> again right now,
> *Naomi*

OCTOBER

My dearest Naomi,

This finds me back from the weekend with you. You looked a little shocked when I walked in, and I can understand why because you'd just received my letter telling you I was coming. It was very, very good to see you. You already know of course, since I told you in person, but still I will say it again and again.

I am up in my room now, just home from school. I was longing to see you on the walk home—so much that it almost hurt.

The weather is balmy, with a nice wind out of the south. There were no clouds in the skies except my memories of you.

I'd better quit thinking about such things or I won't be able to write any more. You made me feel so loved that it continually sends warm circles around my heart.

Thank you.

And I love you,
Eugene

My dearest Eugene,

Greetings of love!

Thank you for a most enjoyable weekend. I can't put into words what those two days with you meant to me. When you left Sunday evening, I went into the house, turned out the light, and ran to the entrance window to watch you go out the lane in your buggy. As your buggy lights disappeared down the road, tears rolled down my cheeks.

This morning I heard someone blowing their horn as they went past on the road, and Mom hollered out, "There they go!" I quickly ran to the window and saw you before you were past Ada's place. I hadn't realized you'd be going past our place or I would've been looking for you.

I feel so empty now, but still when I think of the wonderful time we had and the joy of being with you, it also makes me happy. I guess maybe it's possible to be happy and sad at the same time.

Mom and I fall cleaned the upstairs today. I washed and ironed afterward. Mom is determined to get everything we started done today, so she's ironing now after supper at 7:30.

I still feel threatened by the flu bug, but thankfully it stayed away over the weekend. I think there is a lot of truth to the saying that when you're excited or happy, you're not nearly as apt to be sick or to give in to it as when you are sad or depressed. Oh, groans. I know it's coming now for sure.

Tuesday evening…

I'm still feeling depressed, and I just thought, "If I ever get married to Eugene, I'll be in heaven." That "if I ever" sounds rather hopeless, but a wedding seems such a long way off. The longing for you is very intense right now. To see your smile would be so wonderful. Do you have any idea how handsome you look when you are happy and smiling?

I still have this flu headache, but I went to work anyway. When I came home, I ate two apples with peanut butter. At least I still have my appetite. Peanut butter has some sugar in it, I think, so I felt a little chirped up.

Wednesday…

This is Wednesday morning at 9:30. I had a bad night and don't feel well at all this morning. Last night at 11:00, I woke with an extremely bad headache. I thought my head would split. This morning it isn't quite as bad. Mom said I shouldn't go to work. I'm determined not to miss work though, so I'm planning on going. Maybe I'll feel better by 1:00, when my ride arrives.

Mom went to the sewing this morning, so I'm in the house alone at the moment. I doubt if I'll go tonight to the youth gathering unless I feel a lot better. Tomorrow Mom, Rosanna, Betsy, and I want to go to Bloomington to shop at a neat little dry goods store. The reason is that Elena Marshall has wanted to take us for some time. She says she loves to go down there. It's supposed to be something awesome.

Mom asked this morning, "Do you think you can go tomorrow if you feel so bad?"

I replied, "I'm going regardless how I feel."

Always remember
I love you,
Naomi

My beloved Naomi,

I arrived home from school, took a long jog, and am sitting here writing to you still sweaty. I was greatly pleased and very surprised to find one of your wonderful letters waiting for me. I plopped right down to read it without cleaning up. I was hoping all day for a letter, but I tried to keep my hopes down because I thought another one probably wouldn't come until Friday at the earliest.

It means so much to me that you enjoyed the weekend. I told Lonnie to blow the horn when we went past. They both laughed at me because I was staring out of the truck window at your place. I'm sure I saw you inside the house, and that memory, along with the one of seeing you walk into the house as I was leaving on Sunday evening, still lingers in my mind.

On the way home we stopped in Peoria to go to the home office of the company that makes Lonnie's freedom phone. It's the kind of phone that works like a CB radio, and Lonnie's has been broken for some time. There's no one around their area able to fix it. Anyway, we had a hard time finding the phone place, driving all over that huge city. Once we did find them, they sent us someplace else for the repair. We ended up getting lost again and having to turn back a few times before locating it.

While Lonnie was inside talking with the repair people, I dashed next door to a hardware store for a flashlight purchase. I dropped mine and broke it last weekend when I was home. I'd also been keeping my eye open for a gift shop where I could buy cards because I'm completely out of them. They are very hard to find in our little town. There was no place nearby that sold cards. We did see a shopping mall later with a "Hallmark" sign on one of the stores. Luella spotted it, and Lonnie nearly wrecked as he cut across the lanes to reach the driveway. But we are all still alive, and I am loaded up on cards.

By that time it was 1:00, so we stopped at a Wendy's for lunch. I was starving and eagerly gulped down a burger, fries, and Frosty. Yummy, yummy. Lonnie said he had to have two Frostys to get over the fright Luella gave him as she directed him to the driveway for the card store. Luella, of course, claims it wasn't her fault at all, that she was only pointing toward the store.

Just think—when you next get a card from me—there was almost bloodshed buying the things. What an awful thought, but I'm feeling right awful at the moment.

I miss you,

Eugene

My dearest Eugene,

Mom, Rosanna, Betsy, and I came home from Bloomington at around four this afternoon. We left after five this morning, and my was it a blast! We browsed the stores, bought material, just did this and that and the other. Then we went to Dutch Kitchen for lunch. Betsy and I each ordered a shrimp basket. Betsy managed to eat all of hers, but I couldn't so I brought mine home and Dad ate the rest. Now he won't be hungry for supper, but he doesn't seem to mind. I guess my flu is still not over, as I feel a headache threatening again.

I should have been smart and stayed away from the youth gathering last night, but I decided to go at the last minute. My flu symptoms weren't too bad while we played volleyball. Especially with Don and Joseph Miller playing beside me. Don can be a real cutup, and he kept me laughing with his wisecracks.

We girls went inside early, but the host family offered nothing to eat but homemade ice cream and cinnamon rolls. Those are excellent tasting foods if I'd had other healthy things to eat earlier, but I didn't. Dan had told us to eat supper before we came, but I ignored the instructions since I was feeling yucky. Thankfully things didn't get out of hand, even with not eating. I would have cried if I'd ruined the trip into Bloomington for myself.

Robert was very sympathetic all evening at the gathering, which I thought was nice of him. When we were playing the last game, I must have looked pretty rough because Phillip Yoder said, "Well, Naomi, you can just go sit down and rest and think of Eugene."

Robert said, "You don't have to sit down to think about him, do you?"

And I said, "Certainly not."

It's always nice when people around you understand, especially boys. Please tell Lonnie and Luella "hi" for me.

Late evening…

Here I am again after writing you a letter this afternoon and getting it ready for tomorrow. I don't know exactly why I'm writing now except I'm so lonely for you. I don't know what's the matter with me. It seems so much harder to be apart from you since your trip back. Maybe it's because

I'm still not feeling well. I know it will be a great relief once I don't have this constant headache.

We bought three storybooks on the trip into Bloomington, and I've read one through already. Maybe I shouldn't read with my head throbbing, but it takes my mind off the pain—some of it anyway. I'm lying on my bed, holding my head with one hand, and writing with the other. My room is an absolute, total disaster and does nothing to revive my spirits. I suppose I will get things a little in order before I shut down for the night.

Dad and Mom went to the school meeting since they like to keep up with what's going on.

Friday afternoon...

I didn't go to work after all this morning because I still had my headache. Thankfully, it is somewhat better now. The young folks have something going tonight. They're going to make cider at the Harveys using hand presses. *Yah,* that should be fun, and we'll have cider to drink afterward. Don is driving tonight, and we'll leave right after chores.

How is school going? You haven't written anything about it recently.

I have to work tomorrow for Mrs. Bach because she wants to go somewhere again. That means John to take care of and that awful dog. Somehow I have to make friends with him, but he is a nasty creature with bulging eyes and chops that nearly drag the floor. I guess God made all creatures, and somewhere in the human heart there must be love hidden for all of them.

I long to see
you so much,
Naomi

My dearest Naomi,

Things are exceedingly boring around here. I often try to imagine what you might be doing. I dwell on the sweet memories of our last time together, which tends to make the situation worse instead of better. It seems like years since I've seen you.

My mom wrote yesterday. I followed your suggestion and sent her a fat letter. It's hard to imagine that my school news is interesting to anyone, but she thought it was. And that's about all the news I had to send her. She said she's sending books for me to read, and she also tried to give me a pep talk. Apparently some of my misery must have come through.

Last night the young folks attended services at a street mission fifteen miles from here. The place is open to anyone who needs meals and a bed for the night. There is one catch though. Before anyone stays for the night they have to attend an hour-long gospel service. When we arrived, there were around thirty men sitting inside, looking like a tough bunch. They had the men sitting on one side, and the visitors on the other. One of the young folk boys presented a devotion, and the whole youth group sang for twenty minutes. Afterward, Stanley, one of the married men who came along, gave a thirty-minute sermon.

I think I would like working in a place like that. It would give a worthwhile feeling to help people who have so terribly lost their way. Especially people who are living out on the streets.

I hope you are keeping yourself entertained and that the flu bug has passed on by now. The best to you.

Love you,
Eugene

Jerry and Tina Eicher

Hello, dear Eugene,

How does this find you? Well and happy, I hope.

Don, Dad, and Lester went fishing at the Yoders' pond tonight. They left with the open buggy. Brrr…it's pretty chilly and cloudy. They're planning to fish till late. I can't see what is so fun about fishing, but they were all excited.

Last night was a beautiful evening, but according to how I was feeling it should have been raining cats and dogs. I cried upstairs with my head under the pillow for a long time so Mom couldn't hear me. It must be the aftereffects of that nasty flu spell I had.

To top things off, I had a big disappointment tonight when I arrived home. Boo hoo…no letter from you. I will try to wait patiently.

You might not have much news to write about, but it would've been great just to hear from you. Maybe it is better I don't have you around at the moment since I'm fighting back the tears. But having you here would make them go away, wouldn't it? Yes, it would. Now I'm really crying, and it's all your fault.

I had to struggle against tears more than a few times today, and I almost cried in public, which was a new experience for me. Usually when I'm around people I'm not bothered with the threat of tears. Thankfully things got better as the day progressed. Perhaps I shouldn't be telling you this, lest you think there's something seriously wrong with me or with our relationship. There's not. It's just that I'm so sad and can't really explain why. I hope you can understand.

Church was at Bishop Enos's, and the young folks had a short singing in the afternoon for some of the old people who live in town. Dad didn't want me taking our horse Vick because he's lame, so we hitched up the younger one. I don't think Dad would have let me drive him without Don along. Can you believe that?

I didn't want to go at all, really, not with such sorrow hanging over my head, but I thought it'd look silly if I didn't. When we walked out to the buggy, I wavered again at the thought of the drive into town.

I said to Don, "Listen, I don't feel very well, and I'd rather stay home. So why don't you go by yourself?"

Don shrugged because he didn't care one way or the other either. Betsy, who was also going, threw a fit. But I still wouldn't have gone if Adam and

Brenda, with Julia riding with them, hadn't driven up right then. They saw I wasn't planning to go. Adam said, "Oh, come on, Naomi!" and this and that until I climbed into our buggy. We caravanned to the gathering.

After we arrived, we walked all over town, stopping to sing at only two places because nobody else was at home. So my instincts had been correct. I should have stayed home.

Guess what? We have received a wedding present already. Someone I used to work for gave us a silver tea set. He said he wanted to give it to me when I married, but now he is getting married. They have two of everything, so he thought he'd give me the present now. That's strange since his place is the one I liked to work at the least.

I used to clean for him before I started dating you. His first wife was still living then, and they had the messiest house you ever saw. Anyway, I never thought I'd own something that's made of silver.

Tuesday evening…

I received one of your longed-for letters today. When Mom told me yesterday that it was a mail holiday because of Columbus Day, I was quite disappointed. You don't know how much I look forward to your letters.

You did scare me a little because you sounded so down. Is everything okay? I'm glad you continue writing regardless of how you feel.

When I think of how much you love me, I certainly don't feel worthy of it—more overwhelmed than anything else. I was happy to hear that you think God still forgives us of our faults because He surely does, otherwise there would be little hope for any of us.

The young folks are going to sing on Friday night for an *Englisha* neighbor, Mr. Burns, who has cancer. That should make for an interesting and worthwhile time.

Oh no! I have gotten carried away with my writing. It's past ten already. Nine was supposed to be my self-imposed deadline for bed tonight.

By the way, I don't get bored with your letters, and the longer they are the better. My love will never cease for you, and you should never fear. I also treasure the memories of our times together. I just can't write the way you do, but you have to remember that the very things you treasure about me, I also treasure about you. In a different way, no doubt, but I treasure them all the same.

Jerry and Tina Eicher

I could go on writing if I had the right words, but I don't. So good-night for now.

I love you,
Naomi

Dearest Naomi,

I was surprised and thrilled at finding another letter from you when I arrived home tonight. Your letters mean so much to me, and I look for them with great eagerness. And interestingly enough, the last two got switched around somehow, so I guess the mailman isn't perfect. I also received the card today, which is very beautiful.

Did I tell you the second batch of sparrows from the school project were dead the other morning? They died suddenly overnight for no known reason, so I have given up. There will be no more sparrows.

The mouse is doing fine, though, but we still haven't caught anymore. The children are still looking. Perhaps the survival rate of this one is higher because it is a field mouse. I caught a house mouse in Lonnie's garage last week with a live trap. I put it in with the field mouse. They spat at each other and looked ready for murder, so I didn't dare leave them together even for one night. So that venture failed. I took the house mouse outside and let it go.

Today I had Dena, one of the eight-graders, take some of the minor responsibilities off my shoulders. She had free time and looked bored, so I had her take the first graders to the blackboard to practice writing and recognizing the numbers from 1 to 1000.

Tomorrow I will work with them myself. I prefer that rather than letting someone else do it, but today I had social studies and that's always a hassle. So while I was up front teaching fifth grade social studies, Dena was at the board on the other end of the room writing down numbers for the first graders.

I was trying to keep my eyes on both places at the same time, glancing back and forth. When we had finished checking papers and were ready to read, I told the class to start. While I was looking back at the board, absorbed in watching what they were doing, the fifth-grade class burst out laughing. I quickly snapped my gaze back to them. They were wanting to know who was supposed to read next but noticed I was intent on looking at the first-grade class in back. They got a good laugh out of that.

Little Lydia has had an awful time with her vocabulary, struggling with even the simplest of words. On the fourth lesson this year, her grade was down in the forties. I took her aside that day, telling her that it's time to do something about the problem. The poor girl. I asked her why she doesn't look up the words in the dictionary, and she said, "Because I don't understand what it says." She didn't say it sassily, but in her usual cheerful manner, as if things simply were so and nothing could be done about it.

I have been going over the words with her the last two weeks, showing her how to match them up in the dictionary and explaining the words she doesn't understand. From her improved grade this week, I believe that aid helped. The fact that she doesn't know words shows up in reading class. Today we were reading in social studies, and she didn't know what "rapid" meant.

Well, it's about 6:00 so Luella will have supper ready soon. Tomorrow morning Lonnie and Luella will be fasting because they have communion on Sunday. I'll fast too, even if I'm not participating in communion.

With all my heart
and love,
Eugene

My dearest, beloved Eugene,

This letter finds me tired and feeling so-so. Ada brought us two jugs of cider from the young folks' cider pressing the other night. I knew it was good because I had some that evening. Now Dad wants popcorn to go with it, so I'll bring the popper out soon. This will be a popcorn and cider night around here.

Don went with the young folks to sing at the *Englisha* neighbor's place. I finally gave out, and said I wasn't going since I didn't feel well. I guess I need another good letter from you to cheer me up, but there was none in the mailbox today.

We're supposed to have frost in the morning. The weather is so unpredictable this time of year, we never know what it is going to do next. Tomorrow, if it's still nice, Betsy and I are planning to help Elena Marshall rake her leaves and get her flowerbeds fixed up.

Rumor has it that Richard and Joan are planning to begin milking by spring. He's already doing work on the barn. They moved to a place on the south side of the community. I don't see how in the world they can afford to start milking, but Don said Richard gets $16 an hour for painting jobs, so he must have money saved up. Dad says it's hard for young people to start out farming and make a go of it with the way milk prices are.

Robert's Rosemary had the flu bad enough she had to be in the hospital for a day, but she's older, so maybe that was the reason she had such a bad case. I am good and depressed as I battle the flu bug, but thankfully there is no need for hospitalization. That's not really funny, I know.

I miss you so much. I sit here thinking how nice it would be to see you and have a good talk again. One of the girls who is dating talked with me last Sunday evening. She thinks it's bad when she doesn't get to see her boyfriend throughout the week. I could have laughed at her, but I remember I used to feel the same way. I told her you don't know how glad you can be to see someone until you actually experience a long separation.

I don't know what more to write except to remind you that I love you very, very much.

How I miss you,
Naomi

My dearest Naomi,

"We are troubled on every side, yet not distressed; we are perplexed, but not in despair; persecuted, but not forsaken; cast down, but not destroyed" (2 Corinthians 4:8-9).

It's around noon. I have been at the schoolhouse the whole forenoon working on report cards. Last Saturday Lonnie had me painting the barn buildings, but today he had fieldwork to do. Partly because of that and partly because of report card week, I'm here at work on a Saturday.

School has been in session for six weeks now, which means it's seven weeks since I left Indiana. That seems like ages, dear, and if God hadn't given me the strength to bear it, I know it would have been even harder.

I counted the other day, and there are ten more weeks until Christmas and seventeen weeks of school after that. But who wants to think of that mountain still to climb?

Most of the pupils are getting good grades, but I don't think it's because of me. They are smart pupils. Lydia has really improved in vocabulary for the last two grades sessions. I continue to keep a close eye on her and help where I can. It seems she may be catching on. I sure hope so. Her average in vocabulary for the six weeks came out to sixty-six. Seventy is the dividing line. I sometimes make them redo something that goes below that, but for vocabulary I never have. Mostly because it's in workbook form, and they can use dictionaries so there's no need for second chances.

Yesterday I had a little episode with one of the first graders. Brandon and Mark are always laughing with each other and carrying on while they're supposed to be working. This time they were showing each other their work and having a great laugh over it. I told Mark to quiet down, but I had no sooner turned around then he was going into high gear again. I thought of telling him if he didn't quit I would do something—I wasn't sure what. But a teacher shouldn't threaten, I figured. I didn't say anything, allowing them to carry on while I tried to think what I could do.

I had a spelling class in session, so it wasn't the best time to deal with anything else. When that class was over, I settled on a solution. The children have seats that can be moved around, and Mark sits in the front row. So I walked up behind him while he was carrying on. He didn't see me coming. I took the back of his chair in my hands and turned him around so he faced backward. I whispered in his ear that this was his punishment for not being quiet. Also, I said this way he didn't have to turn around to talk with his friends.

He put his head down on his desk, burying his face in his arms. I left him there for five minutes or so before turning him back around. It worked quite dandily, if I must say so myself. He was quiet for the rest of the day and hasn't had discussions with his classmates during schooltime since.

Sunday afternoon...

It's 4:00, and we had visitors for dinner. They are still downstairs talking with Lonnie and Luella. Tonight some of the young people are attending the singing at the church we went to last month. I'm really looking forward to going again. I think it's the same deal as last time. Some of the young folks aren't going because they want to stay and play volleyball. I want to hear the singing.

One of the visitors today for dinner was a girl who attends Goshen College. She spent some time in Central America working in the missions communities. She could talk some Spanish, she said.

The younger couple had a little girl along, about three years old or so. All during dinner the man made the biggest fuss over her, cooing and giving her attention. She was kind of cute, so I could understand why.

They had communion at church today. They do everything the same as we do except it's in a much shorter time span. Church started at 9:30, which is thirty minutes earlier than usual, with a short devotional following. The bishop got up next, starting right in on the main sermon. He doesn't give the sermon from memory. He read from the twenty-sixth chapter of Matthew, straight through the crucifixion story, doing very little expounding.

When they pass the bread around, two ministers walk through the congregation with plates, breaking off pieces from the loaf and handing the bread to people in their seats. For the wine they did the same thing, two ministers passing the cup, one for the men's side, and one for the women's side.

The foot washing was done in about the same time frame. Everything was over by 12:10, which is much sooner than the usual 4:00 in the afternoon for an Amish communion service.

I don't think I told you that we went for a walk on Thursday with the schoolchildren. It was my attempt at breaking their boredom. That would be *theirs,* not mine. They don't have nearly as much work as I do. On the way, we picked up small things for the nature table—fall leaves, oak branches, and berry twigs.

By the way, I did get more sparrows in again. One of the schoolchildren brought one in yesterday and two today. I should have stood my ground because one died already, the poor thing, but the other two seem to be eating well, so maybe they will survive.

I miss you, dear.

Eugene

Dearest Eugene,

Greetings in our dear Savior's name.

This finds me up in my room writing away. I walked home this afternoon from church soon after the second batch of people were at the tables because I made it in on the first round. You never know how things will go. There have been times when I haven't gotten on until the third table, especially if the house is a little small, and they can't set up a lot of tables.

By the way, your sister Heidi said all the females at their house have been on diets all week, which depressed me. I guess I should go on one, but who likes diets? I'll just try to watch my eating closer. That will do it, hopefully.

I spent some time outside this afternoon leading Laddie around. I can tell from the look in Dad's eyes he's seeing dollar signs from the coming sale of the colt, which has to happen, I know. I've gotten really attached to him, that's all.

There was an *Englisha* boy at church today. One of the girls said his name is Darrell Hooley, and that he's staying at Harvey's place. He wants to join a community and is checking out the possibilities.

Daniel and Lydia are really going on with their courtship. At least according to what the others say. It's said that they're acting like they're already going steady, and I suppose they will be pretty soon. Don said Friday night that he saw them together as much as the other steadies, if not more. I say good for them, as it suits me just fine. I think they make a good pair, and you never had any business dating Lydia in the first place, whatever your excuse was. There, that is said.

Some news events this Sunday were as follows. Sharon, Martha, and Ruth all had cape and apron suits on for the first time. On the singing front, someone must have decided it was time because David Miller sang the praise song for the first time. John Yoder had to start the first line for him, though. David didn't do too badly from then on, but his voice was rather weak. I suppose I'd be a bit weak too if I had to do the song. I miss the power and beauty of your voice when you led the praise song. I cried a little in the middle of the song thinking about it, but then I stopped when I became afraid someone would notice.

Melvin and Johnny were here today as visiting ministers from the other district. Johnny had the first part and Melvin the second. I appreciate the way Johnny preaches. He is meek and includes himself in what he says. He often stresses the point that we are not to be too hard on other people but to look at ourselves first. I often wish I could be more like that. His daughter Barbara is such a good example. You hardly ever hear her talking about or putting other people down to the last notch.

Stan Yoder's family and the Richards are leaving for a sudden Montana trip on Tuesday. It's for a visit to relatives, though I don't know how long they will stay.

Today we had a really beautiful day, with the first frost on the ground this morning. I miss you awfully, especially after the praise song episode. I didn't feel like I could smile all day, and when I did, the attempt felt plastic. We girls sat behind the men, and I watched the young wives as they brought their children to their husbands. I thought how great they had it that they can be together practically all the time. I also thought about what our children would look like, perhaps a little like you or a little like both of us? Would he be calm or active?

I hope it won't be too many weeks until I can see you. What a joy that will be, even though the pain of parting will be hard again.

I love you dearly,
Naomi

My dearest Naomi,

"A bruised reed shall he not break, and the smoking flax shall he not quench" (Isaiah 42:3). I have been repeating this verse a couple of times a day. It's a great comfort to me, showing us how God deals with those He loves.

I received your letter today, the one you wrote on Friday evening. You say so many nice things, all of which warm my heart.

There was a letter from my mom today. I guess she wants to keep checking up on me. But I suppose that's what moms are all about.

I have some questions for you to answer sometime...whenever you get to it.

> No. 1: What do you see as the most important thing that you want out of marriage?

> No. 2: What do you mean when you say "I love you"?

I'm kind of blue right now, but I hold you very close to my heart. Take care, and I will write more some other day.

And I love you,
Eugene

Hello, my dearest Eugene,

Oh, what a day! I feel like I've been run through the mill. We had hay this evening—two loads of it. Dad drove the baler, dropping the hay on the ground. Betsy drove the team, while Don stacked the wagon. Rosanna and I pitched the bales up. There was so much trouble with the baler that we didn't get the whole field done. Now our elevator isn't working, so Don drove right into the barn, throwing the bales up to us in the mow by hand. Talk about work…dragging those bales around. Ugh!

Mom and Betsy helped in the haymow for a while, but Mom is older and Betsy is a young girl, so Don and I ended up doing the second load by ourselves. I guess I shouldn't complain because the bales were lighter than they are sometimes.

Betsy and Larry received their report cards today. Betsy did really well, all A's except for one B. Larry did exactly the opposite: Two D's, and one F, the rest C's. We were all very disappointed, the poor guy. He's different from the rest of us, but I say that even if he isn't so good at school, that doesn't mean he won't be a success in life. He takes a great interest in growing things, and I think he definitely will make a good farmer.

The preachers are having problems with James Yoder again, and this after everyone thought the problem with his Calvinist beliefs had been resolved. I could see when the ministers came downstairs last Sunday morning that something was bothering them. Bishop Enos called a members' meeting after church. He said they hope to settle some of these points satisfactorily with James in the next two weeks.

Melvin's wife told Mom that she has never pitied the ministers more. This seems to be a very hard case for everyone to handle. There are whispers going around that maybe the ministers aren't handling things correctly, but I've decided for myself that I will definitely stand by the ministers. Also, I'll try not to be hard on James or his family, and fast and pray for both.

Earlier in the afternoon, Mom and I drove up to visit Della at the hospital. She seems to be getting along fairly well. She had some sort of opening made in her stomach, like her brother Floyd did the other year, but at least she doesn't have cancer. The problem was a blockage caused by an ulcer, whatever that is.

The mail service is a little twisted, I think. Today I received your card and also a letter. But nevertheless I was glad for both. I just reread them. Thanks so much for the card.

I placed a letter in the mail today and would like to put this one out tomorrow, but I'll wait till Wednesday, I think. That way you'll get a longer letter.

Wednesday morning…

Here I am again. I want to hurry and finish this letter before the mailman goes. This is a very windy, cloudy, rainy, dreary morning, so maybe it'll hurry up and get cold enough to snow.

Dad, Don, and Larry went to the Worthington livestock auction last night, taking two of our cows along. Neither was worth much. Now we are down to milking eight, but still have two heifers who should deliver their calves soon.

My mom picked up your mom yesterday morning. They went to Leann's place for a coffee break, they said. The real reason was Mom wanted to pick up a quilt. I don't know what your mom's reasons for going were. Maybe she just wanted to visit.

Tonight the young folks have a gathering at Monroe's to clean up, since he and his wife have purchased a new place.

We finally got the last load of hay in yesterday evening. Afterward, Rosanna, Betsy, Mom, and I were sitting in the living room resting, discussing, of all things, what names I want to give my children. Rosanna and Betsy were offering all kinds of suggestions. Suddenly Betsy said, "Wouldn't Eugene laugh if he could hear us?"

I'm sure you would have. But it's good that we're planning on having lots of children because we came up with some really nice names for them.

Mom had a letter from one of her sisters in northern Indiana. Their boy Edward is getting worse and worse with his *rumspringa* behavior. He even parked his car right beside the house! Why his parents allow it, I don't know. Rosanna said that if her child parked a car beside the house, she would smash the windshield. But I doubt if she really would, once the time came.

Keep looking up! Remember, my thoughts and prayers are often with you. I'm so lonely without you. I love you with all my heart.

Again, I love you,
Naomi

My dearest Naomi,

Tomorrow the bookmobile is coming, so that meant we had to get all the books in order today. Each child has to have the books at his or her desk ready to turn in. The children took out around 150 books the first time, so that's a lot of books to keep track of. From what I can tell, everyone has the books back at school rather than lost at home somewhere. To help, I had written all the titles belonging to each child on a separate piece of paper. Last week we checked all the pages, and we went through the whole thing again today.

Dena has been doing well with the first graders. She practices and practices with them on the blackboard, working on numbers from 1 to 1000. I've also worked with them some, and they are learning—slowly.

Poor Laverne's asthma has been acting up lately. I don't know if it's the weather or what. He gets to wheezing and coughing so badly. But he's a tough little boy and won't give up. Everyone feels sorry for him. His family takes good care of him. His older sister Velma, who's in the seventh grade, is like a mother hen when it comes to her brother. Laverne talks to me sometimes, but not about his condition. He tries hard to live life as other people do.

This morning Lydia brought a salamander to school. She said her dad caught it and put it into a can for her. She wouldn't touch it. I had to get it out and put the creature in the gallon can where the foxtails are. The can is filled almost to the top with dirt, but I didn't figure it would crawl out.

Then Crystal came in and saw it. She said, "What if that thing gets out? If it does, I'm not coming to school tomorrow."

Of course, you can guess what happened. Just before recess Velma pointed down to the floor—and there it was. It ended up causing a minor panic. Everyone looked to where Velma was pointing, and almost at once several of the girls clambered to the top of their desks. The hardier girls and the boys helped me chase the creature, but it got away. There will be no more salamanders in school.

I had a run-in with Dena today in English class. I didn't know she could be so sure of herself. The class had active and passive verbs. When the subject does the acting it is active, if not it's passive. After marking whether the sentence was active or passive, they were to rewrite the sentence with the opposite voice. Here is the sentence in question: "Several boys have already completed the projects."

Boys are completing the projects, so it is active. The rewrite could possibly be "The projects of several boys have been completed." Dena wrote, "The projects have already been completed by several boys," which I thought was still active.

Dena claimed her version was passive, so now I am doubting myself. Anyway, write me what your opinion is. I would be interested.

With all my love,
Eugene

Jerry and Tina Eicher

My dearest Naomi,

I reread one of your letters from a while back, where you watched the married couples and thought how wonderful they had it being together all the time. Well, that will be wonderful, but we have to wait, I guess.

The news about the trip to Montana I had heard before—maybe you told me. That sounds like fun though.

The bookmobile arrived on schedule today. We had eaten lunch fifteen minutes earlier than usual so we would be ready, but it still came before we were done. I took the lower graders out first. I stayed inside the school-house while the upper graders went by themselves. Four lower graders weren't in school today, so I took their books out myself. I didn't get new books for them though. They didn't tell me to, and it will make less work rounding up books next time the bookmobile comes.

Anything out of the ordinary routine makes extra work, I'm finding out. Even if one student doesn't show up, the next day the lessons have to be explained all over again. Even though most of the grades only have two or three pupils, that still adds up.

Larry, from third grade, has been absent for the past three days. He's the slowest in the class, but a nice boy otherwise. My guess is he's helping out on the farm, but that wasn't the reason given to me.

Because of the bookmobile we skipped arithmetic and reading today, leaving more time to spend on social studies. I also knew the students would want time to get into their new books. Only two of the first grad-ers were in attendance, so I only had phonics class for them. I would have liked to have reading class, but I thought it would be a waste of time with only two here.

We have another decorating project going on. We're coloring three new scenes to hang from the ceiling. Tomorrow we'll start in earnest. On Saturday I should have time to exchange the new cutouts for what's up there now—birds. What I'm putting up is a pumpkin with fruit lying beside it, also a cornstalk and a scarecrow. They're supposed to be Hal-loween scenes, as the Mennonites do that kind of thing—at least around here.

I've never gotten around to telling you how much I enjoyed the singing Sunday evening. This time a group of young people sang—seven girls and eight boys. The sound of their voices was so beautiful. I guess I love music.

Thursday evening...

I came home at 5:00 tonight because I had to gather the eggs. Lonnie and Luella have gone visiting at the hospital. Lonnie's mother has lung cancer and isn't doing well. I didn't receive any letters from you today, so I reread two of your old ones.

It seems I've been working harder to get my subjects through at school the past few days. I'm not sure why. The year I taught four grades, I used to have arithmetic and English class in the forenoon. Now I'm trying to put seven grades through in the same time period. There are, of course, fewer pupils in each grade, which helps.

The three upper grades are getting into some difficult arithmetic work. I think that's mainly what's taking the extra time. They started on decimal points and are struggling to understand how percentages work.

Then to really mess things up, I had to go and give the seventh graders the wrong instructions. While I was explaining the math lesson, I thought something was wrong but couldn't figure out how else to do it. The book gave no instructions for the section, and I'd worked out only one problem. Instead of finding the volume of a sphere, I ended up telling them how to find the area of a circle. I called the class back up, and we got things straightened out.

Another area I struggled with was explaining simple, complex, and compound sentences. A simple sentence has only one clause, a complex two—one dependent and one independent. A compound sentence has two clauses with both being independent. That's how I explained it at first.

But the students were calling simple sentences complex and complex sentences simple. The compounds were not a problem. I figured out that it's almost impossible to tell whether a sentence has two clauses, one dependent and the other independent just by reading it. Rather, you first separate out each clause by identifying it by the subject and verb, then you see whether it can stand on its own. So now we use that approach, and things are going much better. So much for the teacher making things clear.

I wish you were here.

With all my love,
Eugene

Dearly beloved Eugene,

Thought: "Do nothing you don't think Jesus would do." I've been thinking on these words the last couple of days, and I think it's a good motto. It's also very hard to do. I know because I've been trying, and half the time I forget. I get mad at myself, but I think it makes me try all the harder.

Mom is going to northern Indiana tomorrow. Harvey and his family and Eli and his family are going up for a funeral, and they asked both Mom and Dad to go along. Dad is too busy with the farmwork, so he's staying.

I worked for Elena Marshall today. She wants me one day a week for a while until she gets caught up. I didn't promise anything, as I don't know how my schedule will go. It's kind of full already.

Betsy was sick yesterday, throwing up I don't know how many times. Ada came up last night to see if we have any stomach remedies for her children, so they must have it too. Today Betsy must have been some better because she walked to school. I hope it's not something that will get passed around. I, for one, don't want it.

There was a young folks gathering last night, and Don and I went. They had an ice cream social and volleyball, of course. It was held at Harvey's place for the *Englisha* man whom I told you about, Darrell Hooley. He has apparently spoken with Bishop Enos and is serious about joining. He's the funniest guy I've been around in a long time. He had us all laughing at his stories about his work at the hospital.

I didn't get a letter from you today, but one came yesterday. My, you sound blue, and you sure asked some hard questions. As I read over them, I could have said "I don't know" to both of them. I have never analyzed how or what I want in marriage, but I will try now.

"What do I see as the most important thing that I want out of marriage?"

For one thing, you have to realize I'm different from a lot of girls. I was very independent before I met you. And I wasn't so sure what in the world was so great about getting married. Well, you made me change my mind drastically.

I think, though, I'll have to be married for a while before I really know what is the most important thing I want out of marriage. But as for what attracts me to it, the answer is really quite simple—*you.* To be with you, to share everything with you, and to know you even better. That's the best answer I can give for now. Ask me again after we've been married a few years!

"What do I mean when I say 'I love you'?"

Well, I mean just that. *I love you*. Remember that motto you once gave me? "Life's a beautiful mystery…We sometimes forget that lying at the foundation of human life is a beautiful mystery—love. Many try to describe it, many say they understand it, but it belongs to those who live it. So never forget to love."

I agree with that. I can't explain it except to say that my love is a deep affection for you—and even more than that, it's a respect and a faith I have in you. And trust too. I hope that makes sense and answers your question. The truth is, I just love you, and I don't really have the wisdom to explain it. I can only say that I'm grateful to share this beautiful mystery with you.

Now, would you answer these same questions for me?

And on the other topic—you said you were at a loss to know why your pupils are getting good grades. Well, you may have smart pupils, but they also have a very good teacher!

Yours,
Naomi

My dearest Eugene,

Hello. It is late already, like 10:00 p.m., but I will write a few sentences anyway.

I will be babysitting for Chris Van on Monday for a few hours in the forenoon. That's a new job I picked up this week, and think I'll really like it. They have three small children, one of whom is handicapped.

This forenoon I husked corn with Dad, Don, and Larry on the field we didn't use for silage. I enjoyed the work although it tired my arms. It does get me out of the house and into the open fields.

I'm sorry to hear about Laverne's troubles, the poor little guy. I think it's very important for a teacher to really love his pupils because they sense it when you don't.

About the sentence that you and Dena disagreed on. I can kind of see her point too, but I think you are right.

Sunday evening…

None of us went to the hymn singing tonight, which was at Stan Miller's house. Don didn't want to go, and I didn't care one way or another, so here we are. Dad stayed home today from church since he woke with an earache and couldn't hear unless Mom faced him and talked close to his ear.

When we arrived home from church, he could hear better again, so the morning's rest must have done some good. The reason he's under the weather? Yesterday he drove the wagon home from an auction north of Oden, where he purchased a new hay baler. The trip was at least twenty miles, and Dad was chilled to the bone. He could have called a driver to take him up and haul the baler home, but I imagine he wanted to save money.

Elena Marshall came by this afternoon and talked with Mom for a long time about the marriage problems she's having with her husband, Bob. She claims he's verbally abusive when things get tense. I guess they are both receiving counseling from their pastor, so perhaps things will get better for them soon. I think they both need our prayers.

Hearing about marriage problems doesn't improve my feelings tonight.

I felt very lonely, and now I'm a little scared. But don't worry. I know you're a good man and would never abuse me.

All my love and prayers,
Naomi

My dearest Naomi,

"Come unto me, all ye that labour and are heavy laden, and I will give you rest. Take my yoke upon you, and learn of me; for I am meek and lowly of heart: and ye shall find rest unto your souls. For my yoke is easy, and my burden is light" (Matthew 11:28-30). Verses like this are what I fill my mind with when I get discouraged. It's very comforting to know God is always ready to forgive.

The other morning at the schoolhouse I was reading 1 John 1:8, where it says, "If we say that we have no sin, we deceive ourselves, and the truth is not in us." I knew that I couldn't say that I had never sinned. I guess no one else can say it either, so that gives no one the right to think that he or she is better than anyone else.

It's hard for me to face someone in a direct confrontation, and this flaw of mine has shown up in my dealings with the eighth-grade girls. They are both confident of themselves and have no problem questioning my actions if it disagrees with their opinions. This is a good thing, I guess. If I'm wrong, I'm wrong, but if I'm right, I'm right. The difficult part is telling them so. Oh well, I will have to try.

Last Friday night the young folks had a volleyball game at a gym they rent. It costs fifteen dollars for the evening, but when you split the amount between twenty-four people, it isn't too bad. At least that was the plan, but when it came time to figure what each person's share was, no one had pencil and paper. Someone suggested it should be fifty cents, and we'd call it close enough. I tried to do the math in my head and came up with sixty-two or sixty-three cents, so I told them fifty cents wouldn't come close.

They talked a while, and the final decision was to have everyone pay sixty cents. When I got back home and checked it on the calculator, sixty times twenty-four only gives $14.40, so someone had to make up the difference. It was a confusing mess anyway, with people throwing in bills and coins and trying to get their forty cents back. They should come up with a better system.

I caught another mouse at school yesterday, chasing it out from under the schoolhouse bookcase, so now we have two. But don't tell anyone the schoolhouse has mice. They will blame me for setting the thing loose in the first place, and I had nothing to do with it.

This one was a field mouse, so the two were still eyeing each other when I left the schoolhouse. The plan may not work anyway. The sparrows are fine though.

With love,

Eugene

My dearest Eugene,

"I will praise thee, O Lᴏʀᴅ, with my whole heart; I will shew forth all thy marvellous works. I will be glad and rejoice in thee: I will sing praise to thy name, O thou most High" (Psalm 9:1-2).

That says pretty much how I feel tonight. Today I worked for Chris Van, or rather babysat for her in the forenoon. I absolutely loved it. Zack—he's the Down syndrome kid—will be three in February. Florence is a very lively two-year-old. They are both very intelligent, each in their own way. Chris also has a girl named Jeri, who is eleven and was in school. Anyway, all I had to do was play with them. They were so well behaved. They didn't cry or even complain when Chris went out the door. Chris has really impressed me. She and her husband are Christians, and she seems like a very devoted mother.

I think this job will help make my winter a little shorter. Oh yes, they live close to our dentist in Worthington. Chris comes to pick me up and drops me off, so I don't have to worry about a driver.

This afternoon Lydia Gingerich, two of your sisters, and I went school visiting. Kathryn and Aaron teach this year, which you probably know. Kathryn's side of the schoolhouse was all cheery and decorated with flowers. She has the upper graders, and Betsy has had nothing but praises to sing for her teaching. At recess Aaron asked me if you still write to me every day. I told him you hadn't for a good while, but that you wrote a couple times a week. He said you do a lot better than he used to when he dated his wife, Lily, and that he thought that you were a writer—or at least that you like to write.

I think you are a very good writer. You know how to express yourself so that it sounds decent. Not like me at all.

Well, it sounds like Dad got the water motor fixed. It conked out this afternoon. He had to go after a new battery in Worthington while Mom and I did the chores. I don't mind doing chores. It's almost an escape for me. You probably don't understand this, but when I'm in the house day after day after day with only brief trips outdoors, I start feeling like a caged animal.

That man you wrote about who came to dinner and had a fit over his cute little girl. That was really sweet of him. I can imagine you doing that with one of our children. There, I dared say it in a letter, but don't mention it when you see me again. I'm kind of shy about such things, but then you know that already.

Tuesday evening...

I had a great day at work, coming home in plenty of time to help with the chores.

At church things continue to fall apart with the James Yoder situation. He apparently attended an *Englisha* service on Sunday. They say Bishop Enos is almost physically ill over the whole situation.

Mom heard all of this today when they were cleaning at Monroe's new place. Someone even thought that James's wife, Millie, had considered going with James to the *Englisha* church, but she was talked out of it at the last minute by Bishop Enos's wife. Millie claims she just feels numb and doesn't know what to do. I feel so sorry for them all.

Tomorrow forenoon Betsy and I are going to see Mrs. Ballenger to help her clean her flowerbeds, lawn, and windows. Then in the afternoon I have to work for Mrs. Bach. In the evening the young folks are supposed to husk their popcorn plot. Don and I are definitely going since we weren't at the singing. If Don backs out on me, I will drive myself. Husking popcorn in the dark will be fun. It would be even more fun if you were here, so look what you're missing out on. But now I'm being mean.

> I do love you and
> miss you,
> *Naomi*

My dearest Naomi,

I have arrived home from school and was hoping there would be a letter from you. Sure enough there was. I could have jumped up and down if I weren't too big for such things. I don't remember if I got a letter last Saturday, since last week seems so long ago. The letter I received today had the answers to the questions I asked on marriage and love. I was so looking forward to them, but now I'm laughing because you want me to answer them too.

By the way, I like your answers very much. Here are mine.

"What do I see as the most important thing I want out of marriage?"

I just want to be with you all the time. I will never be able to quite get enough of that. The feelings of companionship, the satisfaction of sharing my deepest feelings with you. I get so lonely without you and long for the sharing of our faith together.

"What do I mean when I say that I love you?"

First of all, I'm talking about a deep feeling and longing I have for you. The joy I get from being with you. The commitment that I feel toward you, just as they say "in sickness and health, in joy or sorrow, and in good weather and in bad." The root of my love for you seems to be a thing beyond feeling.

I've often wondered what I saw in you that caught my eye. I don't know for sure. You seemed a girl above all others. A girl I could highly value. It seemed like nothing would be too hard to do for you. It's a great joy to please you, so deeply have I let you into my heart.

I'm by myself tonight. Lonnie and Luella took off for a trip to Fairfield this morning before I got up. They were supposed to be back by 6:00, but it's past that time already. I feel so lonely, of course, and would love to have you here as company, but that goes without saying.

In Mom's last letter it sounded as if you might all be coming out for Thanksgiving. Is this for sure? That would be great, grand, and awesome, and all that. What a plan! That way it won't be as long till Christmas. But now I'm frowning because every time I see you the parting gets worse. But please, do come.

We were having devotions at school the other morning when one of the children said a mouse had run past the basement door and went under the bookcase. I said we'd finish first with our song. I then sent them all back to their seats except Lester and Dennis. We slowly pulled out the bookcase with Lester at the ready, but the mouse still got away from us, running down the side of the wall where the desks are. Everyone jumped out of their seats, as I ran after it. I finally caught it. Now I know we have mice in the schoolhouse, and no one can blame me for it. This old schoolhouse is getting to be the limit.

There are now three mice in the cage. We can't see them because they burrow under the sawdust. The sparrows are still fine.

I love you,
Eugene

My dearest Naomi,

"Charity doth not behave itself unseemly, seeketh not her own" (1 Corinthians 13:5).

I finished reading your letter I received today. As always, I so look forward to them. Sorry to hear about Elena Marshall's troubles. I don't know her that well, but hopefully your parents can help her.

I learned something I didn't know this week from the eighth-grade science books. Yeast, which makes bread dough rise, is really bacteria. When mixed with dough, yeast begins to feed. This produces a gas, which causes the dough to rise. The heat in the oven causes the gas bubbles to expand even further. Interesting.

I now know how to operate the microscope in school. It's one of those big outfits—not just a small handheld one. I often dreamed of working with a large microscope, so I was thrilled to see the school had one. So far I wasn't able to figure out how it works. One of the men from the church came past the schoolhouse on Sunday and showed me how. We stopped in after we returned from singing at the old people's home. I placed one of my hairs on the slide, and it looked strange. Today I gave all the children a chance to look at the hair, which they found interesting.

I wish you knew how the schoolhouse looks. You probably think with all the mice we catch in it that it's tumbledown and all, but it isn't. There are even inside toilets, which the Amish school didn't have.

The building is long and tall with a bell tower on top. It's old, but well kept. Wood siding, slate roof, and the old style windows that go almost from the floor to the ceiling. The back entrance—which we use—has been remodeled when the bathroom was put in, but the front of the school, facing the road, still has the old tall wooden doors.

At some time before the church purchased it, the building must have been used as a community center. Outside, the playground is large enough to play softball and we're surrounded by open farm fields. It's lovely, really.

The young folks are going to Trenton for a volleyball game tonight at the same place we went to last week. This is where they have the inside court. Tomorrow night we are having a wiener roast/teacher's meeting at the schoolhouse. I like their way much better than the Amish method of having teacher's meetings, where you sit down and everyone expresses their concerns publicly. Here I will have the opportunity to speak privately with each set of parents.

On Saturday evening the young folks are having a Halloween party. Everyone is supposed to wear a costume, so I don't know if I'm going or not. I'm still pretty Amish, I guess. I can't imagine myself as a ghost or a goblin. Perhaps a corn shock or a cherry tree, but I don't know how to dress up as those creations.

The children made new name sheets since the old ones were getting boring. Now the schoolhouse windows are freshly adorned with students' names written on drawings of pumpkins, fall leaves, and freshly plowed farmland.

I wish you knew how much I miss you.

I love you,
Eugene

My dearest Eugene,

How are you doing? I'm doing fair.

I worked at Karibos today, and it was a mediocre day. The only excitement I had was when the cat, Patty Paws, started wheezing and coughing. She sounded exactly like ours do when they're going to throw up. I grabbed her, galloped downstairs, and pitched her out the door. She probably thought, "What a miserable human being!"

Both Don and I ended up going to the popcorn husking last night, and it was as great as I expected. Of course, it would have been better with you there…and if the moon had been up. As it was, we had to husk by lantern light. The boys were racing each other to see who could get to the end of the row first. I think they managed to miss more popcorn than anything else.

Don is trapping again this year. Yesterday was the first day of the season, and he caught a nice-sized red fox first thing this morning. He brought it by the house to show us. The poor, pretty thing. They are the cutest creatures. He said he would store the fox in Mom's freezer in the basement, as the prices are really low right now. You can imagine what Mom had to say about that, but I think necessity will likely triumph over her protests.

He's placed traps on the stone-quarry land, and on the farms all around here. He wants to place some on Aden's land yet, which will be as far west as he can go, both because of distance and from other trappers having the rights to the fields.

Your sisters said today that your uncle Ollie's only son has leukemia. They heard it indirectly, so they don't know for sure. I feel very sorry for them if he does.

Your mom said our trip out there is planned for the middle of November. It seems hard to wait that long, but I will try. Remember that I love you and am praying for you.

Late evening…

Hello. Here I am again. I forgot to mail my letter this morning before I went to work, so that's why it's still here. Another of your letters arrived, and I finished reading it on the couch. I liked your answers to the questions quite well indeed. I felt like I could jump, run, and do cartwheels all in a long row. Now wouldn't that be a sight? But when you said you liked my answers, I did let out a whoop. I was afraid you might not like them. As you can see, I have my fears—but often they are short-lived.

I love you ever so much,

Naomi

My dearest Naomi,

I have the egg-gathering duties for tonight, but I sat down and read your letter first. It's good to hear that you are happy. I try to be, but things are boring and rough once school is out. I work on adrenaline all day, and then after 5:00 or so I crash.

I wonder where Aaron gets the idea that I can write well? And it sounds like it must be all over the community that I wrote every day for a while. Ha! They probably all got a good laugh out of that one. Poor homesick Eugene.

It's good to hear of your enjoyment in babysitting the new children. I can certainly share the feeling here with the schoolchildren. They do grow close to my heart.

We were in the Trenton gym last night for the volleyball game. It closes at 9:00, so that gives us time for about three games. I really enjoy playing volleyball, as you know—sort of an Amish thing, I suppose. Afterward, one of the girls asked me if all the boys where I come from can play volleyball. I said, "Yes. It sort of goes with the territory."

I've been wondering for some time how I could get Larry to read at his own level. When he does read storybooks, he picks first-grade-level books. I figured the problem must be he thinks the other books look too difficult.

Today I showed him the reader they read from in class, and then I walked over to the bookshelf and chose a book on Daniel Boone. I told him to try reading it—that it was the same level of reading. He got a big smile on his face, taking the book back to his desk. At next recess he was all excited, talking to me about how interesting it was and showing me how far he had read. So maybe he'll read more at that level. I hope so.

It's time for bed, but I have to tell you how the parent/teacher gathering went tonight. I wish you could have been here. We had the greatest time. Most of the parents waited until we had eaten before they talked with me. Everybody was so nice and is well pleased with how things are going—or at least they said so.

Before we ate, I spoke a few words on how school was going from my perspective. The crowd was large and public speaking is a little scary for me, but I made it through. After my little speech I asked Lonnie to say the blessing for the food. Lonnie and Luella were invited since they are boarding the teacher.

There was also other excitement for the night, but not produced by me. Someone lifted the top on the mouse cage and one escaped. So there was a race on, with a couple of men and boys running after the mouse. I was talking with parents at the time, but ended up going to help. The mouse of course, disappeared, and no one could find it. With no mouse in sight, things eventually quieted down. It reappeared toward the end of the evening, climbing up the bookcase. The ruckus was on again, and one of the men caught it this time, returning the mouse to its home base.

Laverne's mom said the sweetest thing tonight. She said that before Laverne ever saw me he said that he didn't know if he would like a boy teacher or not. Now the other day he said that he sure hopes I teach again next year.

The women all had a fit over how the schoolhouse is decorated. I didn't know it was that big a deal. They were saying amongst themselves they had been so afraid a male teacher would leave the schoolhouse looking bare. Well, fears taken care of.

Goodnight for now. It's well past 10:00.

Sunday…

I'm quite lonesome tonight, but that's not unusual for Sunday evenings. Things are really quiet in the house. I could use a buggy ride about now, with you beside me, not to mention an Amish hymn singing.

I don't feel like writing about school stuff, but I do wish I could tell you how wonderful you are, how comforting and soothing your presence would be, how beautiful you look, and how there is no girl on earth as marvelous as you are. But you're not here, and I probably wouldn't say it if you were. So maybe writing is a blessing in disguise.

I've been reading a book I purchased at the drugstore. It's about body language and has some good points, I think. I find it very interesting that the first graders will show any emotion they feel. If they're happy, they jump up and down. If they're sad, they cry, and if they're bored, they show it. The book says that as a person get older he will begin to wear a mask. I'm sure that's true. I guess it wouldn't work if adults showed every emotion they felt. The book says it's because people get hurt too often. I don't know, but I suppose that's true.

I know I love you, but there are not many ways of showing that right now, book or no book.

Love you, darling.

Eugene

My dearest Eugene,

I finished rereading your wonderful letter with the answers to those marriage questions. I asked Mom the same questions, and she thinks the most important thing is trust or having faith in each other. I have thought over her answer, and I think that could be very true. Because really, once you couldn't trust each other, there wouldn't be much of a marriage. Also, I don't see how you could truly love your partner if you couldn't trust him.

You mentioned another thing that I've often wondered about, and that is what you saw in me that attracted you. Somehow I always thought I should be able to figure that out, but I've never been able to. Now if I know you can't figure it out, I'm sure I can't because you are a lot better at figuring things out then I am. I do know you are the most wonderful person I could have been attracted to.

Well, I have to get this room cleaned before chore time so talk to you later.

Monday morning...

Hello. How does this Monday morning find you? I'm feeling a good deal better than yesterday. I was going to finish this letter, but I was too tired after chores, supper, and dishes.

I have to babysit at 9:30 this morning for a few hours. This afternoon Dad, Don, and I are planning a trip to the Bachs. Dad and Don are putting up their storm windows. The Bachs have these old-fashioned ones that are really heavy, so Don has to go along. I will clean the house while they work outside.

Yesterday was a rainy, dreary day for a Sunday. This morning it's nice again and balmy. James Yoder went to that other church again yesterday. He took the three youngest boys and Dorothy with him. Millie and the rest came to our church. That poor family. It would be such an awful situation to be in.

We ended up at Robert's Friday night on a sudden invitation. Your family was also there. The men were all working on some project outside while the women stayed inside and played Probe. I really enjoyed the game.

What would you like for Christmas? Is there something you really want or need? If there is, please tell me. This isn't proper to ask, I suppose, but I'm at a loss to know what you'd like. I think boys are much harder to shop for than girls.

Monroe and his wife are going to move to their new place tomorrow. Somebody said Daniel might continue boarding at Robert's since he helps on the farm now. I suppose Lydia would be happy, as it's closer to where she lives. By the way, they are going steady.

Sometimes I get the feeling this winter will never end. I sit around imagining what life would be like married to you. That would be quite wonderful, but it doesn't give me any more patience, which I'm in sore need of. Take care of yourself.

With all my heart,
Naomi

NOVEMBER

My beloved Naomi,

Just as the months do onward go.
Just as the seasons surely roll.
So is my love as sure to you.
It's ever binding, ever true.

Two months have gone by, though it seems more like two years. I often wonder if you miss me as much as I do you. Yet I hope you don't sit around and mourn for me. I do enough of that for both of us.

There sure is a big difference between weeks at school. Last week I had to push everything hard to get the lessons through, now today things went smoothly. I even finished early enough that I could work with the first graders for an extra half an hour. I wish I could spend extra time with them more often.

Dena, Dennis, and Laverne were absent today. Dena is on a three-day trip to Michigan. Dennis was sick, but he's supposed to be back tomorrow. Poor Laverne has been taken west to a doctor for treatment. His condition has continued to worsen, to where his skin started to scale badly. The plans are for him to be at the doctor for most of the week. Hopefully he won't have a hard time catching up when he comes back. If they find help for him, it will have been well worth the effort.

On Tuesday the school is planning a trip to the local river for part of the day. The excursion will be to the campground I was at the other Saturday. I hatched up the idea last week and talked with the board last Monday evening. The children are all excited. I didn't tell them where we're going though. I'll make them sweat it out to increase the pleasure of the outing.

Last night we visited Luella's sister's place. She's an old maid, and older than Luella. The topic of interest was her parakeet, which she took great joy in showing me. The thing talks. His name is Billy, and I got to hear him say "Billy talks."

The parrot also says "Billy's tired" and "Billy's naughty," but that wasn't easy to understand. They informed me the only way to teach parakeets to talk is if one person is around them all the time and spends a lot of time talking to them.

I've been having headaches lately, which is very unusual for me. Who knows what's causing it. Perhaps a nasty brain tumor.

Tuesday evening…

It sure gets dark around here early.

I reread your letter with the answers to my questions tonight, enjoying it again. I'll have to remember that you like to be independent.

Lonnie brought up something interesting the other evening at the supper table. He said that when a new idea comes to him, he thinks about it, and even though he might not like the idea, if it's right, he can learn to like it. I thought that was a good way of looking at it.

I've started planning the Christmas program this week. I found one poem I want to use for the introduction, so that's a start. I might try taking a familiar melody we know and putting new words to it.

Around here the schoolchildren have a tradition that on a child's birthday they stick the person under the table. That's been going on at school, but they haven't gotten rough yet, so I haven't forbidden the practice. I figure one has to walk carefully with other people's traditions.

The other morning in arithmetic class, Dora wasn't done with part of her page. We went ahead checking the other papers, and as I read the answers off she was afraid she would remember them so she held her ears closed. That's one honest girl, if you ask me, although I doubt she would have remembered the answers.

I love you, dear.

Eugene

My dearest Eugene,

Greetings.

Elena Marshall stopped by today and spoke with Mom again. She says that when she tries to talk with Bob, he won't listen and just doesn't communicate. He's not ignorant at all, but there isn't much love between them apparently. He won't even kiss her anymore. She said he goes with her to the marriage counselor, but he won't talk there either. I feel sorry for those two. It seems to me that a marriage like they have wouldn't be much of a marriage at all. How sad. I sure am glad Amish people don't have marriages like that.

The information you wrote about the yeast was not new to me, but I suppose I work with such things more than you do. I too have often wanted to operate a microscope. I think that would be very interesting, so perhaps you can show me when we come out before Thanksgiving.

Darrel Hooley still comes to church once in a while, but I'm not sure what his plans for the future are. It must be hard even thinking of joining the Amish if you haven't been raised in the faith. At least it seems so to me.

Today we received a letter from Dad's side of the family. Three of his siblings might come to visit this Saturday. Yippee! Anything to break the boredom around here.

The weather has been seventy degrees two days in a row, which is pretty odd for November. Especially since it's supposed to snow on Friday. Or so the lady I work for told me.

Mom was helping Monroe and his wife move today.

And so it goes around here. I miss you awfully, Eugene.

With all my love,
Naomi

My beloved Naomi,

The weather isn't cooperating at all. It has turned cold and windy, so it's yet to see how the planned outing tomorrow will go. The children are enthused enough about the trip. I informed them tonight on where we're going.

I was looking through the *Pathway Readers* today, searching for poems I could use for Christmas and ran across this one. I won't use it, but I really like it. I think I heard it used for one of the Amish school programs once. Here it is…

> Light after darkness, gain after loss,
> Strength after weakness, crown after cross,
> Sweet after bitter, hope after fears,
> Home after wanderings, praise after tears.
>
> Sheaves after sowing, sun after rain,
> Sight after mystery, peace after pain.
> Joy after sorrow, calm after blast,
> Rest after weariness, sweet rest at last.
>
> Near after distant, gleam after gloom,
> Love after loneliness, life after tomb.
> After long agony, rapture of bliss,
> Right was the pathway, leading to this.
> —FRANCES R. HAVERGAL, 1879

Thursday evening…

When I arrived home from school, a wonderful letter from you was waiting. I quickly headed upstairs to read it. I agree, your mom had a good answer to the question on marriage.

The weather today didn't turn out well, but we still went on our field ′t was cold, with a strong wind blowing. When we arrived at the river, ′ed out to the water, where I expected the air to be much warmer. ′ll. It nearly snapped my ears off, so we stayed around for a few ′ving to look for someplace else to eat our lunch. We found a ′eep ravine that cut the wind off, so it wasn't too bad.

Jerry and Tina Eicher

I'm having fun with the microscope. I looked at a scab, which had blood vessels running all over the place, and at some green leaves, which had many straight lines and were, of course, green.

I love you,

Eugene

My dearest Eugene,

I'm back from babysitting, and it's 9:00 p.m. I was there the whole day, the husband having picked me up at 8:00 this morning. I tell you, I have never met a family I have admired so much. Lee and Chris seem to have a wonderful relationship. He is the exact opposite from her—well, maybe not exactly. She is a little taller than I am, slender, with dark hair, and on the beautiful side. She speaks softly with a very pleasing voice and is somewhat of a perfectionist.

Lee is tall, and not really fat but *big*. He has a booming voice, very hardy, with an outgoing nature and a nice personality. They get along great with each other. Their Christianity struck me immediately. In all the places I've worked, I've never found a family that is as dedicated like they are. They even say grace before meals, which is a very rare thing to see outside the community. Anyway, I have never been happier with a job than this one.

Do you have any idea how happy it makes me that people out there like you so well and want you to teach another year? I am thrilled even though we plan to get married and you won't be going back.

I'm sure I would never be a good speaker, even if I managed somehow to speak in front of a group. I'd collapse afterward, feeling a great relief that it was over. I'd probably fear I didn't say something right. I think it's great that you feel so good about it afterward. I believe you are probably very good at speaking in front of people.

Now it's late, and I should get some sleep. This letter isn't very long, but I will try to write a long one over the weekend.

With all my love,
Naomi

My dearest Naomi,

"Nay, I had not known sin, but by the law" (Romans 7:7). I have spent time looking at this verse, trying to understand it. It's some mystery, and I wonder if anyone understands it. Stan probably has an answer, if I ever get a chance to ask him.

I forgot all about telling you what I wanted for Christmas. You really don't have to bother, and that's naughty to say that boys are harder to buy for than girls. It all depends on the perspective. I'd say don't get anything big. I've been picking up small things here and there for you as I have the chance. Of course, if you want something in particular, please tell me.

I'm still thinking hard on what I want, and all I can come up with are books. You know what my tastes are. I could also use work or dress handkerchiefs, and perhaps a gray shirt would be nice. Does that give you enough options? Oh, and a wife would also be okay.

Luella was making plans at the supper table where to place everyone for the night when you come out for the Thanksgiving trip. She doesn't know yet, but the Sauls are offering to take in several people. I'm sure Luella will have things figured out by the time you arrive. She said everyone is very anxious to meet you. If they stare at you and you pass out from the glory, I promise I will join you on the floor.

We received the news this morning that Lonnie's mother died last night. It was not totally unexpected, but everyone is in mourning around here. There will be no school on Tuesday because of the funeral. I was hoping we could have school the day after Thanksgiving, but I'm doubtful the school board will approve, as they usually take the day off. I would like to get as many school days in as possible, the sooner to meet my quota, plus it gives me something to do.

They are making active plans to ordain a minister at the church. It's still a long process, but by the end of this month they hope to at least have the date of the ordination.

Since I'm not a member, I don't hear everything that goes on, but there is talk that depending on who gets ordained, there may be a split in the church. There is much argument amongst the members on whether to change the rules on allowing photos and musical instruments. I thought only the Amish argue about such things. I guess it just goes to show you.

I'm feeling quite lonesome again, and it would be so good to be home.

I'd love to see you, as well as everyone else. Sundays are long days in which the air itself doesn't seem to move. Things go so slowly.

I think so much of you and love you dearly.

You are so sweet.

Eugene

Jerry and Tina Eicher

Dearest Eugene,

I have finished writing a page for my cousin Malinda's circle letter. I told them I'd like to drop out and asked them if it would be okay if I entered Rosanna in my place. I think there are ten people on the list and she'd like to keep it that way. I decided I can't keep up with my letters to you, let alone writing circle letters. Rosanna isn't writing anyone that I know of, so she might want to, if the others don't object.

Last night we got our first snow, and it has been snowing off and on all day. The temperature was twenty-seven today, and this morning Dad said the wind chill must be close to zero. Brrr! Winter is here from the way it looks.

You said you don't like how early it gets dark out there, but I like it because it seems we get supper finished earlier and Dad doesn't stay outside working as late.

I did get one of your wonderful letters today, and that's usually the first thing I ask about when I get home. "Did I get a letter?"

You said that two months have gone by. I don't keep track because they go too slowly. When I think of all the months that lie ahead, it gets pretty depressing. That's usually what I think of instead of how many have passed.

I wonder how your trip to the river went yesterday. I hope you had nicer weather than we did.

By the way, I don't especially like being independent. Well, maybe sometimes I do. I hardly ever feel independent when I'm with you, and it's not that I want to either. Though I might always get independent sprees, but that's a girl thing, isn't it?

Goodnight for now, and I love you. I think if you'd walk in the house right now I'd give you a big hug regardless.

November 6...

All the above was yesterday. Now it's the next evening, and Dad's relatives have just left. It's only 7:30, so they didn't stay very late.

Our chores are done. Don helped me milk so Dad and Mom could visit. We had eaten supper before chores. I fully enjoyed the day, and I think the others did also. You can enjoy the time better when only a few families come rather than the whole clan. Oh, and they were having a royal time teasing me about getting married!

Grandpa said, "They'll marry on Thanksgiving without any question."

And I said, "He's out in Iowa, you know."

Someone else chimed in with, "Oh, well, you could even get married on a weekend."

Another said it just takes a half day. Gary said, "Not even that long."

Then Grandpa said you probably couldn't get married before school is out, and I said that was right.

Then he very matter-of-factly said, "Oh, so you'll get married next year in June?"

I just sat there and laughed at them. They don't know how right they are.

Dad and his brother Henry made it through their business transaction okay. Dad had borrowed some money. Mom and Dad had been praying that they might be able to pay Henry $1000 today on the $3000 debt and the accompanying interest charges. And wouldn't you know, Dad was able to sell enough hay so he had the money. When Dad handed Henry the check, Henry said, "Well, now, I don't want to make it hard for you."

Then Henry went and removed the interest rate of 5 percent he'd been charging. So now we only have $2000 to get together by Christmas and it's over with. What makes me happier than anything was to see them handle the matter so well because Dad said loans between family members can sometimes cause more problems than they do good.

Don and I plan to make a trip to the east district for church tomorrow at Stan Hochstetler's place. I wanted to visit just for anyhow, and Don agreed, so that's that.

Sunday afternoon…

How I wish I could be sitting beside you downstairs instead of having to write long distance. I did have an enjoyable day with flashes of sadness here and there when your name came up. One thing has cheered me considerably, and that is we have decided on the final date for our trip—the week before Thanksgiving. So I don't have to wait as long as I thought. Just think: I'll get to see you! I'm so anxious to see how everything looks—Lonnie and Luella's place, the schoolhouse, the young folk girls, but most of all you.

James Yoder was not in church today, and Bishop Enos mentioned that we should all pray for the family. I'm certain there were tears in his eyes, the poor man. He seems burdened about the matter, as are Mom and Dad. Excommunication can't be far away if things continue on like this.

Betsy invited James's oldest daughter, Martha, home with her for the afternoon. I suppose she's trying to be extra-friendly with the family's situation the way it is. On my part, I'm trying very hard to be more tolerant of people and refrain from saying anything harsh or unfeeling about anyone. Sometimes I say things without thinking or only think of it afterward. I guess such habits are deeply ingrained and take a long time to break.

I have to babysit again tomorrow.

Take courage, it won't be long now till I see you again. I'm saying that for me as much as for you. Let's not think of the parting on the other side.

Love you,
Naomi

My dearest Eugene,

I received one of your wonderful letters today. When I arrived home from babysitting Mom announced there was one with a mischievous look on her face. I thought at first she was up to something, but it turns out the mailman had dropped the letter at the neighbor's place a mile down the road. They were kind enough to send their oldest girl down after school with the letter. I don't know how it happened, the address was perfectly correct, so don't blame yourself.

Mom and I have the chores to ourselves tonight because Dad and Don are working late baling cornstalks on the farm across the road. It's a poor man's version of straw, which gives you some indication of how the finances are around here.

You should have seen what Larry and his cousins did Saturday, the little rascals. They found some old perfume powder and a tube of cream in the ditch along the road. So armed, they smeared and powdered every one of the cats around the place. Now there are cats walking around smelling like roses. I will have to search the barn after chores to see if I can help the poor creatures. Yuck.

I like the poem you sent along, especially the line "Love after loneliness."

I worked at the Colombos today and dared ask for a raise since I'm the only girl in the community working for $3.00 an hour. Mrs. Colombo was nice about it and readily agreed.

Dad is in the middle of replacing our fixed water motor at the barn. With the one that's on the pump now, we have to run down every time we want water, start it, and then stay there and shut the switch off by hand when the tank is full. That takes fifteen minutes of standing around and waiting.

There will be a work *frolick* tomorrow at Richard and Joan's new place, and both Dad and Don plan to go. I think the young couple is moved into the house, and this is work for an addition to the barn.

Don is out tonight with a proud new purchase of his—a squeaky mouth whistle that is guaranteed to call up foxes, he said. I think he's going by the advertisement and not experience. "Here fox, here fox!" That's really funny. I'm sure the foxes will be way too smart for the little whistle and Don's flashlight with the red lenses, but don't ever tell him I said so. He is quite devoted to the cause.

Tomorrow night Harvey and his family, your folks, and all of us are planning to visit Junior Yoder and sing for him. He had a recent back injury from a fall and has to stay flat on his back for two weeks. Wouldn't that be awful, being flat on your back twenty-four hours a day?

I love you with all my heart and will say goodnight for now. I am quite sleepy. I miss you so much, and I am really looking forward to November 19.

With all my love,
Naomi

My dearest Naomi,

We didn't have school today, as you probably know by what I wrote on Sunday. We attended the funeral of Lonnie's mother, which was over by 11:30, and then we attended the graveside service. They served lunch for everyone at the church. I didn't know many people, so I stuck as close to Lonnie and Luella as I could.

A choir from a church in Wisconsin did all the singing, which is different from how the Amish conduct a funeral with no singing at all. I thought it was nice though. The preacher was also here from the church in Wisconsin. I guess it's a sister church, although I've not seen much visiting back and forth so far.

At the graveside they read a poem Lonnie's mom kept by her bedside during her last weeks of illness. Luella gave me a copy, and I've written it out below.

Keeping My Eyes on Him

Earth's sorrows gather round and toss the soul,
I wonder why, how does one know?
What God has planned, what He would gain,
From all life's sorrow, grief and pain.

I lift my eyes, I cry, I groan,
My face with tears are wet, I moan.
These questions only drive my heart away,
From thoughts of him, of glory's brighter day.

So I will lift my eyes, and seek his face,
Though hidden by the clouds of earthy waste,
Death is the chilly crossing to the sky,
He waits, his arms spread wide I know, to answer why.
—T.T. WILLIAMSON

I'm in the middle of a project at school. I'm cutting out a plaque in the shape of the state of Iowa. I plan to carve or burn in the name of the school, the school year, and the names of all the pupils, along with the teacher. So far getting the letters into the wood has been the hardest part. Lonnie lent me his two soldering tools he had in the garage, but they didn't work.

Jerry and Tina Eicher

Then Duane brought in another tool, which worked okay until it quit for some unexplained reason. Now I'm back to where I started—with nothing. But I will continue trying.

The last sparrow in the nature preserve at school died. Its companion died a week ago. So there you go. No more sparrows, I promise.

Tomorrow night is the first of the wintertime young folk Bible studies. That's something new for me, so I'm anxious to see how a Bible study class goes. Stan is teaching.

With love,
Eugene

My dearest Eugene,

We were supposed to go to Junior Yoder's place tonight, but Enos Byler sent word they had a young folks gathering planned for tonight. So Mom put our visit off until tomorrow night. I'm sitting here waiting for Don to bring the horse out of the barn, at which time I will dash out and help him hitch to the buggy.

I was working at Mrs. Bach's this morning. John says "Hi."

A wonderful letter from you arrived. I can hardly wait for our trip out there. Now the days seem to go much slower than they did before.

Oh, here comes Don, so catch you later.

Thursday evening...

We aren't going to Junior's tonight after all because there is a school meeting.

About an hour ago, Katie Troyer, Joan's mom, walked down from their place and said she wanted to talk with me alone. I was pretty sure what it was about. Well, it turns out I was correct. Joan had asked me the other Sunday, totally innocently, "Is Eugene planning on joining the Mennonites?"

I said, "Of course not."

She said, "Wouldn't it be nice though? Just think, you could join along with him."

We both laughed, but I didn't take her seriously at all. Later I made the mistake of repeating the conversation to Mary Miller. This was against my better judgment, but I didn't think fast enough and the words slipped out. I then made a point of clearly telling Mary that Joan hadn't been serious.

Well, last Sunday evening Don told me the rumor is going around that Richard and Joan where thinking of joining the Mennonites before they had any children to tie them down.

Katie heard about the rumor, but Joan hasn't heard it yet. Of course, they want to keep it that way. But since I seemed to be the source of the rumor, that was why she was coming to me. There is also something else shocking going around, she said, but she didn't say what.

I said I was awfully sorry and repeated the above conversation that I had with Joan, stressing that I had made a point to say Joan wasn't serious. Still I said I was sorry—I should have kept my mouth shut. Katie was very nice about it, thanking me for helping straighten things out. At least she came to me instead of stomping my name in the mud like she could have.

Last night was enjoyable in a way. We girls peeled pears and cut them up. The boys were working out in the barn putting in a floor above the horse stalls. One of the girls said that Paul Mast, who is away for a few weeks, wrote Barbara a six-page letter. I don't think the letter could have been as good as yours even with six pages.

Barbara and I had a chance to talk alone and started confiding in each other about our boyfriends. We found out we are a lot alike in that area. I wouldn't have thought her as being like me at all, but we are in agreement on everything. Both of us have trouble expressing ourselves, and often you ask me what I think about something and I don't know because I've never thought of it before. When I said that to Barbara, she said that's exactly the way it goes with her. And we both hate to make decisions.

The volleyball game afterward was great, as usual. We only played one game by lantern light, and then we had snacks of popcorn and apples. I think everyone was tired because they started leaving well before 10:00, although most of the steady couples were still standing out by their buggies talking when Don and I drove out. I ignored them. It's very much not fair.

I was glad you gave me an idea on what you want for Christmas. I was afraid you would ask me what I want. The reason I don't know what I want is that I'm not really in need of anything. But I guess a small bulletin board and bookends would be nice. You said you've been picking things out for me, so don't go spending a lot more. And I could also use a husband.

About whether Mom and Dad will come out for the trip. Dad is indecisive at the moment.

Dad has a new shed project going on behind our barn. Don and Dad set the posts in today. Larry helped this afternoon after school, but he's too small to be of much good. I did see him carrying boards around for them. Don wanted to finish early enough so he could check his traps well before dark. I don't think the trapping business is very successful this year. But at least it's more successful than the whistle-blowing project was, which produced nothing. But I was nice and didn't rub it in.

I love you and long
to be with you,
Your Naomi

My dearest Naomi,

"They that wait upon the LORD shall renew their strength; they shall mount up with wings as eagles; they shall run, and not be weary; and they shall walk, and not faint" (Isaiah 40:31).

I become more and more convinced I couldn't have found a better girl than you, Naomi. You are wonderful, and in only a week I'll be seeing you. I can hardly wait, and I have so much to show you.

I really enjoyed the Bible study last night. It was so different. They sat around in a circle, read some Scriptures, and had a discussion about them. I even had the nerve to say a few words myself.

The topic was the first ten verses of John, chapter three, on how a person must be born again and how he can have the assurance of salvation. The group leader, Stan, pointed out three ways one can judge whether he is born again.

The first one is in 1 John 5:1: "Whosoever believeth that Jesus is the Christ is born of God." Stan said that is the inward evidence a person can have.

The second verse is 1 John 4:7: "Every one that loveth is born of God." Stan said this is called the "out-going evidence," which people can see.

The third one is 1 John 2:29: "Ye know that every one that doeth righteousness is born of him." Stan said this is the "outward evidence" that we wear on us all the time.

I received an even better impression of Stan than before. He's a young married man and very sincere. He had wonderful thoughts, and he knows his Bible like few people I've known.

I'm going to the volleyball game tonight, so over the weekend I'll get caught up on the news around here.

With love,
Eugene

My dearest Eugene,

I'm so lonely for you. When I think of the coming trip, it does cheer me up some. The weather is cold here and it was snowing earlier—hard, peppery flakes.

Don and Dad are working on our shed today. Tomorrow there is a work *frolick* planned for the men at Monroe's to hang drywall for their house addition.

Last night we finally made it over to Junior Yoder's place. Harvey and some of the young folks were also there. We sang and visited, with Don and me leaving at 9:15 because we were both tired. He was tired from the night before working with a big haul from his traps. Yes, he is more successful than I thought. By the time he was done skinning three foxes and several coons, it was close to 1:00. I was still tired from Wednesday night and from not getting to bed early Thursday.

Poor Junior. He says he has more pain now than he did before the operation.

This forenoon I washed four loads, and they're drying on the line now. Mom is sewing a brown suit for one of Ada's younger girls.

One of our heifers had a calf last night, so we'll see what kind of rodeo we have tonight when we try to milk her for the first time since the birth. I'm not really planning on hanging around for the show, but Dad is usually good with such things.

Well, the weekend is coming up fast. I wish I could be looking forward to seeing you tomorrow here instead of next week in Iowa.

Monday morning…

Dad and Don are outside working on the shed, but Mom and I haven't done a lick of work beyond cleaning the breakfast dishes.

Yesterday we had lots of visitors in church, amongst them some of my circle letter pals. Now that I've met them, I really don't want to stop writing, so I might keep on. Rosanna says she doesn't want to write anyway.

I got to meet one of the girls, Marilyn, for the first time. She really impressed me, and I like her immensely. She is as friendly in person as she is in the letters, and she has a very pleasing soft voice. She's also beautiful, although not in a dashing or empty way. She loves poems and likes to read.

Her sister was also along, and Don thought she was better looking, but I think his taste is tarnished.

Mom told me later that I can no longer say that I'm not outgoing. That shocked me because I never thought of myself as outgoing. I still don't, but maybe I can be, depending on the people who are around me.

Anyway, I really enjoyed those girls, and it's not often I can say that about company because I can get bored quickly. There was also a visiting minister, Wayne Troyer, who could really preach. Bishop Enos had him do the main sermon.

James Yoder was in church yesterday. He and Millie made a trip back to northern Indiana where they came from with a load of our ministers to try to work out their problems. Hopefully this will be a solution for them, as James claims he respects the ministers from there. He also has family in northern Indiana. James and Millie had a meeting with the ministers from there and some from here. But Dad says he doesn't think it did much good. At least from what he heard. Other than to establish the fact that the Indiana ministers agree with our ministers. Surprise, surprise.

They said afterward that his family just pleaded with James to change, especially his mother. His mom didn't even want them to leave to come home until James promised a change. James wouldn't promise, but said he would think some more about it. He is planning to come back to church for now. It seems like the predestination doctrine he picked up is very hard for him to let go of. He repeated his claim while he was in northern Indiana, that he believes he had no more to do with his second spiritual birth than he had to do with his first natural birth.

Well, I'd better get something done around here. I am about as excited about coming out there as I can be. This is probably the last letter you will receive from me before I arrive. So I can probably say see you tomorrow or the next day.

Yippee!

Love you,
Naomi

My dearest Naomi,

Lonnie and Luella's grandchildren are here. They are taking them back home around 3:00, and I'm planning on going along to break the boredom. It's hard telling when we'll get back.

This morning at the breakfast table I dumped the sugar bowl over to start things off. Luella said it's a good thing it wasn't the salt or I'd have bad luck for sure. The next thing was pouring orange juice into the cereal bowl instead of milk. Well, there are those mornings.

I don't know why I'm so blue about everything right now, but I am. Blue, bluesy, and dark blue. This may sound off the wall, but I still want to tell you. If you ever wish to break our engagement, I would understand and hold no hard feelings against you. But please don't ever make any hasty decisions about such things. I would always remember our good times together.

As I said, I'm blue right now, so just ignore the ramblings as they don't mean anything. I was able to write a poem, so perhaps that will help.

Until I see you again,
I love you.
Eugene

Thinking of You

When the days get lonely, and the way is long,
I think of you, love, in your faraway home.
When my heart gets weary, with the toil of the way,
I think of your sweetness, as I travel each day.
When I'm longing to see you, each day is so slow,
When your presence is absent, my heart hangs low.
How our parting does hurt me, and tear at my heart,
All day it's throbbing, smarting, and falling apart.
Life without you is so lonely and drear,
A desert, a wasteland, a shadow that's near.
I struggle, I rise, I gather my strength,
I rally my hope that I will see you at length.

Hello, dearest Eugene,

I'm on cloud nine, maybe cloud ten. Every so often I squeal or get a big grin. Mom says she won't be able to stand me until we leave. I went to the young folks gathering last night just to make time go faster. It was the sewing at Bishop Enos's. Some of the boys were questioning me about when we leave and everything.

Robert asked with a cheesy smile on his face, "Can't you wait, Naomi?"

I said, "No, that's why I came tonight."

He said, "Why? So you can tell us?"

I said, "No. So the time will go faster."

They laughed over that one.

It did seem as if a lot of the young folks were missing. I think some are on a trip to Ohio, but the big hole of course was because you weren't here. The boys became goofy halfway through and tried singing songs by themselves, which was awful. Some of them sang tenor so loud it was overwhelming, and they got off tune. Don said Phillip is one of the worst ones at the yelling, but Don gets loud enough himself, especially when they're all trying to make an impression. If they could control themselves, things would go much better. Their first song was fine, but then the yelling started. I think they could have used your help.

Your last letter got me down a little, the one about me wanting to break our engagement, but I decided to let it go. We all have our bad days, and I'll see you soon, which makes me happy. So I'll just take it all with a grain of salt.

This finds me deep in packing, but I thought I'd finish this letter first. I figured if this was mailed tomorrow you'd get it Monday or Tuesday when I will have been there and gone. I've carefully spaced my letters the last few days so that you don't get any on the Friday and Saturday I'm in Iowa.

I found out some news this morning. Katie came over to borrow something from Mom and said that her son Jonathan has dropped his relationship with Robert's Mary. So that must have been the shocking news she was speaking of a while back. Isn't that something? I thought of them as a fairly stable couple.

I'm just all excited and wonder if I can even sleep tonight. I have lost sleep already from the excitement. I simply can't say how much I look forward to seeing you.

Well, I have to go. I can hardly wait.

Your Naomi

My dearest Naomi,

I am in the depths of despair indeed. The weekend is over, and your van whizzed by the schoolhouse while I was opening the school day. How could the agony get any worse? I don't know, but it did.

It happened during the story hour after lunch. I read a dog story to the children in which two friends, a dog and a wolf, are reunited after a two-year separation. The story concluded with this line: "And no matter what they did after that, it was fun."

I nearly choked up thinking of us and could hardly go on with class time. I'm sure the children thought something was wrong, but they had no idea what it was. Nor will they, as I keep this pain to myself.

I arrived home from school and walked through the house. It seemed like everything still held memories of you. Luella must have noticed. She said quite nicely, "It gets better with time."

When I walked up the stairs I could still see you standing there saying goodbye. I'd better stop this before it gets any worse.

After supper…

I'm back.

I finished your Thanksgiving card this evening, and it will go off in the mail tomorrow. This letter won't go out until Wednesday morning, but I'm still afraid the letter will beat the card, or get there the same time. Anyhow, if it does, you'll know what happened.

By the way, what were you reading in the Bible this morning as you sat beside your mom at the table? For some reason that touched me, and I was wondering.

Well…I might as well go downstairs and read something, as sitting here thinking of you keeps the pain level higher than I want it to be.

With all my heart,
Eugene

My dearest Eugene,

I don't have to go to work today because Chris is having her carpets cleaned. I'm relieved because I feel awfully sad. Last night I cried until there were no more tears left in me. I don't know how long this can keep up, as it's not really making me feel any better. I felt like crying every so often in the van all the way home, but I can't cry in front of people.

On the bright side, it really made me happy to see how well liked you are in Iowa. Dad said he feels this teaching job really was the Lord's will for you. And he wondered if you were being tempted to teach there another year. I said, "Yes, he is, but we might get married instead."

I think Dad liked that answer. He certainly likes you. I told him how depressed you get sometimes, and he thinks you just need more reassurances, maybe over and over again. Well, I can certainly do that, as I love you very much.

I love you,
Naomi

My beloved Naomi,

I stayed at the schoolhouse until 5:30 tonight. It was pitch dark outside by then. I wanted to finish correcting the tests. The seventh and eighth grades had their science test, the third and sixth had an English test, and the fifth and eighth had a social studies test.

They've had a rough week, so perhaps they're sharing in my pain. I'm piled up with schoolwork, as this is report card week. I also want to get the Christmas program typed up so I can hand out the different parts on Monday.

There is also decorating that needs to be done between now and Christmas. As pressed as I am, I should stay home from Bible study tonight, but I'll probably end up going.

The three board members' wives brought in Thanksgiving dinner today, and we had the children file past the table cafeteria style. Everything went well with no spills. Afterward, two of the wives stayed to observe the school in operation. I hope they liked what they saw, but I didn't get to speak to them after school was out. They had to leave immediately for home.

We finished the lunch-hour storybook we were reading today, so that means a new book must be found for next week's story hour. I wish I could find the two books called *The Mystifying Twins* and *The Secret of the Mystifying Twins*. I think the children would enjoy them.

I love you,
Eugene

My dearest Eugene,

I don't feel too thankful today, even though it's Thanksgiving Day. But I know I still have a lot to be thankful for even if you can't be here. I haven't felt like writing much since the trip. I thought if I could just see you again, this loneliness would get better. But it *hasn't* gotten any better. I'm still glad I came for the visit. Before it didn't seem real, but now that I've seen your schoolhouse and Lonnie and Luella's place, it's easy to picture you in that setting.

We will be having Ada and Deborah's families in today, and Mom has fixed a big turkey dinner. It should be ready soon, and I need to help set the table. I think Mom plans to spread the table in the dining room to its maximum length. Whoever doesn't fit will have to sit in the living room—mostly the smaller children.

I counted and reread your letters the last few days to cheer myself—there are thirty-five so far.

Don and Larry have plans to hunt this afternoon with your brothers and some of the other community boys. They are after rabbits, I think.

Tonight the young folks are supposed to be at Melvins'. The girls will wear dark dresses and white aprons and be there by 6:30. That's all I know, but it sounds kind of exciting and strange. I don't really feel like going, but I'm afraid if I stay home I'll just feel worse.

With a heart of longing,
Naomi

My dearest Naomi,

It's around 5:00 on Thanksgiving Day, and I'm by myself in the house, which isn't exactly a pleasant feeling. Lonnie and Luella aren't back yet from their day's activities.

I worked this morning on the report cards before we left for church. It was kind of strange going to church on Thanksgiving Day. I got to wondering what you were doing. I guess your family likely got together somewhere for dinner or had someone over. I could picture you all laughing and talking, which of course didn't help my feelings improve.

After church they had a Thanksgiving dinner for everyone. I'm afraid I'm not very good at hiding my feelings so I looked a little down. I would have gone back up to the schoolhouse and worked to cheer myself up, but there was no one to drive me there. Plus people were talking with me, which was nice. They are wonderful out here.

Ah, Lonnie and Luella just walked in with an invitation to supper somewhere. So there will be something to do this evening at least.

Love you, dearest.

Eugene

My dearest Eugene,

Greetings of Christian love. Don and I went to the Melvins' last night as planned. Some of the older couples were also there, and the Melvins supplied the meal, with Bishop Enos's girls supplying the entertainment. All of the young folks were there except a few of the boys who are in Ohio.

They had a long table set up with benches and had placed numbers on the plates. You pulled numbers out of a hat when you arrived, one hat for the boys and one for the girls. With your number in hand you matched it with the number on the table. The steadies didn't get any numbers, they automatically got to sit in front of each other, the cheapskates.

After we had eaten, slips were passed out to everyone that told us what our assigned duty for the evening was. Then we sang for a while, and one of the boys read a Scripture. That was his assignment. They told us later that if a girl had drawn that slip, a change would have been made, but it worked on the first try. Then Bishop Enos had prayer after the Scripture reading.

There was someone assigned to read a short story, a poem, and ten people to sing together. The singing was a big risk, but they had enough good singers so the sound wasn't too unpleasant. By the way, I was in the group, but I'm not taking any credit. After that, a work crew washed the dishes, and the rest of us sang until 9:30. Don said on the way home that he didn't like any of the evening. He prefers order and certainty, but I enjoyed it. I thought it broke the routine.

Earlier this evening I was sitting at the kitchen table playing Monopoly with Mom and Dad. Dad beat us, like really badly, but that was to be expected. He usually does.

I am so lonely for you I can't put my heart into letter writing, so we'll blame that if you think this is boring. Your card arrived today, and I can't thank you enough. It was beautiful.

I wish you could
have been here,
Naomi

Dearest Naomi,

Some night next week the boys plan more sparrow hunting, and I'm scheduled to go with them. I'm going along for the sport because every little thing helps to make the time go faster. There will be no more sparrows kept at the school though. I have not forgotten my vow.

I've been thinking about all the rumors you said were floating around the community. I can see where you would be afraid of getting into trouble for what you said, but maybe it's not as serious as it may look at first glance. It sounds to me like people are reacting instead of thinking. Your remark really shouldn't have gotten blown so out of proportion, so hopefully it's taken care of by now as Katie passes the word around. You have your own charms. Use them, smile, and you'll be okay.

So do you think Jonathon and Mary will start dating again? My guess would be they will, but if Jonathon really has an issue and can hold out for a while, he might get over her. I know very little about the situation, but I imagine there are other pressures, perhaps from the parents. We'll have to see, I guess.

So you didn't like the piece I wrote about letting you out of our engagement. Well, I shouldn't have, but I was blue, and so it went in.

On Friday evening the youth had their box social. Each girl brought a decorated lunch box with a packed lunch inside for two. It's to raise money for charity, and each boy had to buy a girl's box for five dollars. Inside the box is not only the lunch but a number that tells the boy which girl he will eat the lunch with. The girls chose numbers and matched them with the boys' lunch. I guess that kept certain girls from getting lots of bids and others from getting almost no bids. Too bad you weren't here, but you could just as likely have drawn someone else's number.

After eating we played all kinds of games. None of them too bad except the last one, which I refused to play. They didn't object as the evening was almost over, and there were too many boys anyway. This game had them putting chairs in a circle and the girls sat on the chairs. The boys then stood behind the chairs, with one boy having an empty chair in front of him. He'd wink at a girl, and she was supposed to make a mad dash toward his chair. The boy behind the chair was supposed to keep her from getting away.

So much for getting me involved in *that* game.

Anyway, we're planning to visit the Apostolic church tonight where they have the monthly singings. An event which ought to be enjoyable.

I love you,

Eugene

My dearest Eugene,

It's a Sunday afternoon and "woe to me," I feel like shouting. Why? Because it's so boring here.

I guess there was a little excitement a bit ago. Don came walking down the road with three of his friends. They marched right into the house and straight to the bookshelf without a word to me. All of them must be bookworms. Well, I hope they found something interesting to read. I, at least, have a good book at the moment, which is something to be thankful for. I have started reading *A Man Called Peter* by Catherine Marshall, which I think you have already read. I'm about halfway through.

The weather is rainy and gray, and I'm laughing right now. Just think. I found some humor, but not from the weather. Those three boys went up the stairs a while ago, and the thought just occurred to me. I wonder if they fainted when they walked past my room. Things are pretty messy in there, and I think the door is open. But from the amount of noise they're making, maybe they didn't notice.

Mom and Dad are out somewhere for the evening. I've had a long day and still have a long evening ahead of me.

I have to babysit tomorrow for Lee and Chris's little girl. She's the only one at home for the day as they put Zack in a school/home for special children. They can teach him a lot of things he's not learning at home, and the people there are very devoted. At first I wasn't sure what to think about that, but when Chris explained what a nice place it was and how devoted the sisters are to their charges, I was sure it would be okay. I guess I've grown close to Zack. Another thing Chris said was that they had decided to look for a sign from God. The sign being that if the home accepted him, then this was the way it was supposed to be. They really do miss him though, and so do I.

The boys have left now, and I let our dog inside so I don't feel so alone. He's sitting on the living room floor looking guilty. I'll probably put him out soon, as he doesn't help much anyway.

My cousin Joy wrote a few days ago. She hasn't been married that long and is having a hard time. Yesterday she was home and had time for thinking. In those moments, her heart gets heavy over her responsibilities as a mother and wife, especially caring for the new baby. She enjoys being a wife and mother, but I think I understand what she means, with everything that's going on in the world.

Her husband, Darryl, is often gone evenings till dark. He goes hunting and really enjoys it, but she thinks it has about caught up with her. She thinks it's fair he should get to do some things he likes, but when the baby is fussy, she wants him home. I can understand what she's saying, and I feel sorry for her. Regardless of how much she thinks Darryl should get to do what he likes, she must feel pretty alone sometimes. She probably wants to be brave and doesn't tell Darryl how she feels so that he won't feel bad. If I know her, she'd rather sacrifice than tell him. I think, though, it's a mistake for women not to tell their husbands how they feel. Because if she'd tell him, he'd very likely not go—or at least not as often. But I would also find it hard to say something.

Monday evening…

Richard stopped in while we were eating supper tonight and asked if Dad could come over this evening for an hour and help nail down his pig barn floor. When we arrived, some of the other men from the community were already there. I'd decided to ride along and visit with Joan. I had thought earlier we haven't been neighborly enough since their recent marriage and move, so this gave me a good opportunity. We had a nice visit, and I really enjoyed the drive over with Dad.

Joan told me that Jonathon and Mary had a date again Sunday night. She said that Jonathon visited Mary on Saturday night, asking if she would take him back because he couldn't stand being away from her. I'm so glad for them, as I could imagine how I would feel if you broke off our relationship. I don't think I'd even want to go on living, even if I knew there was a chance of starting again.

I have to think my troubles are pretty minor compared to some other people's. James Yoder has now decided permanently to attend the *Englisha* church, and Millie wants nothing to do with the decision. It must be simply awful to have a family so torn up. It's one thing when you are in *rumspringa*, and you taste of the *Englisha* ways, but it's quite something else once you're married.

Junior Yoder's back is not improving at all, and they think he will need another operation. He is in such pain all the time, and here I complain and feel sorry for myself with my little aches and pains. I think I often get my mind too wrapped up in my own troubles, and I don't think of other people and their problems often enough.

I babysat today for Chris again, and I also agreed to take on another babysitting job she referred me for. This couple wants me mostly in the evenings. I'm quite glad for the job, which will help keep my mind occupied.

Harvey is going to buy or has bought the place where the Stan Yoders are living. They say Adam and Harvey are going into partnership on a large pig project.

Joan asked me what you were planning to do when we get married. I didn't give her a satisfactory answer. Then she asked where we're going to live. I mumbled around, not giving her any information, and she laughed.

With all my love,
Naomi

Beloved Naomi,

I received two of your letters today, and finished reading them with great joy. Here's a little poem for you.

Your Love for Me

Loving you is so complete,
Like healing waters when we meet.
Your tender touch brings back the life,
That living steals with sorrow's knife.

Winter winds may freeze my brow,
And bend with ice the strongest bough.
This world will rend and tear the soul,
It leaves, it bleeds, it breaks the whole.

Yet through it all, I have one hope,
One anchor fast, which holds the rope.
A comfort sweet which knows no storm,
The voice that speaks with clearest form.

My heart is full and overflows,
Each time it thinks and fully knows.
That you will true and faithful be,
To God, to love, to me.

There's a school board meeting at the schoolhouse tonight, and I hope it goes as well as the others have.

I've noticed lately the children don't seem as enthused about school as they used to be. A lot of it might have to do with the fact that it's cold outside, and we have to stay inside for recesses. This morning I asked them if they would be ready for school again after Thanksgiving vacation. The eighth graders both vigorously shook their heads no.

In class nobody acted as if they had the blues too badly until I got to the eighth-grade arithmetic class. The two girls were as sour as lemons. I might as well have been talking to the fence posts outside. It would have done as much good.

I counted your letters and cards tonight. There were thirty-six, so you are doing as well as I am. I have one more sheet to go in this tablet, which will mean that I have written 100 pages—most of them used in letters to you.

The singing last night went well. Everyone sang for fifteen minutes, followed by a group of fifth and sixth graders. They weren't all that great. Six young people—three boys and three girls—sang next, doing very well, I thought, making up for the schoolchildren.

How wonderful it would be to have you around here. I miss you much.

Tuesday evening…

The sunset was beautiful tonight, with the moon on the other horizon full and rising. To see such things increases my loneliness, but I wouldn't miss it. God's creation has such deep and rich beauty.

I'm having an awful time getting through my daily schedule at school, but I managed today. I'm getting good at cutting minutes here and there.

By the way, everyone is asking if they are receiving wedding invitations. I said "Most certainly. Once it happens."

Love you,
Eugene

Dearest Naomi,

I received your letter today that was written on Sunday. In my selfishness, I'm glad you say you're lonely. You're sharing my pain. I go through my worst lonely spells over the weekend when there's little to do and more time to think. I try to stay busy because I feel better when I'm working. I'm hoping after Christmas things will improve. At least everyone claims so around here. They say things go faster downhill, so hopefully time will fly after Christmas.

I received a Thanksgiving card today from my relatives in Ohio. My unmarried aunt Martha is also teaching school this year. She wrote a full page of local news, so that now means I have more letters to write in return.

The children have started coloring the decorations for Christmas. Today we made double bells; tomorrow will be single bells and wreaths. All this will end up hanging from the ceiling. The name sheets in the windows get changed soon, and perhaps manger scenes made and colored. That is if the children have the time. I don't color, but it falls on me to hang everything from the ceiling.

I don't know why it bothers me, as this is winter after all, but it sure gets dark early around here.

Thursday evening…

I was surprised to find a letter from you when I arrived home. I'm not surprised to hear that Jonathon and Mary are dating again. That's kind of how those things go.

Sharon had her last day of school today until sometime in the spring. She's leaving with her parents for sunny Florida. They make the trip every winter, which means all her schoolwork has to be sent back for checking. This, of course, will make extra work for me. But so it goes. I can't say I wasn't warned. The school board told me from the beginning that some of the students do this every year.

I'm alone again tonight, and it's hard telling when Lonnie and Luella will be home. Hopefully they'll be back before I leave for the volleyball game, but I guess it doesn't matter. The house will stay standing by itself.

It had been raining lightly most of the day, changing to an awful downpour around the time school let out. As Lester went out the door, he hollered back, "See you tomorrow on the waves." He's funny sometimes.

Lydia is having problems comprehending her arithmetic. I think if I had more time to spend with her I could improve the situation. We will see what chances can be squeezed into the busy schedule.

The children finished the new name sheets today. It's a picture of a snowman with gloves, holding a shovel and wearing a scarf. Underneath, in the snow, is each child's name. We took the old ones down from the windows and Scotch-taped the new ones up. The manger scenes are done, and Crystal came up with the great idea of coloring angels to fly above Mary, Joseph, and the baby. I hope to get those up later in the week.

So long! I've got to run.

Love you,
Eugene

DECEMBER

Dear Eugene,

I received your altogether wonderful letter. And this can only mean one thing. Such a wonderful letter must have a wonderful guy behind it.

I can understand that you had to eat with a girl at the box social, but that doesn't mean I wasn't a bit jealous. I was glad that you didn't play the other game. Now that might have been trouble. I would have been more than a little jealous.

I didn't have to work yesterday or today. I thought I had to babysit for my new job this afternoon, but the lady wasn't feeling well so she called it off. Mom's at the sewing. Dad and Don are off helping Monroe with something. You are probably eating lunch at the school, as it's 12:30.

I picked your letter up again and reread the poem. The first time it didn't really soak in, but this time it did. It catches my fancy exactly, and I like it very much.

I'll now feel much more like going to the youth gathering tonight, since you've cheered me up. Don said he's not going, that he hates sewing, but he might change his mind since it's just up the road at Bishop Enos's place.

I never coax him to go anywhere. I just tell him he can do exactly as he likes, but that I'm going if I feel like it. A girl can drive her own horse just fine. So there.

I love you,
Naomi

My dearest Eugene,

Tonight on the way home from work I thought, "If only I could at least look forward to seeing you once a week, that would be so great." I arrived home to find a letter from you, and that will have to make do for now, I suppose. I plopped down on the couch and read it through, right then and there.

I really liked how you handled the eighth graders in their sour mood. You must be good with them.

Dad and Mom went to the school meeting tonight, and some of the local young folks came by on the spur of the moment. We played games, laughed a lot, and I served cinnamon rolls I made yesterday. Mom shouldn't complain as we can bake fresh ones tomorrow. At 9:30, Mom and Dad walked in, so the school meeting had let out early for a change. Everyone must have jumped up and scurried for home.

Tomorrow afternoon I have to stay with grumpy John and their nasty dog. I think the dog has learned to tolerate me as a necessary evil in his life.

Oh, Mom said the Christmas school program is scheduled for Thursday evening on December 23. Will you be here? I sure hope so.

Well, it's around 11:00, and I need some sleep. I don't think I'm getting near enough rest, which is my own fault.

I love you very much.
Naomi

My dearest Naomi,

It's still raining buckets around here. Lonnie said this morning people are having trouble with their basements flooding. No schoolchildren arrived on the waves, though.

The volleyball game last night was a flop. So many people showed up to play, we had to take turns rotating in. To top things off, everyone seemed worn out. It must be the rainy weather, as I didn't feel much like playing either, which is strange. I usually enjoy volleyball immensely regardless of the circumstances.

It looks as if we'll have the Christmas program on Friday evening instead of the following Wednesday. The reason is that Dawn, Lester, and Dakota are leaving for Florida on December 20, and I can't afford to lose more participants. There's already too few pupils for a good program without losing three more. I don't know what the great attraction in Florida is—the weather I guess. It sure has gobs of people around here heading south.

The schoolchildren are complaining because they will only have a week–and–a–half vacation over Christmas. I figure they will have to complain, as I need as many schooldays in as possible so I can dismiss earlier in the spring. We're short days already, and there's still the possible snow days ahead.

Lonnie claims Iowa's likely to be swept with snowstorms this year. I can imagine myself sitting snowbound at the schoolhouse with no pupils, losing days like flies dropping from an Amish summer barn spraying.

Either way, I'm planning on leaving here the morning of December 23, at five o'clock and being there in Indiana that evening. My ride has already been scheduled.

Tonight I'm going with Lonnie and Luella for foot treatments—only the treatments aren't for me. Lonnie and Luella's feet are receiving the doctor's attention, while I'm along for the ride. Both think the treatments help their stress levels, but I think it's mostly in their heads. Likely a way for some quack doctor to separate them from their hard-earned money. How can a foot massage have anything to do with stress levels?

Laverne was back in school today after being absent for two days. He's under medication twenty-four hours a day, and I'm sure this has to affect his mind. I mean, it would me. The poor boy. He doesn't seem as sharp as he was at the beginning of the school year.

The school schedule moved along smoothly today, after I anticipated a rough day yesterday. I'm not sure because of what anymore. I forget and I'm not even under medication. I guess you never can tell what's going to happen from one day to the next.

I was looking for a letter from you today, but there was none. Well, tomorrow should bring one, I hope.

We had a nice snowfall this morning, which gave me a chirpy sort of feeling—boyish enthusiasm no doubt. The temperature was moderate, around the mid-twenties, rising during the day, which made for good snowball weather. At noon we went outside and had a grand fight—at least the boys did. The girls weren't too interested. If you would have seen me, you'd think you'll be marrying a youngster. So prepare yourself.

Luella broke her clock today—the one she really likes. It's down in the kitchen being fixed by Lonnie. She said at the supper table that she didn't want Lonnie to try because he would break it even more. Whereupon Lonnie said, "Well, I've fixed a chain on a manure spreader before."

"Like that has anything to do with my clock," Luella retorted.

Now Lonnie is hollering down in the kitchen that he has fixed the clock, but from the noises Luella is making, I don't think she believes him.

Well, so it goes around here.

I love you,

Eugene

Beloved Eugene,

Greetings of Christian love. This finds me wondering what you're doing.

Dad, Mom, Rosanna, and I just finished playing Monopoly. Dad, the usual tyrant, wiped us all out. We are done with the chores, and I am getting ready to head out for the youth supper and hymn singing. Don is staying home. We only have one horse that's on the go, which isn't the young folks', so I'm driving Mom and Dad's horse tonight—Radar. Vick kicked around in his stall this week, landing on the partition and still isn't well enough to use.

We had lots of visitors at church today, and a nice discussion with some of the girls afterward. Your sister Heidi wondered what happens when someone hurts you and you forgive him. Does the hurt disappear? We decided that it does, but the problem is to really forgive someone from your heart.

I don't have any news at all, so this is a short letter. I can hardly wait for Christmas to see you. I miss you so much.

I love you,
Naomi

Dearest Eugene,

It was awful last night, seeing all the steadies leaving early, but I comforted myself with the thought that you would soon be home for at least one weekend.

I don't have to work at my Tuesday job after New Year's Day, which is great, as my schedule is jammed with all the work at home. I don't think Dad's going to milk much after next year, but then he could surprise us all. He keeps talking one way and then the other.

Mom made an eye appointment in Worthington for me, so I'll probably have new glasses when you come home. I'm so afraid I can't find anything decent that I like. Oh well, stop worrying, Naomi!

Tuesday evening…

This finds me tired and worn out. The chores ran late, the cows were out of silage, which I had to throw down by climbing nearly to the top of the silo. We really do need someone else helping around here. But Don can't be everywhere at once, and Rosanna isn't old enough for such things.

Dad and Don have been building forms all day for the sidewalk and steps running from the new shed to the barn. They were also talking about putting in a new hitching post, which will make me happy. Dad came up with the idea today. That way you'd have a nice place to tie up when you visit. And with the new sidewalks around the barn, we won't be wading in mud next spring. From how the weather is acting, we might use them this winter yet.

Dad had a little accident tonight while giving one of the young calves its milk. The calf bucked him hard, and down Dad went. Mom was in the barn at the time. She said he got this rueful grin on his face, but he got right back up anyway. When he told the story at the supper table, he sounded more disgusted than anything and claimed he wasn't hurt.

After Christmas there is another family moving into the community. I've never heard of them, as they are from Ohio. They won't be in our district, so we will see. I'm not sure where their place is. I think up north of here somewhere, near Roy Miller's home.

With a longing heart,
Naomi

Dearest Naomi,

Greetings of love.

I have reread your last two letters this evening since nothing new came in the mail. I think they are very good, and there must also be a wonderful girl behind them. The letter from yesterday was out of order, having gone through Gary, Indiana. The postman must not have been paying attention.

We're working hard decorating the schoolhouse for Christmas. Today the children colored more angels. Tomorrow we'll work on camels and a picture of Mary leaning over Jesus in the manager. We decided that Mary and the angels will go up on strings from the ceiling, with two angels standing on each side. We'll probably put stars on each side, with other stars spread out over the schoolhouse. I started hanging the angels tonight but didn't finish. They look nice though.

We're having a stage from which to perform the Christmas program. The school board was here setting it up last Saturday, and a local tradition was brought to my attention. The school usually has a Christmas tree over the holidays. So I'm going to keep the tradition. No one from home will see it, and I can always say it wasn't my idea. Hopefully that will be okay. Aren't we supposed to honor traditions?

There will be a curtain hanging across the stage that we can pull back and forth for the different scenes. Everything's a bit new for me, but I think I'll like it. One thing I've worked on but haven't been able to improve is the children's singing. That is what it is.

I've been feeling a little sick the last few days, but I haven't stopped working at school. I just can't spare the days. Luella sent along aspirins for when the headaches get too bad. I try not to get too close to the children, which is a bit hard, but will be worth it to keep them from catching whatever I've got.

I'll also be going to Bible study tonight.

Thursday evening…

Whatever bug I had is gone, I think. Last night I told Luella I was sick, but she wouldn't believe me. She told me it was just my imagination. So I said, "Okay, bring me the thermometer and I'll show you."

The temperature was close to 100, but I still went to Bible study. I don't know where the bug went, but I woke up feeling much better this morning.

Getting exercise is a problem for me when I teach school, so I have been trying to jog when I have the chance.

And how is this for a little incident? The other day Brandon took all his books home from school to show his mom, he said. Then he forgot to bring them back the next morning. I told him he still has to do his work, but at home that evening. He came up to class with the others and listened to the lesson. That way he would know what to do when he got home. By afternoon though, this all must have gotten to him because he put his head in his hands and started crying. There wasn't much I could do but wait until he stopped.

We've practiced the Christmas program four times now. There are still places where there could be improvements. Mark and Anthony haven't been to school all week, which will make things hard for them, but I guess everyone will have to make the best of things.

Luella asked me if I wanted to go for a chiropractor treatment for a leg ache that I have. I told her no, at least not for now. I don't like chiropractors—or any doctors for that matter.

Talking about doctors, Mom wrote that they want me to visit a doctor one of their friends has recommended. Someone in Missouri. It's because of my occasional depression problems. I don't know about all that. A doctor's not going to do any good. I think my depression is a result of a thing called life.

We hung all the decorations at school, and things look really nice, if I say so myself. The schoolhouse shines with real Christmas spirit. I'd still like to make more decorations, but it's got to stop somewhere.

Work, work, and more work, but it keeps me sane.

Love you,
Eugene

My dearest Eugene,

Greetings of Christian love.

I will try to write neatly, but I'm very tired so don't expect much. Dad left a gate open in the barn, and our two horses decided to venture forth all the way to the back fields. It was a long walk to get them all in, plus doing our regular chores.

I had my eyes checked this forenoon, and they are about the same as last time. Mom still had me order new glasses with plastic lenses. I never thought I would buy plastic lenses since they scratch so easily, but these are supposed to be 48 percent lighter than glass, so maybe that will make them easier to tolerate.

This afternoon I worked at the Bachs' again. Yesterday she had me there because she wanted to go to town. Today she went to play bridge. I'm learning to tolerate that dog a little better. He actually lifted his chops and looked at me.

The new sidewalks look pretty nice. Tonight I walked all the way around the barn and danced a little jig. You should have seen me! I knew Larry and Don were around somewhere, but I thought they were behind the shop. They weren't. So they got a good laugh out of my antics. Can you imagine me dancing on a concrete sidewalk?

I'm looking forward to Christmas. *Really* looking forward to it.

Your Naomi

My dearest Eugene,

"The LORD bless thee, and keep thee" (Numbers 6:24).

My letters might not be very dependable for a while. I write three times a week, but with everything so hectic I probably won't get them out evenly. I'm going to try though.

The people out there must like Florida a lot. It seems like they are making extra work for you, as if you didn't already have enough.

We had a good day at church yesterday, even with the cold weather. There was a visiting minister whom I liked. He preached the main sermon. He's much younger than Dad, but could he ever talk. Everybody liked him, from what the girls said afterward. I don't think anyone slept while he preached. Not even Katherine Yoder, who, as you know, dozes off right when the first note is sung. Well, that's a little exaggerated.

The minister spoke on grace. I didn't know anyone could preach so much on grace and not get boring, but he did. And I couldn't believe the way he knew his Scripture.

Dad asked afterward, "How can anyone memorize so much?"

At one point he said that grace is a gift and has no strings attached. Like God doesn't say if you do so and so, I will give you grace. The minister said grace is ready for you to take. And he stressed very much that everybody is equal in the eyes of God. We all come to Him with our needs and not to give anything.

The minister said we choose to sin, and he gave anger as an example. When you are out in the barn and something happens, you can get so mad. When the door opens though and someone comes in, you're immediately fine, with the anger all gone. That's because we choose to stop. That wasn't a pleasant thought, but I agree with him.

He also explained the verse to me where it says that if we walk in the Spirit we will not sin. He said, "Sure, while you're in the Spirit you don't sin. It's staying with God that's difficult." He said that being tempted is not sin, it's when we choose to give in to temptation. He had a lot more to say, but I can't remember everything. I do know his sermon was one of the highlights of the day.

Church was at Robert's, and I drove to and from the hymn singing with Don. I'm sure he's starting to eye some girl, but he won't tell me who. It's really none of my business anyway. We used the surrey in the morning, of course, and then Don used his buggy in the evening. He's got a nice horse, but not as nice as yours.

I'm getting a little out of sorts with this mail business. Pretty soon my letters might go to Texas if they're already going through Gary, Indiana.

I hope you are better from your bug.

I love you much,
Naomi

Dear Naomi,

Last night I broke down and went to the chiropractor for my aching leg. Luella kept after me until I gave in. You would have thought I was all broken in pieces from how the chiropractor carried on. And only his healing touch could ever mend the parts. He cracked and pushed and did his thing and called me better for the moment. He claimed my left hip was out of place, as well as three vertebrae in my neck. He said my jogging hasn't been helping things. I'm supposed to go back next week, of which I have no intention of doing.

For the past two mornings we've been practicing the Christmas program with the stage and curtain up. We put the curtain back and forth with every speaker change. I'm not satisfied with the sound of the children's singing, but there doesn't seem to be much I can do about it.

Tomorrow night the young folks will make fruit baskets to pass out when they go Christmas caroling. Then Tuesday evening I have asked Lonnie and Luella to help me hang the last-minute decorations in the schoolhouse windows. Friday night is the program.

I'm hoping you are full of wedding ideas when I come home...or is this too soon?

I love you,
Eugene

My dearest Eugene,

Don dropped me off a few minutes ago from our evening at the young folks' gathering. We were putting shelves in at Monroe's store, and I rather enjoyed it. I worked with the new girl who will be moving into the community. The family is here for a week and will be back permanently after Christmas sometime. Her name is Sarah, and what a girl! She's nice, friendly, witty, and only five months older than I am.

Your sisters weren't there, as well as some of the other young folks. Even with all the young people we have, a few being absent makes a noticeable difference. We almost didn't have the gathering because of the weather. It was raining, cold, and nasty this evening. I think it's been raining all day, and it's still coming down. All the snow on the ground is gone. There's nothing in the fields but brown grass and water running in the ditches.

I worked at Mrs. Bach's this afternoon. Their dog was run over yesterday on the road by some driver speeding by, so no more dog. He was a nasty piece of work, even though he did finally deem me worthy of a look the other day. I felt sorry for Mrs. Bach, who had tears in her eyes while she was telling me the story. Dad had come in the morning to fix her front door, and he told me she cried telling him the story. I guess I would cry too if our dog died. It's just that ours is a nice dog. But I suppose you would get attached to your dog—even if he is nasty.

Yesterday Dad borrowed Richard's Bobcat to pour stone in our mud pit, and Don was helping him grind feed. Anyway, the motor stopped on the Bobcat, and Dad had the loader up. In order to get out, he put his hand out on the frame. Out of habit, he moved the other hand, lowering the loader. The shaft came down right on his hand. He yelled for help, but Don couldn't hear him above the roar of the tractor.

Dad tried to start the motor, but couldn't. After some time, he saw Robert's Joseph coming down the road with their Bobcat, and Dad waved with all his might for him to stop in. Which he did, running first to Dad, and then going for help from Don. Together they pried the loader up far enough so Dad could get his hand out. We think it was under there for a good half hour.

Dad said it seemed like an hour. He came into the house, looking the hand over. No one thinks there are any bones broken. The hand looks gross, but Dad won't go to the doctor. Mom got him to soak the hand in salt water and then bandaged it for him. He went back outside to work, and Don has gone to help make wood for Junior this afternoon.

Junior either has had, or will have, another operation. Anyway, I was Dad's left hand all afternoon. We cleaned the boards from the sidewalks and fixed the one shaft on the single buggy.

I received one of your wonderful letters today. By the way, I'm glad you act like a little boy sometimes because I most certainly don't always act grown up.

It's a little after midnight, so I'd better sign off. How I look forward to Christmas and talking about our wedding.

I love you much,
Naomi

Beloved Naomi,

Greetings of Christian love.

The time is around 4:30, but I'm home from school already. There doesn't seem to be that much work at the school right now, which is strange with the Christmas program coming up. I must have worked ahead further than I thought.

There was no letter from you when I arrived home, which was disappointing to say the least, but maybe the mailman is to blame. I hope it's not for some other reason.

Tomorrow morning will be the last time we practice the program. The children want to practice again Friday morning, but I said no. I think they will be fresher for the evening's presentation if they haven't gone through the program earlier in the day.

Dena wasn't in school today for some reason. I sure hope she shows up for the school program on Friday night, but with her I never can tell.

I checked today on where I am with the first-grade reading schedule because I have been pushing them hard. We still have fifty stories to go and at least sixty-four days to read them in, so I should have time to spare. At least that's better than being behind. The third, fourth, and fifth grades are behind in their arithmetic. I'll have to remember that after Christmas and keep pushing.

It's hard to keep track of everything, but I do know which subjects can be pushed easily and which can't.

I've been thinking about writing a story that has been running through my head the past few days. So far I haven't gotten up enough nerve to try. Where the idea came from, I don't know. It must have fallen out of the sky, although that's not quite possible. The story is about a man who is forbidden to ever see the girl he loves again.

Lonnie and Luella have gone to see their granddaughter, who is in the hospital. They are quite concerned, and there were whispers of bone cancer tonight at the supper table. The doctor's reports aren't back, so perhaps it won't be that at all. Luella is very attached to the girl, as she is to all her grandchildren. Even Lonnie gets into the grandchild thing, though he doesn't like to show it. He says when the grandchildren are around he doesn't get any attention from Luella. On those days, he says, he wishes he were a grandchild.

I had Duane come up to the schoolhouse this morning. We practiced moving the curtains back and forth on the platform. It went okay.

Last night the young folks had a gathering to assemble Christmas fruit baskets. It was held at Saul's, with pizza served. The whole thing lasting until midnight. Whoa…that is the hour Amish dating ceases on a Sunday night, and you weren't even here. What a shame.

I walked home in the pitch-black darkness with the stars ablaze overhead. It was beautiful, to say the least—about as beautiful as you are but not quite. I tried to imagine that you were with me, but I didn't get very far. I hope to see you soon.

With all my heart,

Eugene

Dear Eugene,

Dad and Mom are home late from a two-day trip to northern Indiana. Mom's stepgrandmother's funeral was today.

Guess what she brought back? My wedding dress…or rather the material for it. I still have to sew it, of course.

Mom says the groom is not to know what the material looks like, and that the bride should look fresh and new on the wedding day. She even said you shouldn't know the color of my dress, which I said was a bunch of baloney. I don't stand for such superstition, but then…perhaps I'd better keep it a secret? So don't ask.

She also brought back material for the two witness's dresses. I'll explain how all this came about at Christmas, but seeing that wedding dress material got me all up in the air again.

Love you much,
Naomi

Dearest Naomi,

This is Saturday morning, an hour before we start out on a day trip to an Amish community at Fairfield. I guess I will get to see my kind again, although I don't mind being around Mennonites. Another couple, about the same age as Lonnie and Luella, is traveling with us. At least those are the facts I have been informed of.

The school program is history as of last night. It always seemed so far away, like it would never come, and now it's past. I never did get as scared as I expected I would. So much for fears that don't come to fruition. I think, in fact, from the reaction of the people afterward, that it was a smash hit.

I did get a little nervous when I stood up on the stage to introduce the evening. One of the parents later said I looked calm. Well, perhaps, but that was on the outside.

I wasn't planning to help with the singing but Dena, who was the assigned song leader and the one everyone looks up to for support, didn't show. She sent word she was sick, but I think other reasons were involved—like sabotage. What is it with these emotional girls?

Anyway, the children went into hysterics, especially the other eighth-grade girl, Crystal. I told them to calm down because I would help them sing. I would also lead the songs. So I did, keeping my voice toned down in order to blend in with the children's voices. I kept hoping all night it was working.

Afterward several of the parents said they were glad I helped sing, that my voice didn't really stand out too much.

Below is the program schedule. Each spelled out word has either poems or songs attached to the letter, but you probably know that already. I gave them a taste of an Amish school program. Luella said afterward she had been telling the teachers for years to put on this type of Christmas program, but I guess no one ever would. I'm not sure what they normally do—something about plays—I suppose.

The strange thing is, we placed the Christmas tree right smack in the middle of the platform. That tree had bothered me no end—no matter where I set it in the schoolhouse, there it was. So the solution finally occurred to me. I placed what you don't want to see where everyone sees it, and *voila!* no one sees it.

Jerry and Tina Eicher

As you well know, no Amish bishop would tolerate a Christmas tree anywhere in sight, but there we were, doing a genuine Amish Christmas program with a real Mennonite Christmas tree for all to see. Talk about doing things differently.

I received a whole table full of Christmas gifts. You should have seen the pile, and they made me open them all after the program. I feel richer than the three kings, with others having come bearing the gifts. I'm planning on bringing everything home next week so you can see for yourself.

Christmas Program for Trenton Christian School

First Theme—The Coming of Christ
Poem—Star of Hope
Song—Star of the East
Prophecies read from Genesis…
Prophecies read from the book of Psalms…
Song—Zion's Glad Morning
Prophecies read from Isaiah…
Song—To Us a Child of Hope Is Born
Prophecies read from Jeremiah, Joel, Amos, Micah,
    Zechariah, and Malachi…
Song—He Comes

Second Theme—The Birth of Christ
J - E - S - U - S
B - I - R - T - H
Song—Joy to the World
Poem—Greatest Miracle
Poem—Think of Jesus
Poem—There It Lies
Chorus of How Great Thou Art
Poem—When Christ Was Born
Poem—Bethlehem
Poem—What Shall We Children Bring?
Poem—Sweet Story of Old
Poem—How Great Thou Art
Song—Zion's Glad Morning
Poem—Out from Glory

Poem—The Christmas Story
Poem—God So Loved
Song—Hark, What Mean Those Holy Voices?

Third Theme—The Crucifixion
Poem—Guard of the Grave
Poem—On the Emmaus Road
C - H - R - I - S - T - M - A - S
Song—Faith of our Fathers

Audience will sing Silent Night
Bishop Joe Miller to lead us in closing prayer

Jerry and Tina Eicher

Dearest Naomi,

Greetings of love.

This finds me in the middle of a Sunday afternoon, and I'm starting to get excited about seeing you this week. I should be home by Wednesday evening. Our first plans had been to leave on Thursday, but the school board member who is bringing me out pushed the plans up a day. I wasn't going to tell you, keeping the news a surprise, but perhaps that wouldn't be wise. So…you have been told.

I should also mention this, even though it won't affect our time together during my stay at home. Mom wrote yesterday saying they have an appointment for me with that doctor in Missouri. One of their friends knows him. You know—Amish/Mennonite connections. He's supposed to be good for whatever ails you. I'm skeptical of course, but we shall see. I'll have my arguments with them when I get home.

I hope I haven't been away so long that you've forgotten me.

Love you,

Eugene

A HOME VISIT...

Eugene and Naomi sat on the couch at her parents' place watching the logs burn in the fireplace. Darkness had fallen outside, the last rays of the sun swept from the sky. Snow pelted the windowpanes. Out in the kitchen, the dishes rattled as Naomi's sisters finished washing up after supper.

Naomi reached for Eugene's hand and nestled against his shoulder. "You don't really have to leave again, do you?"

Eugene laughed. "I wish. You know I have to."

"But will this ever end?" A tear crept down Naomi's cheek.

"You know it will," Eugene whispered. "All things come to an end. Lonnie claims we young people have no patience."

"Then I wish I were old so this would be over with."

"I agree," Eugene said. "And we'll be old someday. After we have spent many Christmases together just like this. Warm and cozy inside with our children and someday our grandchildren about us."

Rosanna stuck her head out of the kitchen. "We could use some help, you know. You guys did help eat all day."

Eugene shook his head. "You can have her all winter. I only have her for a few more days."

"Spoiled children!" Rosanna muttered, disappearing.

"I think we'd better go help," Naomi said, getting to her feet. "I do need to live in this house after you leave. And maybe it'll take our minds off the fact that you have to leave."

JANUARY

Hi, dearest Naomi,

It's after the Christmas holidays, but I don't have to tell you. I also don't have to tell you how great and wonderful it was to be with you over the holidays.

And my, how plans have changed in the past few days! Instead of returning with the school board member's family as planned, I will soon be on my way to Missouri by Greyhound bus. Who would have thought I would consent to visit a nutrition doctor?

Mom and Dad had everything arranged when I arrived home, and I didn't spend much time arguing. As you know, since you helped out—on their side. So I guess I figure why not? I don't suppose it can do any harm.

Dad and I are waiting in the Greyhound depot for the bus to St. Louis. Once there, we have to take another bus to the small town where these friends live.

Servicemen in uniform are all over the place. One serviceman is waiting for the same bus we are. I struck up a conversation with him, and he told me he is headed back to his base after the holidays at home.

Later…

We are now on the bus, and you will see the difference in my writing. It's running all over the place from the bouncing. Fifteen minutes ago we boarded. I was sitting on the bench writing when the announcement came over the intercom, and I made a wild scramble for it. Dad took his merry old time. Turns out this was an early bus, with another one following behind. The driver is very aggressive, swerving around cars, and laying it on.

I think I'll try to get some sleep…if I can.

Later…

The time is somewhere between midnight and dawn, and I'm wide awake. How I dislike buses! They whine and carry on, stopping at every little hovel and shack along the road.

I am sitting beside a girl who is presently asleep. She boarded a couple of stops back, escorted to the bus by her boyfriend. They spent a considerable amount of time kissing goodbye before the girl got on.

She picked my row to sit in, as I was one of the few with available seats. After she sat down, she apologized for taking my seat. Perhaps she remembered my feet sticking into the aisle, which I had quickly jerked in when she approached. Anyway, I told her I only paid for one seat, so it was okay.

I asked her if she was married, and she said no but was going to be.

"I know how that feels," I said.

She asked me if I'm engaged, and I said yes.

"When?" she asked.

"Not for a while yet," I said. "And you?"

"June the fourth," she said, all chirpy.

"That's our month too," I said.

She smiled.

I was rubbing my eyes right then, and she probably thought I was crying, which I have plenty of reason to, but I wasn't.

I love you,

Eugene

My Dearest Eugene,

It was so good to have you here over the holidays, and almost good enough to make up for the pain of parting afterward.

I heard that you arrived safely in Missouri. I sure hope the doctor will be able to help. I know you think some of your lows are normal, and you never talk about it much, but it would be great if you could find help. I don't think such things are totally normal, if you want my opinion on the matter.

I should have gotten a letter out yesterday, but there was the hymn singing on Sunday evening and lots of other things to do here on the farm. I guess it's good to stay busy, so I don't feel so lost.

Mom had a dentist appointment for me this morning, and I drove in myself. I used our younger horse so I could go faster. He's still nothing like your horse. My, it was so great to ride with you again while you were home. It made the buggy today feel awfully lonesome and empty. Anyway, there was nothing wrong with my teeth, so they only cleaned them.

Ada and Mom went on a quick trip into Bloomington this afternoon. Elena Marshall stopped by and said she was going and wondered if we wanted to go along. I would have gone with them, but I already had arrangements to babysit this afternoon.

Thank you so much for giving me the nice book for Christmas, and for all the other gifts. I know I already thanked you, but seeing them around the room makes me say it again.

I'm wondering what you're doing right now. It's about 11:00 our time, and your appointment is tomorrow, I think. I so hope it goes well.

I think that maybe this time when you were here was the most wonderful time we have ever spent together.

I love you so much,
Naomi

Dearest Naomi,

God has blessed us with a safe trip so far. We arrived at Dennis and Lucy's place in Missouri after switching buses in St. Louis. Dennis and Lucy are my parents' friends who are recommending this doctor. They are also Mennonites, and Dennis is driving us to the doctor's office.

It's quite a distance away, I am told, and right now we're heading toward Golden City. The doctor's office is still 200 miles away, down close to the Arkansas border, Dennis said.

This seems a long way to go for a doctor, but everyone here is singing his praises. From the sounds of what they say, this doctor can do everything from cure cancer to set broken bones so they look like they've never been broken. I remain skeptical.

Soon after we left St. Louis, while still on the bus, I noticed how much I like the countryside around here. It's beautiful enough to move to—if one would move for such reasons. Mountains would still be nicer, but this is really nice. There are ponds all over the place, even stair-stepping in some spots. I'm not sure what purpose that serves, perhaps it's part of the farming scheme.

I hope you can read this. Writing in a moving car isn't much better than writing in a moving bus.

Next morning…

This finds me in Golden City, Missouri. We stopped here for the night with friends of Dennis and Lucy's. It sure felt good to sleep in a bed again after sitting in that bus all night. I was hoping to see a friend here that I knew from years ago, but he was not home.

I'm putting the card out for you this morning that I picked up in St. Louis. I'd mail these letters if I had extra envelopes, but I only had one along. This trip wasn't planned—remember? I think I'll make a stack of these notes, and mail them all at one time when I arrive back in Iowa.

Yesterday morning while I was still in St. Louis, I walked down and looked up at the Gateway Arch. It was only a couple blocks away, and I was bored waiting at the depot. Someone sure put a lot of work into that stainless steel arch. It was a beautiful sight in the morning sunlight, though I didn't go up, as there wasn't time.

After I walked back I talked with the newspaper man in front of the depot. He said he was a Jew and thinks he will obtain his salvation by keeping the old Mosaic law. I asked him if he can keep the law, and he said, "No, nobody is that perfect."

"Well," I said, "that's the point. That's why Christ came." He became very interested in selling newspapers after that comment.

He was interested though in talking about his troubles. He said he came from Texas, and this was his first day on his newspaper job. He was doing a good job of it, with his round jolly face and cheerful personality.

"Want a paper, sir (or ma'am)?" he'd call out when someone walked by. And regardless if they bought one or not, he'd call after them, "Have a good day, now."

I asked him if he was married, and he said he was, but divorced. They couldn't get along because he worked sixteen-hour days. They also had conflicts from religious differences. He said his wife and he argued and argued until he'd had enough of it. His children were becoming nervous, he said. Personally I don't see how leaving them improved the situation, but I didn't offer my opinion.

He said child support now costs him 500 dollars a month, which is a lot of money. He's behind in the payments, which is understandable since he's been out of a job for some time.

When I boarded the bus, I sat beside an older lady who began pouring out her troubles before we reached the edge of town. For forty-eight hours she had been traveling already, she said, and had lost her second suitcase. Actually it wasn't lost, the suitcase was accidentally placed on another bus by the driver.

She wasn't able to get the connections she needed and had to change bus lines to make better time. Her home is in Pittsburg, Pennsylvania, and she is going to Denver, Colorado, where her son lives with his girlfriend.

At one of the bus stops she sent me in for a soda and gave me enough money to buy one for myself. I guess the soda was a reward for listening to her troubles.

At 10:30...

Here I am again, waiting at the bus depot at Springfield, Missouri, the doctor's visit behind me. Dad left on an earlier bus, so I'm alone now. I didn't get to see any cancer cured or legs made whole, but the doctor does think I suffer from low blood sugar. "Hypoglycemia" is the fancy *Englisha* name for it. The doctor has sent me on my way with strict diet instructions in my pocket and a six week's supply of food supplements.

I have mailed another postcard here in Springfield, this one with the arch in Saint Louis pictured, framed in a sunset scene for background. I liked it a lot and hope you also do.

I will have a four-hour layover in St. Louis, but that was the only connection I could arrange which makes Trenton by tomorrow morning. School is scheduled to start then. I'm keeping the schedule, since we're on a tight one, and will be for the rest of the year. My bus leaves St. Louis at 1:15 a.m., and arrives in Mt. Pleasant at 5:30 a.m. I called Lonnie and Luella from a pay phone, and they will pick me up there. I really hate to make them come out that early in the morning, but so it goes.

In case you don't know what low blood sugar is—and I didn't either—this is how it was explained to me. Your body needs sugar, which you take in by eating, and all is well and good. But what if there is excess sugar ingested? In such cases, the properly functioning pancreas will put out insulin, which burns off the excess sugar. In a malfunctioning pancreas, too much insulin is released, which drives the blood sugar down to unhealthy levels, leaving you kaput. Hence depression.

The solution is to keep your sugar levels low enough where the pancreas doesn't overreact. This makes sense to me, though it means there are diet days ahead. Sugar, red meat, and white flour are to be eliminated—at least from what I can see looking over the diet list. I will give it to Luella when I arrive back in Trenton, and she can do with it what she wishes.

Now, here is the wacky stuff. The doctor said the brain has seven parts, and in some people parts have been damaged. To check your brain status you relax, close your eyes, and picture these colors as someone reads them off to you. You have to be able to see all of the colors: red, orange, yellow, sky blue, dark blue, green, and purple. To his satisfaction, I could picture all of them. I have no idea what would be done if one couldn't.

With all my heart,

Eugene

My dearest Eugene,

Your mom stopped by this morning to tell us your dad was home and that the doctor thinks you have a severe case of low blood sugar. I was very happy to hear they found out what the trouble was, or is, and I sure hope you stick to the special diet the doctor placed you on. Would you write me with the details? Mom would also like to know. She is having trouble with the same thing—she thinks. But of course, she won't go to the doctor. The other morning she nearly fainted getting out of bed, so please take care of yourself. I so wish I could be there to see that you do.

Yesterday Katie stopped by with the news that our grandparents on mom's side are coming tomorrow for a day's visit. Then today we received a letter from Grandma saying they are coming tonight and planning to stay overnight. One of their Mennonite nieces is driving. Well, they aren't here yet, so I suppose Katie will be proven correct.

Mom wondered if she and your mom could go over our wedding guest list and see if there aren't some people we could leave out. I think I'm going to forget about inviting my married cousins, as I never was very close to them anyway. Mom thinks there are way too many guests. So if it's okay with you, I'll let them decide things, as I don't mind. But I'm not saying we'll let them kick off all the people they want to.

I'm about a third of the way through the book you gave me. I like it so far.

Don't forget to take care of yourself. I'm a little worried that you won't, if you haven't detected that yet.

Lovingly,
Naomi

Dearest Naomi,

A welcomed letter arrived from you today, the first since I arrived back. I was hoping you would write on Monday, but it's understandable that you didn't. Anyway, you lifted my spirits, especially after another separation. The months ahead loom pretty high, but Lonnie laughs at me when I moan and complain. I guess older people have a different perspective about time.

We've had two days of school now with only thirteen students in attendance each day. Sharon, Dakota, Norman, Dawn, and Lydia are still in Florida, where it is sunny, I assume, unlike around here. The lower numbers make for less work now, but when they come back the trouble will start.

You should have seen all the glum faces in school on the first day back. They were enjoying their Christmas vacation too much, I guess. Life is what it is. By today though, the eighth graders were in a good mood again. Yesterday you could have fried eggs on their scowls.

Lonnie and Luella picked me up on time at the bus stop, which isn't a surprise. They are a very nice couple. Luella demanded to see my diet sheet at once, and she got busy right away studying the instructions with great diligence. She has already banished all red meat, sugar, and white flour from my diet. The woman has no mercy. She said poor Lonnie also may end up suffering and that he needs a good diet himself.

The poor man was the look of misery tonight while staring at what was on the table, but I suppose he will survive. This may turn out to be a worse thing for him than when his grandchildren come. At least they go home when the weekend is over.

Luella's taking control of this diet feels good to me. I was wondering how I would ever manage on my own, since the diet is strict. I can see though, that I already feel better, and that's after being on the diet for a few days. That could be all my imagination, I know, but we'll hope not. Wouldn't that be great, feeling well all the time? That's not a life I know a whole lot about, I guess. I've learned to live with ups and downs.

I miss you much,

Eugene

Jerry and Tina Eicher

My beloved Eugene,

I'm so lonely I could have bawled all day, and I don't look forward to the weekend at all. Other than the wonderful visit from Grandpa and Grandma and your letters, this must have been one of the longest weeks I've ever lived through.

Yesterday my cousin Barbara drove in with her car around 9:30, with Grandpa, Grandma, and Malinda along. It was such a joy to see them all climbing out. Mom and I raced to give them all hugs, and we talked on the lawn for the longest time. Barbara doesn't wear a covering anymore, and she doesn't dress Amish either, so that was the disappointment of the day.

They stayed overnight and were here until 2:00 in the afternoon. Malinda wanted to visit our school, since she teaches this year, so Rosanna and I went along. She said she was looking for pointers to improve her own teaching. I think she liked the way things were run, but she said they were doing things about the same as she's used to. She did say she's quite troubled by the fact that she still doesn't get along very well with her co-teacher but doesn't know what to do about it.

So I enjoyed their visit, but my highlight today was definitely your second letter and first postcard. I'm so glad the doctor in Missouri turned out to be of some good. Your comments were funny about the expectations they had of him, but you can be thankful he was of some help. Grandma said she wants to know how you get along. They scared me with tales of what diabetics go through, which is what you become if your low blood sugar gets too bad and the pancreas stops working. I think you probably know all this, but it was the first I had heard the information. So please take care of yourself.

The sewing was Wednesday evening for the young folks, and then last night the Millers invited us over for supper. Both events would have been better if you had been here, but I still enjoyed them.

Your trip sounded very interesting with the different people you met and the lovely scenery. How I would have loved to be along, but I'd better not think on that too much or the tears will start again.

Take care of yourself now and stay on that diet.

I love you,
Naomi

My dearest Naomi,

Luella told me that your mom sent her a note along with the Christmas present I brought back. In the note your mom said she hopes the next four months go by as fast as the past four months have. I tell you, older people do have a different perspective on things. Four months? A short time? I guess that's why they can't understand why young people are always in such a hurry.

School attendance continues at a grand total of thirteen, and will stay so for the rest of the week. I can see the royal mess running smack into my face when the missing students arrive again and I'm back up to seventeen.

On Wednesday afternoon I arrived home around 4:00, slept for two hours, trying to catch up on all the lost sleep. I can still hear those bus motors whining in my ears. When I woke up it felt like Thursday morning, only the sun was going down instead of coming up.

The young folks had a practice singing last night, learning some new songs, with the gathering held at Saul's place. I walked up and enjoyed it for an hour or so, excusing myself early so I could get to bed. I told them my eyes felt like sandpaper, and they were quite understanding.

Lonnie and Luella had been invited out for supper, so the house was empty when I came back, which didn't help my loneliness. But I lost my sorrow in sleep, waking up late this morning. That's unusual for me—sleeping through an alarm. I threw my clothing on, made a mad dash downstairs, and arrived in time for breakfast.

Luella has me on the diet, of course, watching over me with a feverish eye, banishing all manner of forbidden foods or even the mention of them. I do feel better, though, so I'm happy.

Saturday…

Another letter arrived today, which is good, though it just makes the longing to be home all the worse. Thanks for the concern over my health. I am abiding by the diet, guided by Luella's firm hand. The woman is doing what I have never been able to do—keep healthy and regimented food in my body. Horror of horrors, I have to eat salads! Not just once a week or once in a blue moon, but every day. How much worse could it get?

Lettuce should be food for rabbits, or horses, or for creatures who wander

Jerry and Tina Eicher

the night, but not for humans. Whoever first thought of lettuce as human food should be banished in chains and shackles to some dark dungeon.

And carrots and celery? I know God made them, but He surely had other usages in mind. Things like bovine consumption. The vegetables crunch between my teeth and rattle my brain with the awful racket of chewing. It is a horrible way to keep life in the body. But I feel better, so what can I say?

Today after school we had some excitement at the farm. I was sitting at the schoolhouse after the children had left, looking out the window, when I saw a coon climbing the trees in the front yard. I wasn't exactly sure what I was seeing because of the distance so I went to check it out. Sure enough it was a coon. I told Luella, who called up to Saul's place to let Duane know. He drove down in the pickup, bringing his rifle and Janie with him, but the coon had disappeared by then.

Janie came up with the idea of looking in the barn under the hay bales. We had moved a few bales when she started hollering, "There he goes! There he goes!"

The coon scurried across the floor, escaped through an open window, and headed off over an open field, with me right behind him. I was determined not to let him get away, but he did a sharp turn toward the back field, getting into the fence row. The others didn't feel like running anymore, and I was gasping for breath, so we let him go. Duane wanted to fire away, but Luella wouldn't let him, which was a wise decision with all the people around.

Lonnie's dad is in the hospital from a bad case of the winter flu, and they went down last night to visit him, taking me along. I only went inside for a few minutes since the visiting rights are restricted with how sick he is. Lonnie said the doctor thinks he's doing okay for an eighty-year-old man.

By the way, the grandchild's test for cancer from before Christmas came back clear. So it was all a big scare, but something to be thankful for nonetheless.

If you want to know where the doctor's office was in Missouri, look on the map clear down by the Arkansas, Oklahoma, Kansas border, in the little town of Powell.

Sunday….

This morning at breakfast poor Lonnie let his feelings be known. I knew there was trouble coming, but I didn't know exactly where it would break over the horizon. He is sure that the quality of his care has diminished considerably since Luella spends so much time on my food preparation. He says he will soon be reduced to skin and bones. If I were in his shoes, I'm sure I'd feel the same way. I told him "I'm sorry" and that Luella doesn't have to do all this work for me.

He laughed but I still know he's at least a little serious about it. What can be done? I don't know. Luella stands over me, making sure I eat everything she puts on my plate, and she checks when I come home from school, questioning whether I've eaten the right things while at school. The diet is very specific with time and items, but not the quantity of the food. I guess what's good for you can be eaten in large amounts. Yuck...

Lonnie complains that the food isn't getting to him. He claimed last night he couldn't get any salad until Luella had served me and had taken some for herself. So it goes, but I am being good...and eating horrible food. That is food which is horribly good. I don't know how else to say it.

The church had a minister's ordination over Christmas while I was gone. There were three men in the lot: Saul, one of the school board members, and Stan, the young man who teaches the youth midweek Bible studies.

They set up the three books like the Amish do, with one of them containing a slip of paper.

Stan drew the book that contained the slip of paper, and he was already ordained by the time I arrived back from Missouri. Today was supposed to be his first time preaching, but he gave his testimony instead. The regular minister filled in the rest of his allotted time. I am beginning to like Stan more and more. He has fire, zeal, and self-confidence. He really believes God has called him to the ministry and chose to confirm it with the draw of the lot. I believe he's right about that.

With all my love,
Eugene

My dearest Eugene,

I arrived home from babysitting to a quiet house. Mom is still down with the flu. She must have been worn out because she has it so hard. I sure hope it doesn't spread any further. Dad seemed cheerful enough when I was out helping with the chores—if that can be used as a guide to flu prediction. I still feel okay, so I will hope for the best. The rest of the family also seems fine.

I served them all supper, and then made chicken broth for Mom. She sat up in bed when I brought it to her, sipping it slowly. The bread didn't get eaten, but at least she has healthy broth in her stomach for the night.

I'm glad to hear that Luella is keeping close tabs on your diet. By the way, we figured out that Mom doesn't have low blood sugar because she went off of sugar and didn't feel any better. She still won't go to a doctor, but she thinks it might be an iron deficiency. We shall see, I guess.

Yesterday I was in Worthington with Mrs. Brown and her two girls. She wanted me to go along to help get their pictures taken. They are the sweetest things and were all dressed up in their Sunday clothes and cute as buttons.

Last night I gave Dad his haircut since Mom was down with the flu. I enjoyed it, although I never thought I would be a good barber. Mom said Dad behaved himself better for me than he does for her. He was afraid I wouldn't do it right, but he held still and the job looks fine to me. Now Don and Larry are next. Can't you just hear them yelling?

There is a young folks gathering tonight at Robert's, with plans to shell the young folks' popcorn. That should be fun—gathering around the barn floor in the lantern light. I just wish you were here.

With lots of love,
Naomi

My dearest Naomi,

Lonnie's dad has taken a turn for the worse, and they have him on an IV now. The house was in a hush tonight when I came home since the news was so unexpected. Well, maybe Lonnie did expect something, even after the doctor gave them such a good word. Both Lonnie and Luella are down at the hospital, but I decided not to go along.

I wonder what you are doing this time of the night, and if you are as lonely as I am. There has been no young folks gathering this week. They don't seem to have as many as we Amish do. It would be nice to have more because it gets kind of old being mostly around children and the senior generation.

I see in your last letter you are concerned I'll end up with diabetes. The doctor in Missouri has already warned me of that danger, which is one of the reasons I'm being so faithful to the diet. I don't want my pancreas giving out, as diabetes would be much worse than hypoglycemia. So rest assured I'm doing what I'm supposed to do, and not only because of the diabetes. I really want to get over the constant blues that sometimes comes upon me. It feels good to be on an even keel, not feeling like a boat rocking up and down on tempestuous seas. It also feels good to know that my frequent depressions were not simply something in my head, as I always figured they were.

We are still missing seven students in school. Three of them should be back next week. None of them should have much trouble catching up except Lydia, so I'll have to see if I can give her extra help.

Crystal was in a really good mood today, which helps. I always worry when the students aren't happy, even when I know it's not my fault. Dena was absent today. For what reason, it's hard to tell. She's sure to be out of sorts the first day she comes back.

With love as usual,

Eugene

My dearest Naomi,

Today is a week since the Christmas holidays, but it seems much longer than that. I sit here thinking about our parting and how lovely and sweet you looked.

I never had the time to tell you over Christmas that my parents have some objections to our wedding this summer. Maybe I shouldn't tell you this now, or ever, as I don't think it matters. Once we're both twenty-one, we can do as we wish. I don't think they're being mean or that they don't approve of you. They didn't really tell me why, nor did I ask. I suspect it has something to do with their fears of our maturity level. I'm the oldest, and this will be their first child who marries. Anyway, please don't worry about it.

On a more humorous note, I think I've found the perfect match for my sister Mary. The boy lives out here, of all places. Not that she needs any help or would ever think of joining the Mennonites, but still, I can't help but think about them being right for each other. He's really a nice boy.

Winter seems to have arrived in force, with the weather changing on a dime. There still hasn't been enough snow for the children to play outside—only cold and bitter wind. Since we're trapped inside, the children are full of energy at recess times. They end up blowing it off during schooltime at their desks, which is not good.

I didn't get a letter from you today, but since one came yesterday I shouldn't complain. When it comes to letters from you, I'm hard to satisfy.

What do you do with your long winter evenings? Do the young folks have much going? What about ice skating? Has that started yet? They don't do any ice skating around here for some strange reason.

Thursday evening…

Today the weather changed again, and it was beautiful outside, the sun bright and warm with almost no wind. At lunch hour I just stood at the corner of the schoolhouse and soaked in the warmth, feeling the stirring of life and love. I guess the young dream a lot, especially when they don't know what lies ahead. I hope life is good to you and me. I think it will be.

The youth mid-week Bible study was enjoyable again. Stan is still leading the class even though he's a minister now, which is great. I like his style of teaching. The topic was on spiritual adoption, and the verses came from Romans 8:15-17. But the discussion didn't stay on adoption. Stan explained that verse 16 speaks of the Spirit bearing witness to our spirit that we are the sons of God, and that whenever the conscience is free of guilt, this clears the way for the believer to feel in fellowship with God.

I spoke up and said that I couldn't agree entirely with the wisdom of using our conscience as a guide, especially on whether we are in fellowship with God. Because there are such variations to the intensity of an individual's conscience. Some people are very sensitive and others are not. It seems to me God has some other standard by which He declares us righteous.

Stan then quoted 2 Corinthians 10:5, the part that says, "And bringing into captivity every thought to the obedience of Christ." I told him I don't think thoughts and conscience are the same thing, which Stan apparently did. So after some discussion, the conclusion was reached that they are not the same. The class felt like the conscience only uses our thoughts to work through, and while thoughts might be under our control, our consciences are not.

Stan wrapped up the discussion by saying that our consciences can be something that can be taught and ought to be under the control of the Holy Spirit. That is a conclusion I agree with. They also agreed that it might take years of being a Christian for the conscience to be properly trained by God.

Stan led the discussion further to Romans 8:17, where it says, "If so be that we suffer with him, that we may be also glorified together." He asked us when we think this glorifying takes place. Someone ventured that heaven likely brought glorification, and Stan agreed that it does, but that we also get a lot of good out of suffering while still on this earth.

Stan used his own life's testimony as an example. He feels that God put him through extra hardships to prepare him for the ministry position he now holds. "If I hadn't gone through those trials," he said, "I wouldn't have anything to tell you when I get up behind the pulpit to speak."

That really touched me.

He also used the example of kindness. Unless we first feel what it's like to be used unkindly by others, it's often very hard to be kind to someone.

He laughed and used me as an example on being separated from our loved ones. "Take Eugene here," he said, "and the fact that he has been away from Naomi for so long. This will likely deepen his love for her because when they get back together, they will remember how it once was without each other. While if they had never been separated, they wouldn't know how that feels."

I thought that was also a good point, although it doesn't really help the current pain a lot.

Surprisingly, a contentious issue here in the church is the assurance of salvation. I thought only Amish churches argued about this. I guess many of the older people here, including Lonnie and Luella, feel that it's wrong to make such statements and that our salvation must be left to the Lord.

Stan, on the other hand, openly advocates saying that one is saved by the work of Christ. The two sides seem to be at each other's throats at the moment, and strangely enough—considering that I am Amish—I am on Stan's side.

I told Lonnie and Luella at the supper table the other night when they asked me about it, that I believe the Scriptures say we can know what Christ has done for us and that this is not a statement of pride. Lonnie said the forefathers never believed so, that they felt God decided such things at the day of judgment.

"We can have a hope," he said, "but we must not tell God what His decision will be."

I think this would be an insecure way to live, but I didn't argue with him. They seem quite happy and content believing as they do.

I love you,
Eugene

My dearest Eugene,

Greetings from a very tired girl. I went to the popcorn shelling at Robert's, after being up reading until midnight last night. Mom said that was tough, so I received no sympathy from her corner. I need to get to bed earlier and will try tonight—after I am done writing this letter.

Your mom heard me talk about the book you gave me last Sunday and asked whether she could read it. So I passed the book on through one of your sisters tonight because I finished it last night.

Once we arrived at Robert's, it was worth the tiredness to be there. Talking and chatting with the other girls cheered me up. The boys started throwing popcorn kernels near the end, but Robert called them down, which was a good thing. Those little things hurt when they hit your neck.

Mom is trying to eat foods that contain large quantities of iron. As pale as she looks, she should go in for an iron shot. At least she should have herself checked out by a doctor, but no way. She will try other things first. She's stubborn that way.

I love you,
Naomi

My dearest Naomi,

I'm very lonesome for you, as usual, especially with the weekend coming up. I'm looking forward to making this all up to you someday by being with you all the time.

Lonnie's dad passed away last night. The funeral will be on Sunday, so I really won't have too much leisure time over the weekend. I've been doing the chores for the last two evenings so Lonnie and Luella could spend all the time they need with family.

The children are playing inside games at school, many of which I've never seen before. Today the boys and girls divided up into groups after secretly numbering off each group. Everyone guesses who in the other group has their number by writing down three choices. Those with hits in the three tries get a point. If there are too many ties toward the end, they take it down to one guess per round.

By some coincidence, the sixth graders, Dennis and Jackie, had the same numbers the first three rounds. Jackie threw a fit when Dennis kept guessing her on his first round. She threatened to quit the game. They are regular sweethearts. I mean, it's no secret to anyone because of the way they act. So it was natural to me that Dennis should pick her.

I convinced Jackie to try another round, and Dennis didn't pick her, nor did she have his number, so she calmed down. Girls are strange sometimes.

It's too bad you weren't here because I would have picked you every time.

With love,
Eugene

My dearest Eugene,

I forgot to ask you in my last letter if you could tell Luella that Mom and I really appreciated her letter. Luella listed your full diet, in case you don't know what she wrote about. Even though Mom won't be using the diet now, at least I know what you're eating. It sounds healthy even if the food doesn't taste good. You were funny with the cuisine descriptions, but you must keep on the diet!

I wonder how Lonnie's dad is by now.

I received your letter and card today, which was a nice surprise. That card is beautiful. Thank you.

I hope your school attendance gets better soon.

I arrived back from a tramp through the back fields. One doesn't get as much exercise in the winter when there's no outside field work, so I took time for a long walk. Plus, it's snowing nicely. I filled the bird feeder while I was outside, as the snow is staying on the ground now. We have the usual barn sparrows who use the feeder—the pesky things—plus black-capped chickadees, cardinals, a pair of wrens, and I even saw a house finch tonight.

It was a nice walk, bundled up as I was in one of Dad's pants, the legs rolled up under my dress, and the three coats I squeezed into, with a big scarf topping off the outfit. You would have laughed, I know, but you might as well get used to this if you're going to marry me. I love long walks in the snowy fields.

Oh, I wish I could be with you tomorrow. A long buggy drive home from church with you at the reins would be just the thing a girl needs.

With all my love,
Naomi

Hi, dearest Naomi,

Here's another letter from me. I received two from you today, which is irritating when they pile up like that. I know it's the mail's fault, not yours, but there I sat for three whole days sweating it out, waiting for another letter, and then two come at once. Patience, Eugene, patience.

I'm a little nervous, I guess, thinking about what I wrote you a few letters back—that my parents have objections to our marriage this summer. I really shouldn't have told you that. They had the right to express their fears without my passing it on to you. I think it's perfectly normal for parents to have fears about their children and when they should marry. On my part, I never expect to find anyone better than you or someone who suits me better. They won't object to our wedding next year. I really wouldn't worry about it.

And please don't get nervous around them, either. I really should have kept my big mouth shut. I can imagine you'll try to act extra nice and end up all tense and out of sorts. They really do love you.

Dawn, Norman, and Dakota are back in school and scrambling to catch up. I'm also scrambling to get checking their schoolwork done in the evenings so they can see by the next morning if there are any problems.

The chairman of the school board brought an electric typewriter to the schoolhouse tonight. I felt like a little boy with a new toy. The thing is a whiz compared with the old manual typewriter I was using. I think Noah had the manual one along on the ark with him and left it in Iowa.

Tuesday...

The eighth graders have run into problems with their arithmetic. This takes extra time in class, which runs other things shorter, but so it goes. Try explaining how to find the area of a rectangle, the volume of a rectangle, the circumference of a circle, the area of a circle, the volume of a cylinder, the volume of a sphere, the area of a sphere, and then its outside surface area. And doing all this in a few fifteen-minute time slots. Anyway, we survived.

The new typewriter will surely have me spoiled by the end of the term. It will be difficult going back to the old manual typewriters at home after this luxurious machine. Here you only touch the keys instead of pounding down with great vigor.

On an unrelated subject, when I write Miller on your letters, I have often thought what a wonderful name that was and what a shame you should lose it someday. But how can I help it that I love you?

With all my heart,

Eugene

Jerry and Tina Eicher

Dearest Eugene,

This is not going to be an easy letter to write. Nor will it be easy for you to read. The truth is, I don't think we should marry this summer. I think waiting will be better for all concerned, and I don't want you to try to persuade me differently because I have thought about this a great deal, and prayed, and, yes, cried too. Maybe if we wait your mom will eventually be ready to let you go (although part of me doubts she'll ever be ready). And maybe by that time they would think me mature enough and worthy of being your wife (although part of me doubts that too). I'm feeling so bad about this, but I'm in such confusion and agony, and you are so far away that I can't see or talk with you.

Did you really have to teach at that school? This is never going to end, or so it feels. I can't tell you how confusing this all is or how many tears I've cried since I received that last letter. And yes, you should have told me about it. I'm so glad you did. If we love each other, we must tell each other these things and work them through. Only how? That seems to be the problem. For now, though, we had better call the wedding off. I just can't think what else to do.

What really hurts is that your parents don't approve of me or think me worthy of you. That cuts all the way down to the heart. I don't think I can live like that—with my husband's parents thinking their son messed up by planning to marry me.

Maybe you can find yourself a nice, wonderful Mennonite girl out there somewhere who will meet their approval. And there are a few girls around here your mom seems to think are great. I'm sure you can do much better than you are doing with me.

I don't want you to think that anyone put me up to this because they didn't. I've thought this out myself, and it seems the best thing to do.

And I still love you,
Naomi

My dearest Naomi,

I arrived home with the high hopes of finding a letter from you, but of course there was none. The rest of the day suddenly seemed exceedingly boring until I remembered there was Bible study tonight, which helped a little.

The best thing I could do was reread some of your old letters. I get so lonesome for you out here on these flat plains. As I reread your letters, I see a lot of places where I made blunders in the things I wrote you. I hope you have patience with me because I will try to improve myself as time goes on.

It does seem harder this way, with us apart and trying to write letters. I hope this venture wasn't some big mistake, some dream I ran after trying to do something interesting with my life. I know a farmer's life is also interesting, so I'm not knocking that. I do plan to settle down after my next year of teaching. We should have plenty of time then to work this out and to enjoy our lives together.

And please tell me how you feel. Don't try to protect my feelings. Improving oneself can be painful, I know, so I don't want to shy away from that.

This morning Lonnie and Luella took one of their friends to the airport in Chicago. I would have loved to go along for the drive as I've never been in Chicago, but work comes before pleasure. I guess I should act like the children do—taking off at the slightest excuse. Perhaps if they would see the teacher act like they do, they would know how it feels. I get so exasperated. If they even have a sore throat or *say* they do, they stay home. Sickness follows all of them around like the plague, jumping out from dark corners to drag the poor pupils home from the schoolhouse. Am I being nasty? Yes, I suppose I am. I will quit now and think nice thoughts about them.

Anyhow, Lonnie and Luella had to leave at 4:00 this morning, which left me by myself for breakfast. Luella said that Janie could come up and fix breakfast for me. I said no she wouldn't, and Luella said yes she would. After we went around the circle a few times, Luella gave in and left me with detailed instructions on where things are. I think the poor woman is afraid I will burn down her kitchen. She'll probably be expecting bowls to be melted to the burners, at the very least, and grease spots all the way to the ceiling. Perhaps I should play some trick on her, but I can't think of anything good enough that wouldn't be courting disaster, so I will leave the joke department to others more skilled than I am.

Luella left all the food items on the counter for me, so I heated the water for the oatmeal, toasted a piece of bread, and set the bacon out to be fried. While the pan was warming, I tossed in a piece of butter, and the house promptly filled with smoke. It was no trick either, just stupid of me. I quickly opened all the kitchen windows and waved a towel around. If Janie had been driving by on the road, I'm sure she would have come racing in to save Luella's kitchen from the hands of the clumsy schoolteacher.

Luella usually prepares poached eggs for breakfast, but I took the opportunity to fry the eggs. Hopefully that isn't breaking the diet rules or it will create a stink when Luella comes back. I tried to hide the evidence so there wouldn't be a discussion on the virtues of poached versus fried eggs. Lonnie likes his eggs poached, and that's fine with me, but if Luella finds out my preference, she will think she has to make fried eggs every morning.

I washed the frying pan to remove the evidence, but I couldn't do anything about the small kettle that shows no signs of poached eggs. So I placed the kettle close to the sink, figuring Luella would think I had cleaned it, but it didn't work out that way. When I arrived home from school, one of the first things out of her mouth was, "Eugene, did you fry your eggs?"

Now she's going to fry my eggs every morning, end of discussion, and no amount of argument would persuade her otherwise.

At the supper table, Lonnie joined in the discussion of poached versus fried eggs. Fried eggs are very unhealthy, he said. I countered with one of my dad's arguments, which isn't much of any argument, it's more of a joke. Dad always said that poached eggs take forty years to digest. Lonnie laughed himself silly over that, and we left the discussion on friendly terms.

Thursday...

I arrived home from school and still no letter. Monday was the last time I received a letter, so I hope nothing is wrong. Sorry for my worries, and I hope I don't pressure you to write all the time. It's just that your letters are such a joy and pleasure.

There is an ice skating planned tonight for the youth, and I'm going, of course. It's been almost a year since I've been on skates. Hopefully, I still know how and won't go sliding around on my knees or bottom. I do so wish you and your cheerful smile could be here.

The Bible study last night was on the fifteenth chapter of John, the first eight verses. The main point Stan made was that Christ is the one true vine, but there are many other vines one can be attached to.

Someone asked the question concerning verse 2: "Can a branch that is broken off be grafted back in?" Stan thought that it could.

Someone else asked what the purging was in the last part of verse 2. Stan said that the way he defines purging is trouble that God sends into our lives to purify us. He feels that if trouble comes from our own mistakes there isn't much purifying value in it, but if trouble comes from doing good, this has value with God. The way to tell the difference, he said, is the issue of control. If we can stop our troubles by changing our ways, then we are producing the troubles ourselves. Otherwise, it's from God and we need to submit.

Stan commented on verse 7, that instead of being so concerned with asking things of God, we should be sure we meet the two stated conditions. First—"if we abide in Jesus," and second—"if Jesus' words abide in us." After that we can ask what we will and trust that God will answer our prayers according to what is best for us. All this seems more interesting in a group discussion, but I wanted to share it with you.

Luella visited school today for the first time. She was there from the time we started until noon. I'm sure there were plenty of faults to see if she compared me to their other teachers, but she didn't say anything negative. Maybe she was just being nice.

I love you,
Eugene

My dearest Eugene,

I'm wondering if you've received my letter yet since your last letter sounded so cheerful. The tension in my chest is something awful. I wish I hadn't written the letter, but I did. So I guess I'll look on the bright side of things and hope I brought something up that needed to be dealt with.

Last night the young folks had a skating party at Benny Miller's pond. I went to break myself out of my blues. Don was busy at home and couldn't make the drive. I was reminded at the gathering of how much I love our young people. They had lanterns set all around the pond and most of the ice shoveled off. We played prisoner's base for a while and then just skated for the fun of it.

You seem so far away, as if I haven't seen you in years, and yet Christmas hasn't been that long ago.

Today I didn't have to work, so I caught up on the ironing and mending. There's not much to do on the farm in the winter other than chores. Dad keeps cutting back on the milk cows when one goes dry. I'm not sure what his plans are. Everything feels all mixed up right now.

I filled the bird feeders and watched the birds for a while until I got too cold standing outside. They are lovely creatures to watch, their perky little jumps and their feathers all fluffed in the cold. It brought tears to my eyes, but I was really crying for other reasons. The birds normally cheer me up.

Mom wants to make coffee ice cream tonight as a treat for Dad. It's his birthday tomorrow, and she wants to catch him by surprise. I don't think it will work. I saw him looking in the cupboards this morning after Mom had left the kitchen. I think he knows she's making something for him. Ice cream can't be far from his suspicions.

I have to babysit tomorrow, likely till midnight, which I'm glad for. It gives me something to do.

Friday…

I don't know what to write tonight. It's after midnight already, and I feel very awful for writing that letter. Another of your letters arrived today, but I don't think you've received the nasty one yet. What you say softens my heart, but what's done is done. I just hope I don't hurt you too much.

I should never have let my mind blow things so out of proportion.

And I thank you in advance for being understanding. I can already tell you are going to be. Let me assure you that after I wrote the letter I felt so bad I was physically ill.

I was afraid you'd respond in a letter and say that we should break our relationship, and that you wouldn't ever write or speak to me again. And I wouldn't have blamed you in the least.

I realize that I was withdrawing from your family, especially on Sundays when I would see your mom. How warped my mind must be.

Last night at the supper table Dad didn't agree with me at all when I shared what I had written. By the way, he claimed to be totally surprised by the coffee ice cream. We made the ice cream in the basement while he was doing the chores. We cleaned everything before he got back inside.

Anyway, he feels that you have no ulterior motives of any sort, and that your parents are just having the normal worries that all parents do. So I feel much better about all of this. Hopefully I have done no lasting damage.

It's so good to think again that our love has value for its own sake. I get messed up when things move beyond that. Please forgive me? And thanks ahead of time for the patience that I know you will have.

I really want to tell you what a wonderful person I think you are. I could never find a more special man to marry than you.

I love you,
Naomi

My beloved Naomi,

This finds me home from church and wondering very much how things are going around your place. It would be so wonderful to spend Sunday afternoon with you.

Stan preached his first sermon today, and I saw a couple people there who normally don't show up, so perhaps he was the attraction. He does preach differently from the other ministers—more personal and engaging.

I asked Lonnie and Luella afterward what they thought. They said they hope things start going better in church now that a new preacher has been ordained, and that they approved of the sermon.

This Mennonite church has a balcony and I sat up there today so I could see how the people reacted to Stan's sermon, but also because I get bored, and this was something different.

Yesterday I made a batch of cookies for the same bored reasons. It's a low state of affairs when a man spends his Saturday morning inside the house and in the kitchen. Just kidding…but they tasted good. Lonnie agreed, so there. Luella fussed a little about it. These cookies weren't on my diet, so I had to promise her I'd only eat a couple and that they were for Lonnie.

Luella pulled the last joke on me though. After Lonnie had eaten his cookies, he left for the other farm down the road to do the chores. After a while Luella called him on the Freedom telephone he always carries with him, and when he answered she told him she wanted to make sure he was still alive.

Ha…ha…They thought that was really funny. And so it goes around here.

Monday evening…

I'm so glad I didn't mail the Sunday letter this morning. At least I can include another one with it. I cannot begin to express my sorrow over your last letter. For some reason I felt as if I had spoken things I shouldn't have, but the shock of your letter was still hard to take.

Is there nothing I can do to persuade you? I'm so sorry for how my parents feel, and that I even told you. Where do all these suspicions come from anyway? Please reconsider. At least wait until I get back, and we can talk about this properly.

Now I'm kind of at a loss. What does one do? Surely you don't want me to discontinue writing my letters. Your letter didn't sound like that, so I'll take a chance and hope this can be worked out.

My heart hurts all over, but I comfort myself that you do love me and that love can win out in the end, even when the circumstances are difficult and the road hard. But if I had known it would be this hard, I don't know if I ever would have come out here to teach. May God forgive me if something happens to separate us. That would be too much to bear.

Well, I will cry my agony alone tonight and keep hope alive in my heart because you haven't cut things off completely. Hopefully your next letter will bear better news.

As always, I do love you.

Eugene

My dearest Eugene,

I wonder what your first lessons are this morning at school…and whether you received the nasty letter yet. I can't say how sorry I am, and I'm now afflicted with great waves of fear. What if you aren't understanding and sink into a depression over this? I have chills running up and down my back at the very thought. But I must not let my mind blow things up. You are an understanding man, you really are.

Hopefully, all your Florida students are back in class by now. The people from Iowa must like the sunshine down south. I'm still enjoying the snow, thank you very much. The birds are especially cute this morning, and I think they are very thankful for my kind attention.

There was bad news at church yesterday. James Yoder has somehow convinced Millie and the children to join him at that *Englisha* church he's been going to. Dad said he thinks excommunication talks are already under way. Bishop Enos looked very troubled yesterday, sitting there on the front benches with the other ministers. I can only say that I'm glad I'm not in the ministers' shoes.

My wrist is still hurting from a fall I took at the skating get-together. I think it will be okay. It wasn't that serious. That's why I didn't mention anything in the last letter, so don't worry about this, please.

Your mom spoke with me after church on Sunday, and I know my neck was turning all kinds of colors. I sure hope you didn't write her about my letter. It's bad enough just knowing I wrote it. If she finds out, I'll never be able to talk to her again from sheer embarrassment.

Your mom said she thinks you are doing much better, now that the diet has had time to take effect. I agree with her. Your letters are so cheerful and much brighter than they were before Christmas. You might say it's just my imagination, but I don't think so.

Then she gave me a funny get well card from your sisters. They knew about the wrist sprain. There were three pieces of candy taped inside, along with the words "Hope you get better soon" and "These candy pills will help speed you on your way." Signed, "The Mast skunks."

That made me laugh, and I feel even more embarrassed for my wild imaginations.

And you aren't the only one getting mad at the mail service. I won't get a letter for a couple of days, and then *kerbang!* there are two. I enjoy them anyway, so don't stop writing.

Also, what is so nice about Miller? There is nothing wrong with Mast at all. I'd change my whole name for you.

You will think this is very dumb, but here it goes. Do you think it would be okay if I called you Sweetheart sometimes? Somehow I got the notion it might not be proper to call a man that. I like it very much when you call me Sweetheart, or any other endearment for that matter. Anyway, I've often called you that to myself.

I love you,

Naomi

My beloved Naomi,

I'm home from school and trying to keep breathing, hoping for good news in the mail. I still can't believe how stupid I was, and I don't blame you one bit for thinking and saying what you did.

As for school, Norman and Dakota are still behind with their schoolwork from being gone so long. I was checking their papers late tonight and, hopefully, by tomorrow things will be back to normal for those two.

Anthony wasn't in school again today, and his brother Larry said that he doesn't think he's really sick, but that he wanted to stay to watch his dad unload corn. I can well believe it by the way Larry was grinning. I figured he was talking from experience and was enjoying his brother's day off in his thoughts. He was receiving way too much pleasure out of the absence for my comfort level.

There's definitely a flu bug going around, and I know from personal experience. Dawn threw up all over her desk today. The girl was still purple in the face when I looked up, so I raced over with the wastebasket in the vain hope the next discharge could be caught before it hit the floor. Nope, it didn't work, and I got the job of cleaning it all up. I almost used the wastebasket for reasons other than what wastebaskets are intended for. Yuck…yuck…and double yuck!

There is no phone in the schoolhouse to call the parents, so I didn't know what to do about getting Dawn home. I went ahead and called for fourth-grade English class, and when Lester came up he whispered that his brother Mark was acting as if he wanted to throw up. I raced back with the wastebasket and asked Mark if he was feeling sick.

"No," he said, though he looked it.

I left the wastebasket there for good measure, with clear instructions where vomit belongs. Perhaps a boy can hit a wastebasket, but thankfully we never found out. He did start crying after a while, and when I asked him what was wrong, he said he had chills. The poor boy really was sick, his forehead hot to my touch. I felt sorry for him and got his coat from the rack.

Crystal soon came up with a solution, suggesting that she walk down and call from Lonnie and Luella's place. Next time I'll think of that sooner. Within twenty minutes two very worried mothers came tearing into the schoolyard.

Some weeks the work piles up, and then the next there seems to be plenty of time for everything on the schedule. I guess this way I appreciate the good weeks.

I'm presently enjoying seventh- and eighth-grade English. Since this is the second time teaching through the books, teaching involves only a refresher course each day before the class. We are into first person, second person, third person, adjectives, adverbs, predicate adverbs, and predicate adjectives.

Take care, and I will keep waiting for good news from your pen.

Love you,
Eugene

Jerry and Tina Eicher

My dearest Eugene,

How are you feeling by this time? Hopefully better than I am. I have a cold/cough, and a big one at that. I think it's what has been going around the community, and it sure leaves one feeling pretty rotten. Apparently this all contributed to my missed appointment this morning. I was dreamily working out in the kitchen, baking a cake, when Mrs. Vanhorn, one of my housecleaning bosses, pulled into the driveway. Suddenly I remembered my job with her. Mom went out to speak with Mrs. Vanhorn to explain while I raced upstairs to get ready in a jiffy.

Mrs. Vanhorn was very nice, of course, but that wasn't the only thing that went wrong. I had told Mrs. Beck I would babysit for her this afternoon, and I didn't remember that appointment when Mrs. Vanhorn asked me to work late. I arrived home to find out that Mrs. Beck came past to say that she wasn't feeling well herself and didn't need me, so things worked out. This is the first time I have been so forgetful in a long time, but it leaves me with worry pimples for days afterward.

Dad went to the work *frolick* today. They are laying block for Stan Yoder's basement.

Richard and Joan still haven't moved into the upper part of their house. They are still living in the basement. At least they are married and together, compared to some other people who shall remained unnamed.

I miss you so much.

Love you,

Your Miss Forgetful
Naomi

My dearest Naomi,

I am rereading your letter, and I think I can breathe again. How wonderful that you have forgiven me for my stupid blunder. And you can call me Sweetheart all you want. I suppose that will have to wait until I get back home again. It will sound better face-to-face than in letters.

Thursday evening...

Things are in a state of shock around here. The bishop of the church passed away yesterday totally unexpectedly! School is called off out of respect for him. The chairman of the school board called last night and told me the news.

Lonnie and Luella walk around here like pale ghosts. They told me at the breakfast table what this could mean for the church. Another bishop will have to be ordained soon, and they fear Stan will get the office. This would be a disaster from their point of view, as the bishop has a lot of power to take the church in whatever direction he wishes.

They could probably tolerate Stan continuing in his office as a minister if his co-minister got the bishopric, but not if Stan does. No one has come right out and said it, but the fears of a church split are pretty strong, and the bishop still has to be buried.

On other matters, I continue to be amazed at how fast the eighth-grade girls can change their moods. There are days when they are so out of sorts they bring the proverbial thunderclouds with high winds and rain right into the schoolhouse. They challenge me on everything I say and make life miserable in general.

Then the next day they are all smiles, agreeable, accommodating, and sunshine and roses. On those days I can say what I want, and they absorb it without backfiring. I even got them to work on a poster today and received not a word of complaint. Beats me what I did differently. I told Luella I think it takes an angel to get along with those girls. She laughed and said I might as well get used to it. Whatever that meant.

With a happy heart,

Eugene

My beloved Eugene,

Whew! I finished giving Dad another haircut, even though he just had one a couple weeks ago. I think he likes the attention. And he likes to tease me the whole time. Once he yelled so loud I thought I took his ear off or something. Then when I gave him the mirror at the end, he studied his hair for the longest time and then said, "Why, it's all crooked. I can't even go out of the house like this." He is terrible, that's what he is.

Mom wanted my help in the kitchen afterward, so it was late before I got back up to my room. I reread your letter, taking more time to absorb things this time. It must have been written just after you read the awful one. I am so sorry, but you sure seem to have taken things well. It warms my heart that you didn't fall apart. I think you'll make a wonderful husband, and it wasn't your fault. I bear plenty of blame myself.

Your sister Mary had new glasses last Sunday, and I forgot to tell you. I think they are close to the same color of mine, and about the same size as the others she had. I think she looks great in them.

How are you feeling by now? And how's the diet?

Love you,
Naomi

My beloved Naomi,

Here I am again, and another week of school is completed. Now for the lonesome weekend ahead and the longings to be with you. Sunday will be four weeks since I've seen you last, and they have been long, weary weeks.

How sweet it would be to see you this weekend, taking the buggy out on Sunday afternoon for a drive. We couldn't stop anywhere with the snow and cold, but just to have you with me would be enough.

That was a nice little line about Richard and Joan still not having their house but being able to be together. I share your feelings exactly.

We had school today with only eleven pupils. I suppose it was because of the bishop's funeral preparations. So I decided to leave the Friday Bible classes off the schedule. I also put the seventh- and eighth-grade science classes together since there was just one pupil per grade.

I went ahead with spelling, but with so many gone this will mean a lot of repeating next week.

I send much love your
way as always,
Eugene

My dearest Eugene,

Greetings of love.

Dad and Don are digging postholes for the fence beside the sidewalk. It has to be frozen ground they're digging through, but Dad says it needs to be done. I think he wants something to do, as the winter blahs have settled in around here.

Mahlons had church on Sunday, and the hymn singing in the evening. I had a sore throat and couldn't sing very well, but I still attended with Don.

Sarah, the new girl I like so much, sat beside me, and at the end she asked me why I was sad. I shrugged. Adam Yoder must have been listening on the boys' bench because he said, "She's lonely" really loud.

He was right in a way. When you're not here I don't feel very well taken care of, but I know it's not your fault. I wouldn't want you away from your school teaching just so you could be with me. But the loneliness has been bad lately. I shed some tears the last two nights and told myself, "Brace up, Naomi! You're acting like a baby."

Julia, Joseph Burkholder, Elaine, and Robert all asked about you yesterday. I think Joseph and Elaine really make a good couple. Joseph was stretched out on the couch Sunday afternoon leaning on his elbow when I walked in. Elaine was curled up beside him on the corner of the couch. They seemed so at ease with each other, and it made me happy for them… but all the more lonesome for you.

Elaine told me later that Joseph also gets depressed sometimes, and he doesn't know why. Joseph told her that maybe he should go on your diet. Elaine asks more often about you and is more sympathetic than any of the other girls. I really think a lot of her.

Missing you awfully,
Naomi

My dearest Naomi,

The last day of January. *Whee!* February here I come.

I've been reading of your hair-cutting ventures with much interest. So I get a barber in the marriage deal? Well, that suits me fine as long as you cut straight. And it sounds like your dad is keeping tabs. That was funny.

Guess what? I saw a girl yesterday that could have been your twin. She looked so much like you, I could have cried. She was a little shorter and she had freckles, otherwise—there you were.

She was at the funeral, hanging really close to the boy she was with. I hardly ever saw them apart so I figured they were likely married. This evening I mentioned to Luella that I had seen someone at the funeral who looked like you. Luella had a vague recollection of the couple, but she was certain they weren't married. They wouldn't have hung around each other all day, she said, if that had been the case.

I said, "Sounds like someone is a little bitter," which set Luella off, and she had to prove her point by calling down to Saul's house. Janie knew the couple, and she also knew they weren't married. So Luella rubbed that in really good.

Luella also asked Janie if the girl had looked like you. Janie said, "Yes, she sure did."

I wish you were here—not somebody who looked like you.

Tuesday…

Last night was the school board meeting, and things went fairly well. I had a lot of items to ask them about, and it took time. All three of them commented on how different I seem and act since I've been on this diet. They brought it up, so there must be something to it. I know I feel better, but I hadn't thought it was that noticeable a difference.

They seem very certain they want me back next year. I told them no because I want to get married.

Crystal's dad is the chairman of the school board, and he told me last night they have been noticing how moody Crystal is lately, and that I was not to take it personally. She acts the same way at home, and they think it's just part of growing up. A phase perhaps. He said his wife went through the same thing and even came close to blacking out at times when she was

Crystal's age. After her first baby, the mood swings cleared up. This is all good to know, but I don't think I've been taking her moods personally.

It's very scary to be out here, not knowing what the next letter will hold. So I try to sit tight and hold my breath and hope for the best.

I love you,

Eugene

FEBRUARY

My dearest Eugene,

I have finished washing the supper dishes, and Mom and Dad are in the living room eating popcorn. I think I'll scribble this letter quickly and then join them.

Yesterday I received a letter from an old friend, Beth Miller, from northern Indiana, whom I had written to on an impulse. I was thrilled when she wrote back, as I hadn't expected to hear from her. The letter wasn't anything you would be interested in, just girl talk and catching up on news.

It tickles me the way you and the eighth-grade girls get along. I agree with you on girls having moods. I'm a champion on changing mine from one minute to the next, so you have been warned.

This weather is unbelievable. It's warm, the sun is out, and there's plenty of mud again. I'm sort of glad it isn't snowing because this way I won't miss babysitting days. It's good to get out of the house, and I love all the children I care for.

I want to help on the farm as much as I can, but there's not that much to do right now. Don helps with the little building projects Dad has going on, and I help with the chores when I can.

Tomorrow is the sewing at Ben Troyer's place. I'll attend the evening youth gathering to break the monotony and loneliness, but I will stay away from the women's get-together during the day. I don't feel up to their chatter about babies and husbands.

Don't let me depress you just because I'm down. Your letters help so much! I'll sign off now. Perhaps popcorn will fortify my soul.

I love you so much,
Sweetheart.
Naomi

Dearest Naomi,

> I have this thought within my heart,
> That gives me hope when we're apart.
> I dream our paths again will cross,
> And that our love can bear the loss.
> Were life to take these hopes from me,
> I'd still believe someday your face I'll see.

I'm home from school, and it looks as if winter has finally arrived to stay. It's snowing and blowing outside like a wild man, and with this flat country there is little to stop the wind.

Yesterday was Groundhog Day, but I don't think any groundhog was stupid enough to come out of his hole. If by chance he did, he certainly saw no shadow as it was cloudy and dreary all day.

Things at school are drifting into the winter doldrums. I carry on, placing each foot in front of the other, smiling when I can. Hopefully, now that the snow has come, the children will have more inspiration to play outside.

I asked the school board on Monday night if they would plan some sort of excursion for the end of this month. We need a spirit lift of some sort, and they said they would look into it.

Last Saturday I worked on a bulletin board where we can have an arithmetic contest for the children. I placed parallel lines across the entire board. Each pupil has a peg and has to work his way upward on the board. The starting point is 85 percent, and to advance the student must get an equal or higher grade. Some lines are designated as mountains, rivers, deserts, and canyons. They must have 100 percent to cross those.

Last night was the monthly youth singing instead of regular Bible study. They do this so everyone can attend some gatherings, but not many adults showed. We sang a while then Stan talked about the songs and the history behind both the writer and his work. He spoke on Isaac Watts, who, he said, could write poems from his youth. Stan said there is the story of a time when Isaac's family was having prayer at devotions, and Isaac started to laugh while they were on their knees. Afterwards, they wanted to know what was so funny. Isaac claimed he had seen a mouse climb up a rope and had composed this poem on the spot.

A mouse for lack of better stairs,
Ran up a rope to say his prayers.

I love you,
Eugene

My beloved Eugene,

I finished helping Mom clean the kitchen from the supper dishes, and now the evening has settled in on us. It's lonesome around here, but what is new about that?

Today Mom took a bunch of us into Worthington for shopping. Ada, Rosanna, Betsy, Mary, and Esther all went along. Mom hired a handicapped man as our driver. He apparently knows you. His name is Gene Roberts, and he was the limit. I think he was trying to scare us by zipping through tight spaces and around corners. We girls held our breath, and then when the danger was past we'd giggle. Finally Gene laughed and said, "It's dangerous riding with me."

When we were loading in the morning, he told Ada's oldest girl that she had to sit on his lap since the van was too full. Thankfully Rosanna knew he was kidding and giggled. Gene got a big grin on his face. Then after he picked us up from the shopping mall, he told me the same thing.

I told him, "Eugene wouldn't like that, you know."

"I'll fix Eugene," he said. "I'll write and tell him I saw you walking around the mall with a dark, handsome fellow. What do you think of that?"

I said, "Not much."

It must have been the tone of my voice because he really laughed. Then he got serious and asked how you were getting along in school. I think he likes you, and he turned out to be a nice man.

I wrote on my mirror the other evening, "Life is the pits. Being lonely is enough to drive someone out of her mind."

The next day when I arrived home from work, my writing was all cleaned up, so Mom must have gotten to it. She didn't say anything for a while, so I figured she at least sympathized with me. Then after supper she gave me this little note, and I have sent a copy along. I went up to my room and cried for a while. I am so blessed to have such a wonderful family.

I still miss you,
Naomi

Think on these things....

You have good health,
And religious freedom,

There are clothes on your back, food in the house,
    and you have a nice home.
There is a boyfriend who loves you and cares about you.
You have jobs—not too many, but yet some.
There is a wedding to look forward to—some girls
    don't, you know.
Life could be the pits if you let it be.
But look up and be thankful.

    —Mom

Eugene, my dearest,

I wonder what you're doing this evening. We finished supper, topping it off with homemade ice cream and cherry pie. Now what should a girl do just having eaten too much? I don't know, but I can see the pounds gathering, which is a serious no-no, so we will have to do something about this.

About my budding barbershop business, remember, I'm only cutting Dad's hair. Don would never dream of letting me touch his, so I really doubt if I'm qualified to cut yours.

I also wish the girl you saw who looked like me would have been me. How great that would have been. And I don't agree that you have to act differently once you're married, and you can tell Luella that I am on your side. So there.

When the school board remarked how differently you act since you've been to the doctor, you didn't say whether they meant you were happier, but I assumed so. I am very glad to hear this news.

I feel sorry for Crystal and her problems. I can sympathize, although I've never gone through the exact same thing. Sometimes it's hard to be female and go through the touchy and grouchy times. Don't say you weren't warned, but perhaps you'd better blame God because He seems to have made us all that way.

My enthusiasm for the wedding isn't exactly spoiled, it just doesn't seem real sometimes because you're not here to plan with.

Monday evening…

Yesterday morning on the way to church we picked up Darrel Hooley, who is staying at Harvey's again. Anna spoke with Mom on Saturday to see if we could take him, as they needed to be elsewhere. He rode with Rosanna and me in the backseat of the surrey. He can talk up a storm! He's a little older than you and funny as all get out. He told us all about his life in the *Englisha* world as a medical intern.

He said he talked with Bishop Enos the other week again about joining the Amish, and that Bishop Enos was still open to the idea. When we dropped him back off at Harvey's after church he said, "See ya next Sunday." So maybe he *is* planning on joining.

He said if only the Amish young people knew that worldly things make nobody happy, none of them would ever leave. I agree with that. Another subject we talked about was the government, and Darrel got all fired up.

"It's dumb, the government is," he said in English, and then he tried to say it in German. "*Da ovvahrichkeit ist dumm.*" It was funny, but he got most of the words right so he must have practiced at Harvey's. I told him how to say it, and he repeated the words several times. Dad laughed in the front seat, and now Darrell wants everyone to talk to him only in German so he can learn the language faster.

I told him about you, and he wanted your address so he can write. It caught his fancy, I think, that I date a schoolteacher. Maybe he thought all Amish people were farmers. I gave him your address, so if he writes, that's what it's about.

Don and I picked him up for the hymn singing in the evening, but you don't have to be jealous. There is no danger, and next Sunday Harvey's young folks should be able to drive him again. That is, if he stays. But I don't doubt him, I guess. He seems sincere.

There was a load of visiting young people here yesterday from Ohio. Most of them I didn't know. They stayed around all afternoon and joined us for the hymn singing. That was nice, although it produced a crowded building in the evening. The plus side was the singing sounded much better with so many extra voices.

I went for another of my long, snowy walks yesterday afternoon, using two coats this time and wrapping up in my scarf. I'm not sure what those walks do for me, but I felt more cheerful afterward. There's something about an open, snow-covered field all frozen over, the summer's grass buried out of sight, everything so still and forgotten that gives me courage and hope. It quiets my soul and reminds me that spring will come again.

I ventured farther this time, down past our property line on the south fence. Don had told me once there was a lane back there that leads to abandoned railroad tracks. I found the lane and the old railroad tracks. It was something to stand there and imagine the engines puffing along, pulling their long strings of cars behind them. Now there is nothing but the old railroad bed—and the snow covering it.

At the singing I wanted to lead a song that fit my feelings, but I couldn't find anything at first. Then I remembered the song you love so much, "Does Jesus Care?" I gave out the number when the English singing time came around, even though I was sitting on the front row facing the boys. It hit the spot exactly.

Darrel said on the way home in the buggy, "Thank you for leading that song."

I told him, "That's one of Eugene's favorites."

He said, "Then he has good taste, this Eugene of yours."

When I was getting ready to leave after the hymn singing, Robert asked how often I hear from you. I said matter-of-factly, "Three letters a week."

His eyes got wide and his mouth dropped open.

I about cracked up laughing.

Robert asked, "How does he know what to write, and how many pages does he write?"

"Oh, he does okay," I said and left it at that.

Please don't think you're strange because you're different than some boys. I like you that way, and surprising someone like Robert is a great delight.

I think I wrote you that James Yoder has persuaded Millie to attend the *Englisha* church. She doesn't want to go, she claims, but said that she is his wife and wants to be submissive where he leads her spiritually. Dad didn't think that was a good idea at all, and it will likely get both of them excommunicated before this is over with.

Betsy and Rosanna suggested some school things you might try to liven up the dark winter days. They said a lunch exchange is usually exciting for the children. I guess you draw numbers to decide who gets whose lunch. They also said a "come as you are" day can be interesting.

Well, it is 9:30, and I have written enough to have bored you out of your wits. As for myself, I am extremely annoyed with our dog. He is howling at the moon and won't quit. Perhaps Dad will go outside soon and talk some sense into his head.

Oh yes, Mom received a letter today from her youngest sister, Sharon. She had her eleventh child at home on Thursday. It's a girl called Catherine Beth.

As you can probably tell from this letter, I'm feeling a bit more cheerful, and it's about time. I'm sure glad you're feeling so well, so perhaps I should start eating what you eat. It sounds horrible, but very good for a person.

I love you so much,

Naomi

Hi, dearest Naomi,

I've been running a temperature all day but kept going with aspirin. I've felt funny for the past two days, but who knows exactly where the trouble started? Probably from cleaning all that vomit from the school-house floor. Can you imagine how many germs were in the air?

Stan had the main sermon yesterday for the first time, and lots of older people were crying. I thought it was because they were being touched by the sermon, but Luella said afterward it was because they missed Bishop Joe. There seems to be a lot of fear that Stan will take the bishop's place.

The sermon was on the love chapter in 1 Corinthians, and I thought it was a good message. But what would an Amish boy know about Mennonite problems?

Luella and I went over the diet last night and decided to keep on with the entire thing for a while yet. The question was the red meat, salt, and nuts, which the instructions said could be introduced slowly at this point. But I'm feeling so much better I hate to rock the boat.

Tuesday....

I arrived home from school as usual, and another long evening lies ahead. I'm feeling some better, although my eyes still look bloodshot.

Since the weather changed the last two days, we've been playing outside, and the children are in a much better mood. Outside play seems to remove the jitters from their mental and physical body systems.

On Friday we have a school Valentine's Day party planned. Crystal, Dena, and Velma are in charge, and I'm playing along because this is what they're used to. It also breaks the monotony, as does my funny writing. That would be my attempts to copy your handwriting in portions of this letter. You can see I am very bored. I think the results look better than my normal handwriting, but not better than yours.

The electric typewriter at the school has me completely spoiled. I noticed this again when Lonnie wanted me to type a paper for him the other evening. I sat down at the manual typewriter they have here at the house and saw at once that I've lost much of my speed, which isn't good. Perhaps if one is Amish, one had better act Amish. But I'm still going to use the other typewriter. It's simply too tempting.

At school we have started a countdown. There are sixty-three days of school still to go, which translates into twelve maybe eleven weeks, not counting this one.

This winter reminds me of the time when you weren't old enough to date, and I was waiting for spring when you would be. April finally came around, and I could ask you home on a Sunday night. I hope this winter isn't as long, but it feels so. April did finally arrive back then, and I took you home. You were, by the way, worth every minute of the wait.

I love you,

Eugene

Jerry and Tina Eicher

Hello, dearest Eugene,

I was quite puzzled today after receiving this envelope in the mail with very odd writing on it. I figured it wasn't from you and didn't use scissors to open it. Then a strange little note fell out with your writing on it. Thanks for the nice surprise.

Afterward, I laid the little note on the counter. Larry ran by and picked it up and read, "Hi, Sweetheart," right out loud! The little rascal! Dad heard and chuckled for a long time. Tonight I complained about Larry at the supper table, and he piped up. "Yeah, it said 'Hi, Sweetheart!'" Anyway, I laughed with them.

Last night I decided I had enough of Ranger's howling and got bundled up and went downstairs to let him into the barn. That was what he wanted apparently. So tonight I made sure he was in the barn before I went to bed. No howling Ranger!

Mom went over to Katie Troyer's to help quilt this afternoon. Rosanna and I drove into the grocery store in Worthington. I let Rosanna drive. She'll drive like Don, I think, hugging the side of the road as if her life depended on it. The rest of the day I worked on our quilt. My fingers are a mess, but I love the way it's turning out.

Well, I should get to bed, I'm pretty tired.

Love you so much,
Naomi

My dearest Naomi,

Whee! What has come over you—starting songs at the singing? I wish I had been there to hear this. What a shame to have missed the grand occasion.

You wouldn't have started the song to impress that Darrell fellow? This sounds quite suspicious and dangerous to me. And you have given him my address. I guess I can be nice and respond. That is—if he writes. He's probably a nice fellow and all, and I'm sure you're laughing at me right now. But you are very far away, and you were very much with him.

You never have to worry about your letters getting long and boring. I don't think anything from you could be boring, and I read the long ones twice.

Well…I love you.

Eugene

Jerry and Tina Eicher

Hi, dearest Eugene,

I'm sitting here in my room eating peanut butter cookies. Oh yes, and writing. I sure don't know what to expect in your letters anymore. Secret notes written on the inside, and now you try to copy my handwriting. But I do like your version of a return address: "Who knows?" That's funny and creative.

Yesterday I arrived home from work and right away had to leave for another babysitting job, so the rest of the family was on their own for the chores. Mom can help if she needs to. And I, after a long evening, arrived home around 10:30.

The one-year-old wouldn't go to sleep and still hadn't settled down when the couple arrived home. Then when I arrived here, all the doors were locked. I had a notion to knock really loud to get Mom or Dad out of bed, but instead I was a nice person and went in through the basement.

It was pitch-black and Ranger was down there, which I didn't know. He gave his friendly growl, rubbing up against me, and I nearly jumped out of my skin. Thankfully, I didn't scream.

Some of the women are taking a trip to northern Indiana on Tuesday. I think I'm going along and might have a chance to look up my old friend Jolene.

Stick to your diet now and hang tight because I can see a big difference in your letters. It makes me feel better if I know you're happy and feeling well.

Your Naomi

Hi, dearest Naomi,

Many thanks for the Valentine's card. It even came early!

Our school Valentine's party went well. I didn't think anyone acted enthused beforehand so I was afraid the day would turn out a dud. Then in the morning they all tramped in holding a bunch of cards and started to pass them out right away. They were all laughing and talking and having a great time.

The real party didn't start until 1:30, and everyone had to wait to open their cards until then. I figured they would draw numbers on who exchanged cards but that wasn't the plan.

Velma informed me, "Everyone just gives everybody a card."

That sounded like a lot of card giving to me, but they turned out to be little, itty bitty cards, so there wasn't that much work involved in making them.

They made me stand in front of the school and start the whole affair off with unwrapping my presents. Then they all joined in. I received a round toy ball, a sort of Rubik's cube imitation, except this is much easier to solve, a watch pen, a box of mixed nuts, and a little octopus that crawls up the wall by itself.

I felt pretty rotten that I hadn't purchased any presents for them, but I didn't know I was supposed to be involved. It was a great time though, and broke up the winter blues for one day at least.

I'm glad you like my new writing ventures, including the new return address with the misshapen letters. I figured you would open the letter in great joy, hoping it was a new boyfriend or something. I know…I really am bored.

I told Lonnie and Luella what I planned to do and showed them the address. They were highly amused and thought it a grand idea. Lonnie even said I should take it to another town to mail so the post office stamp wouldn't be Trenton, but I was too lazy for that. Luella did ask me today how the trick went. I told her, "We're still dating." She thought that was pretty funny.

I love you,

Eugene

Hello, dearest Eugene,

This has been a long, weary day, with Mom and I quilting the whole day. We finished in time for the chores, but I can hardly write now as my fingertips are all chopped up. I'm not the best quilter in the world, let me tell you. So hopefully you aren't marrying me for that reason.

Dad is down with the flu—hard. He couldn't even get out to the barn all day.

Harvey and his family have gone to Florida for a quick trip with Harvey's brother, who is Mennonite. They had an offer to go along and couldn't resist. So we are picking up Darrell tomorrow morning for church, and we are also visiting the other district for a change. Your jealousies are amusing, but let me assure you there is no need to worry.

I sure hope Dad is better by tomorrow morning or we will have to go to church by ourselves. Either way, Darrell is riding with us. But I am being very wicked, aren't I?

Sunday evening…

What a day—and a very enjoyable one. Dad was able to go to church, and we picked up Darrell for the long haul over to the East district. We visited and laughed all the way. He's a real corker. He teased me about the wedding and said he wants to be invited when it happens. In fact, he wants to have a part in it. I didn't make any promises, of course, as it's a long way in the future, and this could shuffle our table waiter plans.

Darrell said he wants to join the Amish in the West district since Harvey and his family live here, but that Bishop Enos's East district is the nicest. I agree, and Darrell must be observant to have figured that out already. He said he wants to live in the East district if he ever gets married Amish. I laughed but he sounded serious.

And listen to this. Brenda, whom I would guess is getting married this summer, whispered to me after church that they had an accident at their house the other Sunday night. Adam saw her wedding dress. Personally I think she wanted him to see it, but that just goes to show that old wives fables aren't really true because Brenda and Adam are one of the nicest couples around and deeply in love.

Don couldn't go to the singing tonight, so I had to pick up Darrell by myself. I hope you don't mind, as it wasn't planned. Believe me, there is nothing romantic about driving a man to the singing and back. Darrell said he would offer to drive, but that he didn't want to end up in the ditch. He's practicing some with the buggy at Harvey's house, but he said he's still stomping the brake pedal and pressing the gas as if it were a car, even while he's holding the reins.

I thought that was pretty funny, but I guess that's how it would go if you were used to driving a car all your life. Have you ever wondered what the *Englisha* life is like? I really haven't, but from what Darrell says it's not all that interesting. I suppose it all depends on what you grow up with. I know that I babysit for some nice *Englisha* people.

Well, it's time to blow out the kerosene lamp and get some shut-eye. There is another long day ahead of me tomorrow, but it has been a good Sunday.

I love you,

Naomi

Jerry and Tina Eicher

Dearest Naomi,

I'm still racking my brains at school trying to come up with interesting things to brighten these winter days. At least the children's Valentine's Day party helped, with the aftereffects still lingering.

There are plans now for a lunch exchange next week, which your sisters suggested. I'll make the announcement tomorrow so the kids can look forward to it.

In March we have an appointment to visit a maple sugar camp, with the school board members' wives getting those plans together.

I've started having devotions a little differently. I used to read out of the Bible storybook, but I've switched to a book called *Stories from Grandma's Attic* by Arleta Richardson. I think the interest level has definitely picked up.

It sounds as if you should have fun tomorrow when you take the trip to northern Indiana. I'd be interested in a full account of the day.

Remember the Rubik's cube ball I received for Valentine's Day? Well, the thing is causing marital disharmony at the house. Luella became addicted to it on Saturday evening, trying and trying to solve the puzzle without success. The next morning at the breakfast table I was told the whole sad tale.

Apparently the time for bed had arrived. They had their devotions, and then Lonnie got into bed. Luella, however, returned to the living room to puzzle over the cube. Lonnie called out that she should come to bed, and that he was cold without someone warm beside him in bed. Luella wouldn't do it though. She was determined to solve the puzzle. Eventually she gave in and got into bed with him. I told Lonnie that I didn't have anyone to warm up my bed. He told me, "Yeah, but you're used to it."

On Sunday night down at Saul's place, Luella went through the whole story again, adding details she had left out in the first telling. Suffice it to say the whole house was roaring with laughter. The cube is still alive and well, but I saw Lonnie looking sideways at it tonight.

The seventh graders, Velma and Jared, had fun with prepositional phrases in English class. You can get strange results if you put them in the wrong place, and they amused themselves in class until they had me laughing.

> The boy came after the dog *with the freckled face.*
> The lady pushed the baby, *with gray hair.*
> He wrote me that I should come visit *in a letter.*

There's a birthday party tonight for one of the youth. That should be fun, but there's always the pain of having to scrounge for food at such places. I don't want to create a fuss. There is usually something around to eat, if the people are into rabbit food, which a surprising number of folks are. Life is the pits, as they like to say around here. I will have to be careful not to say that around home.

Monday…

My skies are gray and seldom blue,
This heart so aches and longs for you.
Oh, darling dear, your face I see,
Come whisper loving things to me.
Across the miles, I wait, I look, I hear,
The sounds of love when you draw near.

Your Darrell Hooley wrote me a nice letter today, but I am quite suspicious of him. Are you sure he has no designs on you? And this thing about him having a part in our wedding. I don't know, but I will be civil and reply to his letter. He did sound sincere in his desire to join the Amish, or is his enthusiasm just his *Englisha*-born ability to express his emotions better? He's probably not any more excited than what we are about things, but the difference is that we keep it all inside.

The eighth-grade girls were in top notch mood today. It produces a more pleasant atmosphere at school than when they stalk around like thunderclouds ready to unload their torrential rains. I'm trying to figure out what trips the switch—or if there even is a switch.

If I force them to do something they don't want to, they will flare up, but an hour later be back in a good mood. Other times, the bad mood comes when there has been little conflict all day. It's like walking a tightrope, but perhaps the end of the school week has something to do with the good mood. Who knows?

You are in my dreams as always.

With love,
Eugene

Hi, Eugene,

I'm going to have to scribble fast and furious if I want to get this out in time for the mailman. I'm back from my first job, and I have to work another one at noon.

We had an enjoyable trip to northern Indiana. The load consisted of eleven girls, along with Myron in his nice van. There was Ada, Esther, Mary, Rosanna, Betsy, Erma, Kathryn, Rachel, Amy, Susie, and myself.

We visited one of their schools the first day and ate our lunch there. The way the children behaved didn't impress me at all. Your school was a miracle in comparison. We then dropped off all the girls, except Esther, who stayed at the school and planned to go home with the teacher.

I had directions from Mom to Grandpa's place. They live about two miles from Nappanee. But first we surprised Mom's sister Laura with a quick visit, and then Dad's sister Katie, and then Jolene, before going on to Grandpa's. Rosanna and Betsy stayed with me at Grandpa's for the night. We walked back to Laura's place for supper since they all live on the same road.

Anyway, I was glad I saw Jolene and her son Lawrence. She's still the same and as slender as ever.

I miss you so much,

Naomi

My dearest Eugene,

I feel like typing, so that's why this letter is different. I guess I also get tired of doing the same thing every time.

I had a boring day, with your letter as the lone exception. I had a good laugh over Luella's addiction to the Rubik's cube ball. Did she ever solve it? I hope so for poor Lonnie's sake!

A lady who says she knows you stopped by today to talk with Mom. Her name is Betty Daniels. I don't know how they got on the subject, but Mom must have told her that you were my boyfriend because they called me outside to shake hands with her. Mrs. Daniels said her husband thinks a lot of you, and that he isn't usually so taken with somebody.

Now I'm going to bring up a subject that will probably not please you, but I have put it off long enough, so here it goes. Mom wants to have the wedding at Wayne Helmuth's. She claims she spoke with your mom and that she agrees. I can see their point, as it will make things much easier to manage, with all the extra space at Wayne's place.

Mom said she doesn't think we realize everything that's involved in a wedding, and how many things the cooks need. And Mom would know because of all the weddings she's served in as cook.

Dad's first reaction was no. He said he wanted to have it on our home place, but he listened to Mom's explanation and ended up agreeing with her. I know you said you wouldn't be able to relax if the wedding was held at Wayne's, but just think of everybody else who will be there, and they are all people we know, so perhaps that will help.

I think this would take a load off my parents' shoulders. The unhandy thing, of course, is that Mom will have to make plans for the date right away because one of Wayne's children might also get married around the same time. This would mean spilling the beans, but Mom thinks Wayne's family will keep quiet.

I told Mom to wait until I received your permission before saying anything to Wayne. I sure hope this is okay, as it's hard getting caught between my mom and my boyfriend.

I'm not looking forward to the coming weekend, since this pain and loneliness make for lousy living. I seem also to have acquired the gift of sarcasm—at least Mom claims so. I do look forward to your return with great anticipation.

And my typing is greatly lacking, don't you think?

I love you,

Naomi

Hi, dearest Naomi,

What in the world are you up to with this Darrel Hooley guy? First, he wants to have a part in our wedding, which takes a lot of nerve. He must feel quite comfortable around you because you drive him around in the buggy. And it really doesn't make any difference who was driving. I'm sure he was enjoying himself.

Well, I will now calm down—or try to. But you had better not be getting ideas about him or else. I wish I hadn't mailed a letter back to him, but then perhaps it was for the best. I might now say things I shouldn't.

At least I still have humor in the house to amuse me. I came home and Luella had a bottle of aspirin and a fever thermometer taped to her little desk mailbox. That's where she puts my letters from you when they come. This was supposed to be for my reaction since there were no letters today. I didn't tell her about Darrel Hooley or she would have brought out the hot water bottle and warm towels.

Luella has her sinuses blocked right now and is hard of hearing, so I sneaked up behind her after supper with a glass of water. I stuck my arm around a corner and poured water into her collar. She about hit the ceiling and looked ready to kill me, so I don't think I'm good at practical jokes. I had better leave those to her to pull off.

Tomorrow will be the monthly singing at the Apostolic church. Last month I missed it because of Lonnie's dad's funeral. Both Luella and Lonnie are planning to go with us, as they enjoy that type of singing.

The Apostolic churches are few in number, Lonnie told me, but they have some connection to the Anabaptist people. He didn't know exactly how, and I haven't been able to find out.

I hope you and Mr. Hooley enjoy your buggy rides together. Hopefully the wheels fall off next time.

With love,
Eugene

Jerry and Tina Eicher

Good morning, Eugene,

How are you feeling these days? I hope better than I am. I've had a cold since Saturday and a very bad headache since Sunday. I think the walk home from church in the cold air didn't help things, but I enjoyed it anyway.

There was a members meeting after church, and Bishop Enos was nice about things, but he said he had concerns that need to be addressed. Personally, I can totally see his point.

Number one, there has been parts singing happening in church on Sunday mornings. He didn't say this, but that had to be the men singing bass. I think I've heard it myself a few times. Bishop Enos said that we have part singing allowed for Sunday evening, and that it's supposed to stay there.

Secondly, Bishop Enos said there have been songs brought into the Sunday evening hymn singings that carry a beat, which tempts people to tap their feet and sway along to the tune. He mentioned "There Is a Way" as an example of such a song. He said the words are fine, but that he'd rather have songs that don't take away from the words.

Thirdly, there is the continued issue with some of the youth boys' haircuts. Bishop Dan said he looked down the row of boys this morning and could only find one boy who hadn't done something with his hair. He said it doesn't matter if you call it thinning, or clipping, or tapering—it's all wrong. Men's hair is supposed to be cut straight off and that's it.

I can fully support Bishop Enos in these matters, and I am glad you don't fall for any of the new things that come in. At least you haven't so far, and I hope it stays that way even if you're teaching in a Mennonite district.

Tonight some of the young folks are singing for Myron Clark's wife, who has cancer. Not everyone is coming because there isn't room at the hospital. Don is going, but as sick as I am, I'm sticking close to home.

Darrell wasn't in church Sunday, which I can't understand. He sure talked like he was staying around the last time I spoke with him. I hope there is a good reason for his absence, and that he hasn't changed his mind. I think it would be a shame if he gave up joining the Amish so easily.

With all my love,
Naomi

My beloved Naomi,

I'm still trying to catch my breath. The booklet you sent me is absolutely wonderful. I feel like jumping up and down like a little kid. And if you were here, I would give you hug. So a letter hug has been sent back your way.

That was nice of Betty Daniels to put in a good word for me. But you already knew I was wonderful, right? Just kidding. I'm actually an awful person, but I would like to give them a wedding invitation because they are good friends of mine. We will have to see, I guess. I know we can't invite all our friends.

You didn't have to be so scared about my agreeing to have the wedding at Wayne Helmuth's place. I don't exactly like the idea, but it's okay. Your parents are making the wedding, so they get the final decision on such things.

I know what you are talking about when you say that you dread the weekends. I haven't enjoyed them since I came out here, and here's a little poem about that.

> The weekend days that come to me,
> Have little life and joy to see.
> They lack the spark and love I knew,
> When I could share them all with you.

Oh, Luella never did solve the Rubik's ball. She gave up trying, so Lonnie is a happy man.

Wednesday…

It seems like the weeks around here are meant to be an endurance test of sorts, and here I am in the middle of another one. Yet the weekends are even worse, so I will stop complaining now. Anyway, it's my own fault I'm out here.

How are you and Mr. Darrell Hooley getting along? Any buggy rides planned for this weekend? I don't own a car or I would offer a Mennonite girl a ride to church. Just joking—well, sort of. And you shouldn't drive him to the hymn singings by yourself.

At the moment I'm at the house by myself. I forget where Luella said they would be at. Perhaps some doctor's appointment, although they both looked healthy this morning.

I still haven't shaken the flu, but it's not really that bad so I haven't been saying much. It will blow over soon, I suppose. At least I didn't have to call off any days of school.

I forgot to mention the hymn singing went well Sunday night. My foggy head kind of spits information out at odd times, and sometimes days after the fact. They had a four-man quartet singing, harmonizing beautifully. The tenor went so high I thought he'd rupture himself. I didn't know a man could sing such high notes. They were pure blasts of joyous sound.

A group of fourth graders also sang, which made our school singing sound like dragging a bag of feed across the barn floor.

I keep reading deeper into the booklet you sent. I'm enjoying all the nice little things you say. Where did you find the time to put this together for me? It's really wonderful. I hope you didn't show it to Mr. Hooley first.

Yes, I am being nasty, but I will try to be sweet now.

Lonnie and Luella have invited me along next Sunday when they travel to the Amish community in Fairfield. That should be interesting, although I don't think it will involve Amish church attendance.

I love you,

Eugene

Hello, dearest Eugene,

This finds me reclining in my room at 9:40 this Wednesday evening. I'm laughing so hard the whole bed is shaking. You are very funny when you're jealous. At the risk of greater fury from your end, I am thoroughly enjoying it. How mean is that of me? But you really have nothing to worry about. Mr. Hooley is no threat to you. He's just a nice person and very sincere. He won't be stealing your girl, even if he wanted to, which he doesn't. You'll have to believe me on that.

I finished reading a romantic story out of the *Good Housekeeping* magazine one of the ladies I work for sent home. She gave me two back issues. Anyway, the stories made me lonelier for you, Sweetheart. So you have no cause for concern.

Mom was at the quilting today, and she spoke with Mildred Helmuth. She said they do have a wedding planned for the last week of May. That would leave one of the first weeks of June open for us, if you agree to having the wedding there.

Oh, the reason Darrel wasn't there on Sunday is because he had to babysit for a niece or nephew. So it looks like he still plans to continue coming.

I wrote a letter to Jolene today, thanking her for the good time we had on the trip. I like letters to friends better than I do these circle letters, which get kind of impersonal. Of course, writing to you is even better than letters to friends.

Thank you for the poem in your last letter. If I could write like that, the words would mean the same thing. I miss you much.

Lots of love,
Naomi

Hi, dearest Naomi,

Greetings from the great flatlands of Iowa. My pride has been greatly mortified and dragged in the dust again by Luella's hand. This woman is a terror, not only of the high seas but of dwelling places on the dry land.

I had only arrived home from Bible study two nights ago, crawling safely into bed, when a little noise started around my desk. I ignored it the first time, trying to get my sleep, but it continued, rattling and buzzing away, sounding like a little mouse making a nest in my desk drawer.

I leaped out of bed with my flashlight and went after the thing, determined to give the mouse at least a good scare before it made off. Naturally it quit the minute I got up.

I opened the door into the hall and shone the light around, but there was nothing there. I checked in the closet to no avail. Climbing back into bed, I snuggled under the covers—and here came the mouse again, digging merrily away. Starting then stopping.

This time I tiptoed out of bed and stood beside the wall, listening. The supposed mouse kept repeating itself every so often, the sound seeming to come from inside the wall. I checked the attic again, but the sound came from the wall toward my room. So I figured it must be inside the wall, and there was little I could do about it other than pound the drywall and try to scare the thing away.

I figured that would awaken Lonnie and Luella, but something had to be done, so I pounded a couple of times and quiet came to my room. The next morning at the breakfast table I told the tale and received vehement denials from both Lonnie and Luella to even the possibility of mice being in the house. But Luella was glad a reasonable explanation for my pounding had now been presented. They had wondered whether I was losing my mind from loneliness.

"Anyhow," Luella said, "first it's your alarm clock, and now it's mice in the wall."

She was referring to the trouble I've been having with my alarm clock.

Lonnie suggested the noise might come from the furnace pipes, but I knew it didn't. Mice and furnace pipes rattling are not the same sound. Not even close.

I asked them if I could call them next time instead of pounding on the walls, and they agreed.

Then last night, sure enough, I was heading for the bed and the mouse takes off, vigorously digging away in the wall. I grabbed my flashlight and searched carefully again. There was nothing to be found, so I went to the stairwell and called down to the living room, hoping they were still up.

"Am I supposed to come up?" Lonnie called back, a few minutes later.

"If you want to hear it," I said.

He grunted something and came up the stairs and stood beside my desk to listen. Soon the supposed mouse took off again, just digging away.

"It sounds as if it's coming from under your desk," Lonnie said.

And it did, indeed. So I took a hold of the desk, pulling it away from the wall. And what should fall out but a plastic dish with a spool of thread spinning inside.

I traced the thread out under the door and down over the open stairwell. It didn't take much imagination to assume who was at the other end. I could have died from humiliation. Lonnie split into gales of laughter, holding his sides from the pain. I went downstairs from a lack of anything better to do, and there was Luella, seated on the floor, her back against the wall, literally in tears she was laughing so hard.

She pulled the string again with one hand to add insult to injury. Finally able to speak, she asked me if the furnace pipes were having problems again. That woman is the limit!

Saturday morn…

I kept this letter over one day so I could show it to Lonnie and Luella. Luella read it out loud at the breakfast table. There were places where she had to stop reading, she was laughing so hard.

Love you,
Eugene

Good morning, my prince!

It's a gorgeous Saturday morning, and I feel rather peppy. I see Don is hauling manure from the barn, which means plowing is coming soon if the weather gets any warmer. I hope or the stink will overwhelm us all.

I quick-cleaned the basement this morning, and now I'll have to do something with my room.

I'm glad you liked that booklet. I was afraid you hadn't received it because it took so long to get there.

Well, I have to get this out to the mailbox and get to work.

I love you,
Naomi

My dearest Naomi,

This finds us in the Amish community at 4:31 p.m. I'm presently bored half to death. I must have misunderstood about the church attendance because we did go after all. That part was good, and I also enjoyed visiting the school yesterday. It's very similar to ours at home, with two teachers, one for the lower grades and one for the upper.

After church I could almost picture you sitting across on the girls' side, and me checking to see if you were ready to leave. When I went out to the barn with all the horses there, I wished mine would have been amongst them so I could hitch the horse to the buggy and pick you up at the sidewalk.

This afternoon I took a walk down the road out of sheer boredom. After I had gone a ways, this young couple pulls up in their buggy and the guy yells out, "You want a ride?"

"No," I said, "I'm not really going anywhere."

"Well," he said, "our house is just down the road a piece. Stop in and have some popcorn when you get there." So that's what I did.

They had only been married last year, they told me, and had a little girl in the crib. I assumed it was their child, but the man said they were taking care of her for his brother-in-law.

I was really looking forward to the youth hymn singing, but they said it wasn't a good idea for visitors to attend right then, as they were having problems with their wild young folks. There was a smaller group of decent young folks who got together, they said, and I guess I should have gone there, but I didn't. My enthusiasm had left me at that point.

Oh, you don't have to worry about me becoming wild or cutting my hair in ways that are against the *ordnung*. I look the same boring way I always have.

Monday evening…

I'm in a perfect fury. I came home from school to find your letter taped to the inside of the mailbox, where I had to work twenty minutes to extract it. As soon as I pulled the door open, I knew what was up. Of course, Luella was close at hand to go into gales of laughter. You can't get around that woman.

And here's another example of how well my jokes fly. On the way home last night I asked Lonnie and Luella if they would have stayed till midnight if I had wanted to take an Amish girl home. Luella turned around in her seat and glared at me, and they both shouted, "No!"

"You could have walked home," Luella said.

For crying out loud, I was only teasing.

Ha! But I did get to pay you back for your Hooley rides. Several of the girls picked me up last night for the ride to the youth gathering. But, as usual, my jokes aren't that great. I didn't even enjoy the ride.

With lots of love,

Eugene

Hi, dearest Eugene,

I hope your cold is gone by now. I'm still feeling a little run over from the attack of the flu again on Saturday night. I woke up with a headache, which got progressively worse all day.

Church was at Abe Miller's, and after lunch I told Mom we needed to go home as soon as possible. She hurried through helping in the kitchen, and then told Dad to get the buggy ready. After a good nap and two aspirins, I was ready for the evening hymn singing, but I still felt rough during the night.

I worked on a new dress this forenoon and had the care of John Bach this afternoon. We didn't make it back until after chores, so Mom had to help Dad.

Rosanna went to see the doctor today about a problem she's had for some time. She was diagnosed with a heart murmur. Dr. Roland wants her to see a specialist, but they don't know yet if much can be done anyway. Mom thinks the murmur was probably there since childhood, as she would have these spells growing up when it was hard to breathe.

I don't remember anyone ever saying anything, so perhaps it wasn't as bad as what the problem has become.

Well, I seriously need to get my sleep.

I love you,
Naomi

MARCH

My dearest Naomi,

How does this find you? I hope all is well. I'm thinking of you often. You are so very far away.

No letter arrived today, but there was one from home, which is second best, I guess. My sister Susie said she thinks you are working on your wedding dress but are keeping things under wraps. Is this so? Are you going to show the dress to me when I get home or will the old ways prevail? I don't know that I care either way, although it would be nice to see the dress for the first time on the morning of the wedding.

Also, one of the table waiters I wanted didn't work out. I received a letter from Louis yesterday saying that other things might interfere. That can only mean one thing, he is getting married. So we now have a vacancy.

I also received another letter today from your buggy friend, Darrell Hooley. This is a portion of what he had to say:

> You have a really sweet girl, Eugene. She is a bubble of fun and a joy to be around. I don't get to see her that often, as Harvey's young folks usually cart me around. But the times she and her brother have picked me up for the hymn singings I have thoroughly enjoyed myself. She is one of the funniest Amish girls I have met. I was telling them on the way home of the problem we have keeping our car windshields clean with bugs hitting them all the time, and how Amish buggies are much gentler on the nightlife.
>
> She said, "Well, you'd go splat too if you hit an *Englisha's* car at fifty-five miles an hour."
>
> Thanks so much for sharing her with me.

255

Sounds like you know him quite well. But I did write a nice letter back to him, and I hope he continues coming to church.

The school has the maple sugar camp tour coming up next week. It's been planned for over a month, with the school board members' wives in charge. When Loretta picked up her children today, she brought me a firm date.

This news is a bit late, but the lunch exchange went well last week. Everyone seemed to enjoy it, but I didn't take part because of my strict diet. Plus, who wants to eat only rabbit food?

I have the calendar you gave me for Christmas hanging at the school, and people are still commenting on it. It's really nice, and both the words and pictures are beautiful. Thanks again.

I've lost track how many times I've read through the booklet you made for me. It means a lot to me, and it's wonderful that you love me.

You are a dear.

Eugene

My dearest Eugene,

What a gorgeous day and so springlike. Yesterday Dad tilled the garden, and I think Mom is going to plant lettuce and radishes today. Between the two of us, it shouldn't take too long.

I have to work this afternoon, and then tonight is the sewing at Enos Byler's place. Mom didn't go as she has too much work. Don and I are taking Darrell this evening. I still can't believe you are jealous of him, but you seem to be, so I will try to behave myself. Not that I haven't already been extra careful. We don't do anything but talk. All he does is sit on the other side of the buggy with Don between us.

I drove to the grocery store in Worthington this morning. Mom wanted me to buy meat, which they usually have on sale on Wednesdays. When I told the manager I needed ten pounds, he leaned over the counter and whispered, "It's not on sale today, but I'll let you have it for ninety-nine cents a pound if you don't tell anyone."

I smiled and said I wouldn't.

He then asked, "Do you want it wrapped or are you eating it here?"

That took me by surprise and I laughed. He's older and not good looking, but a little crazy.

My wedding dress is progressing rapidly and is going well. I don't think I'll show it to you, and not for superstitious reasons. I just think it feels better.

I can't wait for the wedding though. Summer still seems a very long way off, but we will have all our time together again, which will be wonderful. The ladies I babysit for weren't very happy when I hinted about getting married, but they will get over it.

Thursday evening…

This finds me very lonely for your company. Last night Darrell drove Don and me to the sewing in his car. We were going to drive with our buggy, but none of our horses were fit at the moment for such a long trip. In case you wonder, Darrell still keeps his car at Harvey's. We parked our feeble horse there.

The sewing was nice and boring, but Darrel was interesting. He played a singing tape for us on the way over and back, and it was very beautiful.

When we arrived at Harvey's home around 9:30, we sat in the car and talked until 11:30. Darrell couldn't stop talking, and neither of us objected.

Don agreed with me today that the best part was when he told us about his experiences in the Church of God he used to attend. An *Englisha* person has such a different way of looking at things. They have so many options and choices, it almost made me dizzy hearing about them.

Darrell says our lifestyle is much better though—that the world can drive a person almost insane trying to figure out what is right and wrong. I sure hope he makes it through with his plans to join.

Tomorrow night the young folk girls are invited to Richard and Joan's place, as Joan wants us there for an evening while her sister is visiting. I'm going to pick up Mary Troyer, as she doesn't have a ride. I think our horse should be well enough for the short trip.

On Saturday I have to take care of John Bach during the day, and then I babysit for Chris in the evening, so I'm busy.

That story of the racket you heard in your room was hilarious. Maybe, just maybe, Luella doesn't have enough work to do. I think though, they probably do it to cheer you up.

Love you, Sweetheart.

Naomi

My beloved Naomi,

The weather has been very nice the last while, and this finds me in the middle of a Sunday afternoon thinking of you, wondering where you're at, who you're with, and how you're feeling.

According to the calendar, we are now halfway between the time I came back for Christmas and the time I return. Hope flickers dim and the cold winds blow. I sure hope we make it through this okay. The world is a scary place and gets scarier as time goes by. I never would have thought home could feel so far away.

Darrell wrote me another letter and told me he was over to the bishop's the other night again, and he might start baptismal classes this fall if things continue going well. Harvey and his family are offering him a long-term place to stay even though their house is already quite full. He seemed touched by their gesture and concern for his well-being.

Stan had the main sermon today. He really has a gift for public speaking, and his sermons are enjoyable. It must be an accomplishment to speak before a crowd for almost an hour with such ease.

Lydia is back from Florida, which leaves Sharon and Dena still down there. I hope they come back before too long. Dena is due back in two weeks. Sharon, I'm not sure.

It has started raining outside, which fits my mood better than the sunshine did. Tonight is the hymn singing, and Lonnie and Luella have something planned for later this afternoon. Anything that helps make the time go faster is fine with me.

Today I read the letter you sent to Saul's girls, which was an extra bonus. The little note on the outside of my last letter was cute: "Luella, don't hide me."

Stay sweet now.

With all my heart,
Eugene

My dearest Eugene,

This is Sunday afternoon at 3:30. I'm sitting upstairs at my desk with the windows open and eating a banana. At least I don't have a headache. I guess I should have stayed at Everetts', where church was today. The girls wanted me to, but I came home with Mom and Dad.

Darrell rode with us this morning, as the Harvey family buggies were all full. He stayed at Everetts' for the afternoon and was upstairs with the boys when I left. I suppose Don and I will bring him home from the hymn singing, unless Harvey's young folks have room.

A load of visiting youth from Central Ohio were here, but there was no one along I knew.

I started reading a book yesterday at work that I'm really liking. It's called *For Women Only*. Chris asked me if I wanted to bring the book home, so I did. It's a Christian book about how women should treat their husbands in marriage. I'm not going to tell you what it says, but I'll try to practice it someday.

I miss you awfully, and it would be such a beautiful day for a walk with you. Most of the snow is gone, which means no more walks in the snow this winter. I could cry.

I love you,
Naomi

Dearest Naomi,

I came in from a long jog down the road. I love the feeling of accomplishment, even if the great apostle Paul said that bodily exercise profits little. I wonder if he ever jogged a few miles for exercise? Perhaps when he was running away from the Romans, but I doubt if that qualifies.

I received a welcome letter from you today, with more news on Mr. Hooley. Well, I shall have to make my peace with the matter, and he is a nice person, even though I have never met him. And I am only half serious, but I think you knew that all along.

Remember I told you that I read the letter you wrote to Saul's girls? Well, now they want to read one of yours written to me. It's only fair, they said, and wouldn't back off the point. I gave them one yesterday—and yes, it's one you wouldn't object to. It's appropriate, shall we say. Now we'll have to see what feedback they give me. I'm sure it will be good, as your letters are wonderful.

I started checking Lydia's back schoolwork tonight, and I am hoping to be done by the end of this week. She brought in great armloads of schoolwork she completed while in Florida. Most of the papers are well done, I must say. The grades on what I've checked are on par with the work she does here, so I'm happy.

Lydia had sent me a card while she was in Florida. The front of the postcard pictures one of the long bridges from Key West, and she had written on the back, "From the Sunny South. We will be back toward the end of February sometime. Mom is not sure yet, but I'm getting along okay with my studies. I hope I'm on the same page you guys are. See you, and I'd better go, Lydia."

She's the only student who bothered writing me from sunny Florida. Sniff, sniff.

You are likely having a good time at the youth gathering tonight, and I'm sitting at home with two old people—*nice* old people, if they aren't up to tricks. I think the winter weather has worn them out, as there have been no new tricks lately.

Stay sweet and dear for me.

Tuesday evening…

Here I am again, with the weather turning colder. Lonnie said tonight it's supposed to go even lower. Mentioning tricks yesterday must have made me suspicious because I discreetly studied their faces at the supper table, hoping to see any signs of budding stunts and perhaps nip them in the bud. They both looked sad though, which was troubling. I think these church problems are wearing them down. I don't think they agree with Stan's preaching.

Last night I entertained myself with a romance book from the school library. I suppose either Crystal or Dena must have chosen it because I can't imagine any of the others reading such things. Unless Velma did, which is possible.

Anyway, the romance book didn't do much for me except bring back memories of you. I doggedly kept on reading. There was a tender scene where the girl finds the boy she loves crushed under a piece of farm machinery. She holds his head while she thinks he's dying. (He doesn't, of course.) I think I was supposed to cry at that spot, but I didn't. I haven't cried in what seems like ages. Probably because I know it will make me feel worse afterward. I end up feeling all numb and frozen inside, I think I need you to thaw me out again. No other girl can do that like you can.

I'm also enclosing a copy of a letter from my sister, who must be having the winter doldrums and decided to write me. I thought you would find the letter interesting.

With much love,

Eugene

March 1

Dear brother Eugene,

Good morning. It sure is a beautiful day outside, and I will quickly scribble a few lines to let you know how we're faring. I had written you a letter once before, but Mom made me destroy it because I had written a couple of spooky stories we heard. She was afraid if you read them you might hear more queer noises in the walls. That story was really funny, and we sure got a kick out of it.

We have the flu bug around here, with two of the boys flat on their backs with sniffles and gasping for air. The whole community has what some are calling the "Pleasant

Flu," and apparently once you get it, you have the hardest time shaking it off.

Joe had it last week and got tired of lying around on his backside, so he armed himself with a bright idea. Out he went and took the syringe he uses for his dogs and gave himself a penicillin shot from the stock Dad keeps for the pigs. He was a little sore the next day, but it sure pepped him up. Harvey got the greatest kick out of that story, and Joe hasn't heard the end of it yet.

Oh, you might catch the germ if you read this letter, so you'd better hold it pretty far away from your face while reading, and it probably would be wise to disinfect your hands before touching your face. I guess I should have mentioned this at the start, but I figured you probably wouldn't count this letter precious enough to hold close and tight to your face. Not like you would if it came from someone else. Hah…

Dad is having problems with another kidney stone. He always tries to flush it out by drinking a lot of cider. He is in the bedroom right now, lying down. I guess he really has a lot of pain.

Did you hear about James Yoder? Millie has now joined him, and things have gone from bad to worse. He claims he will buy a van this week, but we don't know if that's true or not.

The big news around here is that Susie and Mom are on a diet again. Oh, please don't mention that I told you because if you ask them, they are not on a diet. But they told me this was the last time they would ever be on one. You can suit yourself about which version to believe. What it really boils down to is that Susie wants to be a toothpick for her friend Rosemary's wedding this summer.

Harvey and his family and the young folks around here were invited over to your beloved's place the other evening for supper. They brought along the young man, Darrell Hooley, who is staying at Harvey's place. This is the boy who is seriously considering joining the Amish. I'm sure

Naomi has told you about him. He's a riot and had us all rolling on the floor. Not really, but you know what I mean.

Well, I had better get some work done around here or Mom will be tight on my tail.

As always,
Mary

Hi, dearest Eugene,

Oddle dee doodle dee…I'm in a tense, hurrying mood. Do you ever get in moods like that? I especially do if my day has been spent sewing. I'm still working on my dress, and my shoulders are knotted from the tension.

Yesterday Mom, Rosanna, and I were over at your place working on the quilt your mom is making for us. I like it very much. The other women acted like it was just the usual thing, but I kept thinking, "This is *our* quilt, this is *our* quilt," and I had shivers going up and down my back.

Your sisters gave me an invitation to stay for the night, and I said, "Why not? Just for the anyhow!" I enjoyed it immensely. Your family has been very nice to me, and hope it's not because you lectured them. I didn't pick up anything like that from them, so everything should be okay.

Dad wanted extra silage tonight, and I threw down fifty forks full, plus gave the cows hay. So I feel like superwoman tonight, but I needed some kind of good feeling after getting stuck earlier out in the barnyard mud trying to get one of the cows inside. By slowly pulling on one foot at a time, I got out. *Blech.* Thankfully there was no one around to laugh at me.

It's fine if you find a couple from out there to replace Louis and Martha as table waiters. I think so many of the table waiters are my age or were picked by me, that I'm glad you get to pick one of the couples yourself. My cousin Danny is in for sure, as I received his letter of confirmation last week.

I want to tell you again how different your letters are from what they used to be. You must feel a lot better. They are more cheerful, humorous, and reassuring to me. They never fail to make me feel better.

I'm missing you greatly.

Love you so much,
Naomi

Dearest Naomi,

I can hardly believe it, but it's snowing outside. If the weather doesn't decide to change, it will spoil our maple sugar trip on Friday. That would be a shame indeed. Of greater concern, though, are the snow days that may close the school and that, in turn, pushes back my return home.

I finally pulled a trick on Luella for all the agony she has caused me. Tonight when I arrived home the house was still and quiet. I seized the opportunity for the fertile plan rolling around in my head. I checked upstairs to be sure, but there was no Luella cleaning the corners of the bedrooms.

A glance out the window confirmed the pickup was gone. So I headed back downstairs. I found the liquid I needed in the refrigerator—blood-red beet juice, and set the can on the kitchen table. It took a couple of drawers to find an old white rag, which I wrapped around my hand.

I heard the pickup truck come into the driveway, so I spilled a liberal portion of beet juice on the rag and then over my lunch bucket. It was pretty authentic, I thought, so I sat down at the table and practiced my groans.

Oh no. There was the beet juice still on the table, and Luella was almost at the door. The quick dash across the floor left drips, which wasn't good for the eventual cleanup, but it was good for effect. I sat back down, grabbed my beet-red rag, and groaned.

"Hi, Eugene," she said as she entered. "You're home already."

I deepened the groan, and the poor woman went white.

"What happened?" she whispered. She couldn't take her eyes off my bandaged hand. Then she let out a shriek and said, "I'll get Lonnie!"

That's the problem with my jokes—they always get too serious. They get serious and I can't keep a straight face. Just as she was ready to turn and get Lonnie, I broke out in laughter and unrolled the rag. "It was a joke!" I said.

Luella didn't laugh. I don't think she believed me until she ran her hand over my arm and found nothing wrong.

"You are a rascal!" she said. "Now clean up my kitchen. What am I going to do with you!"

I got to work cleaning the kitchen, leaving it better than I found it. She looked pleased about that at least.

Thursday...

You must have been feeling pretty mean and ornery when you wrote the letter I received today. My poor head went round and round trying to follow the writing written in circles on the page instead of on the lines. Well, I'll have to seek out my bags of tricks again.

Ah, I will try writing this backward. So the rest of this letter will have to held up to the mirror to read.

I asked Delmar, one of the young folks here, if he would consider being a table waiter at our wedding. He didn't know what that was, but he gladly agreed when I explained. I then asked Janie, and she was delighted. So if that holds, we'll have the missing table waiter couple.

The young people here are really enthused about coming to the wedding. Two or three even said they were coming with or without an invitation.

Well, I'm tired of backward writing, so take care.

Love you,

Eugene

My dearest Eugene,

What an evening! I bring you greetings from the Miller hospital. At least that's the way it seems around here. Mom and Dad, Rosanna, and Larry are all in bed sick, so I did the chores tonight by myself. I was kicked by a cow, but thankfully I didn't lose my temper. There was too much to do for wasting energy on anger.

I don't think I like cows that well, but I will be choring alone for another day from the looks of things. Never fear though, I will survive.

I tried a little experiment tonight by combing my hair differently after I washed it. Of course, you've only seen it done the way I always do it, but I think you would have liked the new way. But Mom happened to come up the stairs right then, so I quickly undid my handiwork. She wouldn't have liked it. I liked it because I think it sort of made my face look longer. I might try it again some evening once this sickness has blown over. That is, unless I myself am laid low and gasping for breath, as your sister Mary describes flu victims at her house. That was a hilarious letter. And don't you ever try what your brother did. Injecting his own penicillin. I declare, you guys could kill yourselves.

I would so love to speak with you and spend a weekend together for a change. Patience, patience, Naomi.

I love you,
Naomi

Hi, dearest Naomi,

I had a hectic day at school, with the third- and fifth-graders getting jammed up in arithmetic. That threw everything into a turmoil, and I had to struggle to keep the other classes on schedule.

The children must have sensed the stress level rising because they looked befuddled, and I think parts of their brains shut down. I wonder why that is? I tried speaking slower and softer, which seemed to help. Anyway, we made it through the day.

Luella hasn't been feeling well, so her motivation for tricks has been low. Then tonight she was in high form again, but this time I stayed one step ahead of her.

She had a note taped in the mailbox, but there was no letter from you. I ignored the note and asked, "Where is Naomi's letter?"

"You have to hunt for it," she said. "It's a treasure hunt. Isn't Naomi's letter worth the effort?"

I could see myself hunting through house and barn for hours while she rolled on the kitchen floor in hysterics, so I determined brain power would overcome this obstacle.

"I'll figure it out," I said, heading upstairs.

"Suit yourself," she said, laughing. "You'll need supper soon for all the hunting still to come."

"Very funny," I said from the top of the stairs.

So where was the letter? That was the question. Logic told me Luella would end up in my bedroom somewhere. I followed my hunch, turning things upside down in my room, pulling out drawers, looking in my bed, and sure enough, there it was under the pillow.

Being the kind and good-hearted soul that I am, I couldn't bear spoiling all her fun, so I meandered back downstairs with a mean look on my face to begin the treasure hunt. She did run me out to the barns, and the pole barns, and the manure spreader. But I also found two letters along the way, one from my grandparents in Canada, and the other from Mary again.

I stormed upstairs waving the two letters, while Luella laughed in the kitchen. It felt better this way, and I guess I needed the exercise anyway.

I agree the diet might be affecting my mind for the better. But I will now cease my ranting about Mr. Hooley. He seems to be a nice person from his letters, and that will be the end of the matter.

The letter from Mary said they greatly enjoyed your overnight stay, which was good to hear.

I wouldn't mind seeing you in your new hairstyle, if you know what I mean. Just don't go out in public, please. Right now it would be good seeing you in whatever hairstyle you are pleased to wear.

Thanks for the little card you sent with the words "everyone is lonely without you." I can say the same thing for you.

Remember I told you I gave Saul's girls one of your letters to read? Well, they have brought it back and are not satisfied. Janie said she wants one of the *juicy* ones to read. I said, no, she's not getting any, and that was the end of that.

Love you,
Eugene

Jerry and Tina Eicher

Dearest Eugene,

I will write quickly before the time arrives to wash cow udders. I'm still choring by myself, and things are in a hectic mess.

Dad did drag himself out of bed to attend church yesterday, and now he's paying for it. The rest of the family stayed home, and all this afternoon Mom has been puttering around in the kitchen. She *must* be feeling better. I think she may attempt supper for the two of us. Dad and the others will do good if they keep chicken soup down.

I thought about taking Darrell to the singing by myself, just to tease you, but Harvey's young folks took him. I had to rush to get ready with all the ill people around, but I made it in time. Afterward, I had a chance to speak with Esther about the table waiter spot for her. She said she didn't really want to be with Jacob, which is fine with me. I told her I was sorry, that I thought they were about ready to begin seeing each other. She said they were not.

I thought right away that Esther must have turned Jacob down for some reason because there were tears in her eyes. She said it might be best if I place her with someone else. Then Mom told me today that she heard Jacob had asked some other girl home, and he was turned down. Apparently he tried to hide his indiscretion from Esther, but thankfully she found out.

It would be hard to respect a boy like that—who flits around from girl to girl, like a bee testing the flowers. We girls might be pretty like flowers, but we have hearts instead of nectar.

The book *For Women Only* turned out to be for married not unmarried women, so I stopped reading until such time when I need it—like after the wedding.

I love you a lot,
Naomi

Dearest Naomi,

"Humpidy dumpity," it's another Wednesday evening, and I am bored silly. Job, in the Old Testament, said, "Man that is born of a woman is of few days, and full of trouble" (Job 14:1). I think he knew what he was talking about.

My problem with the eighth-grade girls shows no improvement, no matter how hard I try. I don't seem to have the knack of getting along with either of them. There are clashes, and then there are more clashes. First it was Crystal and Dena, but with Dena gone to Florida for two weeks, Velma has joined arms with Crystal. But I will try to be nice and hope the storm blows over.

I'm on the second to last page of my writing tablet, and this would be the second 100-page tablet I have gone through, scribbling on both sides of the page. I'll need to purchase a new writing tablet, perhaps this time buying one that has pages with lines because how many boys scribble on paper without lines? Plus, that's what you use.

Thursday...

Everyone was supposed to wear a green clothing item at school today for St. Patrick's day. That was a new one on me, but I wore my green shirt. How cute I must have looked.

Today there was no letter, but there really wasn't one due. Just hoping, I guess.

At noon I made the usual announcement for the game after lunch hour. I said, "We will be playing Cowboys and Indians, and the first graders and me will be the cowboys."

Right away I knew that hadn't been said right, but I hoped no one else noticed. On the way outside, Velma got this grin on her face. "Teacher," she said, "it's supposed to be 'the first graders and I.'"

"I know," I said, thoroughly embarrassed. Crystal giggled all the way out the door.

Saul's second girl, Amanda, had her first date on Tuesday night with a boy from Arkansas. He has called a few times, Luella said, sort of breaking the ground before traveling up here. I hope they make a success of it. All three of Saul's girls are nice to be around.

Marylyn and Janie must have some of the same blood in them that you do. They love to go for walks along the road on cold nights after dark, arm-in-arm, marching between the two farms that must be close to half a mile apart. Luella claims that Saul has told them not to, but they won't listen. I guess he's afraid someone will pick them up sometime, but I have a hard time imagining such a thing in this calm farming country.

We are having a volleyball game tonight. Thankfully this week has gone by faster, mainly because there has been something going every night since Sunday. Now I'm on the verge of losing too much sleep.

Every week that passes brings me one step closer to seeing you again, and I can hardly wait.

With many longings
to see you,
Eugene

My dearest Eugene,

I will try to write slowly before I leave for my babysitting job. I'm not feeling quite up to par yet. Yesterday morning when I got up in time for chores I thought I felt queer and weak. When I looked into the mirror—wow! My face was bright red and felt very hot.

So I was in bed the whole day, and Mom helped with the chores. I guess the flu is all over the community, as I heard some of the *Englisha* schools were shut down.

Tuesday evening Harvey and his wife, along with their young folks, Darrell, and your family, were here. I coughed practically all evening, but I figured it would blow over by morning. Thankfully, the evening only consisted of sitting around the living room talking. About quarter after nine, Harvey said, "Well, we'd better be gettin' on home."

Dad said, "What's the big rush? You don't have any cows bellowing in the morning."

Harvey said, "No, but I have a wife who does."

Anna glared at him while everyone laughed because we all know Harvey doesn't like to get up in the morning.

They started talking about how early they get up. Harvey said he has to get out of bed around five or five thirty.

Dad said, "That's sounds about right for you, but we farmers have to get up at four thirty."

Harvey said, "That's not true. I don't believe you."

Dad said, "Well, sometimes…like in the summer."

"So you're not getting up at four thirty right now?" Harvey demanded.

We all laughed as Dad admitted that he wasn't. Your dad then jumped up and grabbed his coat.

"We'd better get out of here," he told your mom. "Before they start asking us what time we get up."

They had us all laughing, as you can see, which hurt my head until I had to hold it in my hands.

Ah, here comes my ride, so I will write more later.

Friday…

Today was a much better day even though I was alone at work most of the time. I feel like a firecracker right now, which might explain why the rest of this letter consists of really short paragraphs.

A wonderful letter was waiting from you when I arrived home. Thank you for the card. You are a pretty marvelous guy, you know.

About the hairstyle—that lasted only for a few moments, and I don't think you would have liked it anyway.

There is good news from Rosanna's appointment with the heart specialist, Dr. Dickson. She does not have a heart murmur after all. The problem has to do with one of her heart valves. The doctor said a lot of people have the problem, and it's absolutely nothing to worry about.

He did notice that she's very tense and asked her questions about what could be causing it. Rosanna told him that she didn't know, that perhaps it was just life in general. Anyway, the good news is that there's nothing to worry about.

I chored again tonight, even though I still have a cough. Doing the work felt good. I think the smell of the barn has a therapeutic effect on a person when he or she feels low. There's something about hearing the cows move about with their soft lowing and smelling the fresh silage that makes things right in the world.

Keep me tuned on what Luella and you pull off next. That treasure hunt was good. I liked how you played along.

By the way, if you have any cousins we could put with Julia for the table waiter list, that would be fine.

Sunday is *ordnungs* church at Richards. *Groan.*

I love you,
Naomi

My dearest Naomi,

It's 8:15 on a Saturday evening, and we're back from a day at the Mennonite Relief Sale in Iowa City. It was a monstrous affair, requiring that we leave the house this morning at 6:30 to be there in time for the duties Lonnie and Luella were assigned. The local church was involved, with some of the young folks taking kitchen duty, but no one had assigned me to anything so I was left to explore all day.

The Mennonite Central Committee has yearly auctions in the different states where they raise money for their mission activities. They had rented a huge building in downtown Iowa City for the event. There were people running everywhere. Food stands, religious stalls, and auction items were spread out in the domed center.

I didn't see any Amish people, but there were Mennonites of all kinds. An older couple had a stall set up with huge posters of nuclear bombs dropping on Hiroshima with "Stop Nuclear Proliferation" written across the top. I didn't talk with them because they looked a little scary. I didn't know Mennonites were involved in political issues.

I went on a book-buying spree since they had several used-book stands around. Now I have a dozen books, which will be a welcome diversion when the weekend comes around. One is a Reader's Digest condensed book, with a story in it I haven't read yet. It looks like some sort of a terrorist plot. Probably not something I should be reading, but I'm bored.

A day like this is hard on me since I see all the delicious food that can't be eaten. With how much better I feel though, I count the cost and consider the price to be worth it. I did get to eat an excellent plate of cod, but no French fries or potato chips. I had a bowl of salad, which was a poor substitute for the absolutely beautiful and heavenly pecan pies I just walked past. I nearly fainted from desire but kept moving.

Lonnie nearly moved me to tears at the supper table tonight. He said he looked around several times today and caught sight of me in the crowd. "There goes my boy," he said to himself.

Sunday…

"For God is my record, how greatly I long after you…" This comes from Philippians the first chapter, verse 8, which Stan preached out of today. I know it doesn't apply the way I used it, but perhaps the great apostle would understand.

Stan said the apostle Paul could have joy in adverse circumstances even while he was in prison, and that surely prison would be one of the worst places one could be in.

Me, being the nasty fellow that I am, asked this question in silence: "What about Iowa?"

Would you believe that it's snowing and blowing outside? I have never seen the likes for this time of the year. I see a snow day coming and running my school schedule flat over, leaving me bored to tears while I sit in the house with nothing to do.

What are you doing today? Do you think of me as much as I do of you? Hardly. That would take a thousand thoughts, all run together until they wrap themselves around each other twice over.

Tomorrow is the planned day for the sugar camp trip. I wonder if the snowstorm will postpone things. I know the children will be disappointed for sure.

I have enclosed a crazy little poem. Please don't laugh, as it's very boring around here.

> With a dingle and a dong, will I come along,
> On the day that I leave, dear Iowa's sun.
> With a bang and a clang sounds my voice while I sang.
> Thinking of my Indiana hun'.
> With a hop and a leap will I cross the old creek,
> Where the memories are thick all around.
> With a flap I will fly and sail through the sky,
> And in the fields of your farm come down.

With love,
Eugene

My dearest Eugene,

Well, *ordnungs* church is over with, and there is bad news. James Yoder and his wife will be excommunicated on communion morning. Besides that, there was the usual *ordnung* reminders, but I don't think too many people were listening with that shocker hanging over their heads.

Bishop Enos told us afterward the vote was unanimous to excommunicate, as both James and Millie now attend regularly at the *Englisha* church. Apparently it's not even a regular *Englisha* church like what Chris Van attends, but some cult-like operation that claims to be the only true church. Some people can really mess up their lives, is all I can say.

Don and I took Darrell to the youth supper and singing. It was raining most of the day, and Darrell slipped three times trying to climb up the buggy steps. I think he might have been teasing us, but it was funny watching him. *Englisha* people are much more expressive than the Amish are. Darrell was flapping his arms around after each slip, trying to keep his balance.

I made a trip to the grocery store in Worthington this morning after I had the laundry pinned on the line. When I returned, a snow shower had come in from the north, turning our wash into a frozen mess. Mom and Rosanna ran out to help me. Together we hauled it all into the basement to dry. The lines aren't very long down there, so that's what we've been doing all afternoon, keeping the stove hot and changing the laundry. I took the last pieces off a few minutes ago.

Tomorrow, Dad's brother Henry and his son from northern Indiana are stopping in for overnight. Henry wrote and made the plans a while back. I think they have business down south somewhere, and it's too far for a one-day trip.

I miss you so much. At the singings, once the last song is sung, the steadies go out, bang, bang, bang. The lucky ducks. I get jealous now and then. Oh well. I guess it isn't too awfully long anymore.

I love you,
Naomi

My dearest Naomi,

This finds us on our way to the Amish community in Fairfield again. Lonnie and Luella wanted to go for the viewing of an older Amish person they know, and I'm going along for lack of anything better to do. They picked me up at the schoolhouse right after 3:30.

That was a bummer of a letter you sent, all clipped up into small pieces. Was that for saying I was bored or are you becoming another Luella? Her influence apparently reached out to Indiana. She laughed at my misery while I worked at the kitchen table, trying to tape the pieces all back together. At least for my trick you only had to hold my letter up to a mirror. I had to use Scotch tape, and suffered the death of many brain cells while in heavy labor before the rest could receive the tonic of your tender love.

Luella said that at least there's no danger of you not being able to handle me, which was apparently a comforting thought to her. I would say from the looks of the incoming fire that she is correct. Please, from now on, only engage the scissors for their proper usage.

Later...

We are driving out of a feed mill/country store here in Amish country, and I have made the purchase of a new, black felt hat. They actually had the size rims required by our *ordnung,* so I will store it safely somewhere for the wedding.

I expected to pay over $40, but the bill came to $26.25 with tax. That's still plenty to spend on a hat that can only be worn on Sundays, but so it goes.

We're sitting in a restaurant waiting for our orders. The day doesn't feel complete without having seen you. I can hardly wait until it will be different.

About my diet. I imagine I will have to stay off of most sugar for the rest of my life, which isn't a pleasant thought, but perhaps you'll help me. Ha, ha...

Besides the sugar, I was supposed to stay off salt for six weeks, and also all meats except chicken and fish. Staying off the salt was really worse than the sugar. But I have been doing that strictly for the assigned time, and I am now allowed to slack off if I want to. Luella and I have had our consultations and plan to allow salt—the absence of which created tremendous cooking problems for her. The sugar restrictions stay, as I never want to go back to feeling like I used to. I had no idea one could feel so levelheaded most of the time.

Tuesday evening...

We arrived back after midnight. The viewing was at the person's home, of course, since it was an Amish funeral. After we passed through the line, Lonnie and Luella stayed for a while to visit. They had a group of young folks come in and sing *Englisha* songs for an hour. Their singing wasn't quite like home, since they didn't sing in parts like we do in special circumstances. When the girls go high, most of the boys can't follow, which creates its own unique sound. Sort of a cross between a file on metal and a dog with his tail caught in the door. You can't quite get that male bellow in gear like you can with the German songs on Sunday mornings.

By the way, April 22 is the anniversary of our engagement. It will have been a whole year, and I won't even be home to celebrate with you.

I noticed at the viewing how different the Amish boys who are in *rumspringa* look compared to ours. They have long hair down to their shoulders. Some even have what the *Englisha* call afros—I think—great fluffy expansions of hair that circle the head, as if a pumpkin had been carved out and perched over the ears.

We didn't do the maple sugar camp tour yesterday on account of snow and cold. It has been rescheduled for next Monday, but who knows with this weather.

Larry wasn't in school on Monday. His brother Byron claimed he had a setback, but he was perfectly healthy last week, so how could it have been a setback? What probably really happened is that there's a new batch of chickens on the farm to tend.

Next Monday night is school board meeting, and I will find out then when my homecoming date is. I hope for good news.

A boy from one of the neighboring Mennonite churches has offered to take me on a day trip into Chicago for a Saturday of sightseeing. He must know I'm bored and had his compassion stirred. We are scheduled to leave at 6:30, and we are coming back whenever we're done.

This Friday will be another school auction similar to the one when you

Jerry and Tina Eicher

visited before Thanksgiving. Only larger this time, from the sounds of it. It's the school's main source of funds for operations. I must say, the last one was an awful lot of fun, plus you were here.

Remember the board I made for the last auction? It was shaped like the state of Iowa and had all of this year's schoolchildren's names burned into it? It sold for $85 in the last auction. I'm making another one. My contribution to the cause, so to speak.

I was planning to make an extra board to permanently hang on the schoolhouse wall when someone suggested that one should be made for all the school years back to 1957. That's a good idea but outside of my ability. So I will leave the project alone, and will also not hang one on the wall lest someone think one year is being exalted above the others.

Love you,

Eugene

My dearest Eugene,

Good morning. It's beautiful and cold. Henry and his son, Isaac, were here for the night and left early this morning. I made popcorn for them and served cider. They had already eaten supper when they arrived around 7:00. It was good to have them here, and good listening to Dad and his brother talking. I liked the chatter of their voices more than anything, since they didn't really say much beyond catching up on the news from people they both know.

Isaac played a game of chess with me. The boy is a whiz and beat me soundly in forty-five minutes. Too bad he doesn't live around here so I could learn from him.

Rosanna went to the hospital for an electrocardiogram of her heart. This was to confirm Dr. Dickson's diagnosis of a prolapsed valve, which proved to be correct. They knew the valve was nothing to worry about, and the test was simply a double check.

I find your problems with the eighth-grade girls amusing, and now Velma has joined in. There's no worry really. Girls are temperamental. It's the afflictions of our femininity. Maybe God didn't want men to have things too easy.

Why in the world do you think you have to change the lines on your letter writing paper? I don't mind your writing at all. In fact, I think you write neater than any boy's writing I have seen. Anyway, I don't think boys should write as nicely as girls. It wouldn't be right. And if you like pages without lines, I don't see any reason why you should change. The important thing is that I couldn't do without your letters, so however you write—don't stop.

I miss you,
Naomi

Hi, dearest Naomi,

At school we're trying to get everything arranged so the studies come out right at the end of the year. At present, I still don't know when the last day of school will be, so that might affect things. I should also review some of the subjects. Getting through the books sooner rather than later would be for the best, if I can manage.

If the school board agrees to the closing date I hope for, I will be coming home April 30. If not, then the week after. If I hadn't lost the two days in January when I went to the doctor in Missouri, the thirtieth would be a sure thing. But that's how things go, and the trip was well worth it. I used to wonder why other people didn't battle with depression as I did, since everyone seemed so happy. Now I know, and it feels good to avoid those crushing lows.

Tonight is Bible study as usual. Each week brings me closer to being with you and walking the roads of home. In the night hours I can imagine your eyes lit up with love and can hear your voice speaking to me. I awaken in sorrow to know that it's just a dream. But soon, my darling, it will not be.

Thursday evening…

This finds me home from school and reading your wonderful letter. Not that it takes the place of your presence, but it helps. The fancy stationary was nice. You've never used that kind before. Are you preparing me for the homecoming? A forewarning of all your sweetness and tender love?

You're likely to fall over from shock at this news, but I am getting along much better with the eighth-grade girls. I'm still puzzled as to the reason, but that's not surprising. I know one thing, it makes for a much more pleasant atmosphere without two grumpy girls stalking the schoolhouse.

Last night the Bible study was held fifty miles from here, which entailed a long drive down. I traveled in a station wagon with three other boys, the driver being the fellow who is taking me to Chicago on Saturday.

We must have all had the talking urge because we jabbered like a bunch of girls all the way down and back. Before we crawled into the car to come back, there was a snowball fight in the yard with the youth from the other vehicles. Sort of a strange ending to a Bible study, but it was fun.

Tonight there will be a volleyball game for the youth. Enjoyable, indeed, and it helps make the evening go faster. There is little to do around the house, and since I have no car or buggy, where could I go?

Friday evening…

I'm in a rush tonight trying to get ready for the school auction, which starts in an hour.

I was surprised to find a letter from you today. So you must have decided to write on Wednesday instead of Thursday.

So you think I should keep the lineless pages. Don't worry, I wouldn't have changed if I hadn't wanted to. I was getting bored with the blank pages, and this helps keep the writing straighter. Also, the pages fill up faster.

Sharon has been back in school for the past two days and is catching up nicely. She returned all tanned and cheery from her stay in Florida. I'll finish checking her back work over the weekend. Her grades certainly haven't suffered from what I've checked so far. That's not surprising. She's a smart girl.

Sweet dreams,

Eugene

My dearest Eugene,

I don't want you to tell anyone this, but Robert and Beth have plans for the middle of May this year, and Adam and Brenda for the last part of May, which leaves the first part of June open for us without interfering with anyone else. Does that sound okay for a wedding date?

Brenda also wants us to be table waiters at her wedding. I told her that I can't imagine you would object, but let me know if you do. And again, not even a whisper of this to anyone. Mom was only told because of the need to coordinate the use of Wayne Helmuth's place as the wedding site.

The new girl, Sarah, and I had a long talk Sunday night after the hymn singing. She was so sympathetic with my tale of loneliness and said she thinks you must be a wonderful person. I told her she was right. I am thankful for a friend who truly seems to understand what I'm going through.

Rumor has it that Sarah was dumped by her boyfriend in their old community. I have a hard time imagining that. She is quite a stunning beauty and handles herself very well around boys. Much better than I do. I think it's more likely she dumped him.

I liked the "dingle" poem, and I could understand it just fine. I dreamed last night that you arrived home, and it was so good to see you again.

Sometimes I think I'll go berserk with all the wedding stuff, and you not here to talk things over with. Plus, my sisters act like it's their wedding with all their advice and criticism. I finally teased Rosanna and Betsy that if they keep this up, they won't be invited.

Sunday...

This was fast day prior to communion, so some of us didn't eat breakfast. It does the soul good, I think—the afflicting part, even when I got a headache out of the deal.

I forgot to mention yesterday that I got that tricky letter of yours. Mom brought in the mail and told me there was no letter for me. I calmly accepted the fact since it fit the day anyway, then Mom opened her letter from Luella, and you had mailed yours along with hers. That wasn't very nice, but the letter was.

Larry and Delmar from out your way will need vests for their role as table waiters. Can you find out if they have black suits? I hope so because nothing else will look very good with brown shirts.

Well, so long.

I miss you awfully,

Naomi

My greatly loved Naomi,

Whoopee! I get to come home the last week of April. Let the day come! And just four more Sundays without you, and then we'll be together!

I won't have put in the amount of school days I need, but the board said I have done favors for them, so they can do one for me. This goes against my sense of responsibility, but they said I shouldn't allow the missed days to bother me. So I won't, but I will rather think of seeing you.

Last night I was at the chairman of the school board's house for supper. They invited the other two board members, but only one could come. We talked about the school year and how we first met. One of them said they were scared when I was hired that I would turn out to be an Amish boy out on a wild spree of some kind.

I can see the reason for the fear, but it was quite groundless, as you well know.

The chairman's wife brought out the letter I had written inquiring about the job and asked me if I wanted them to read it out loud. I said, "Sure."

When she was done one of them said, "I always liked that he asked about wages last."

We all laughed, and I left them uninformed of the fact I had done so on purpose. Not that money was a big concern to me, but it's amazing what will impress people.

This afternoon I'm going up to Saul's place where four of us boys have gotten a wild idea into our heads—we will sing together as a quartet. And I can't even sing that well. Saul's girls claim we blend well, but I don't believe them. Plus, it takes more than blending together. One must also be able to carry a tune.

Tonight there is a pizza supper for the young folks, and I will attend, even though I can't eat a lot of pizza—just a piece or so.

Monday evening...

I have finished filing my income tax. Yes, I must still do so in the state of Iowa. I have been waiting for the state forms from Indiana because I must file in both states, and those arrived today.

The preschool students were in attendance today for the first time.

They do that here—the next year's first graders attend for the last month. All of them were really quiet, coloring in their books and looking around the room like they were scared half to death.

We left for the maple sugar camp this morning around 9:00, arriving back after 11:00 sometime. The farm gave us a tour of the place. It's set back in the hills north of here, with miles of tubing running from tree to tree and then down to the boiling vats.

They gave us samples on the way out, and I even tasted a small bit of the sweetness. No negative reaction so far, but I'll have to watch such temptations carefully.

Tonight on the walk home from school some of Saul's clan approached in their pickup truck. They asked if I wanted to accompany them. There was a skunk caught in a trap, and they were on the way to shoot it. I said "Sure" and leaped into the truck.

They raced across the bumpy field to a ravine where the trap was. I stayed on the truck to watch the action, but even then the smell drifted up to me. Hopefully a bath and a new change of clothing will knock out the smell. But I have no way of telling since Luella isn't home to ask, and one could hardly smell himself under such circumstances.

This evening there is a birthday party for Erma, Saul's youngest girl. That means I'll be out tonight and tomorrow night as well.

Hang tight there. I should be home soon.

With much love,

Eugene

My dearest Naomi,

Here I am again. Just the same old thing and the same longing to be home.

I had been getting reports from some of the students about note passing during school hours. No names, just whispers at recess time and over lunch. I figured most schools have such things, and I can't be watching them all the time in order to catch it.

Still, I went through the desks tonight and found piles of notes in Jackie and Dakota's desks. Beats me why they didn't destroy them since they surely heard the same whispers I heard.

None of the other desks had any, so I figured that was about the extent of things. Both of them sit toward the back and across from each other. I kept a good eye on them today and didn't see any note passing, but they were cutting up quite a bit, which had to be distracting to the students around them trying to study.

I decided to handle it by moving both girls' desks up front. They didn't have anything to say but hung their heads and complied.

Lester then pops up and said he didn't pass any notes. I said, "That's good to hear, but I didn't say you did."

Dakota quickly raised her hand and said that Lester *had* passed notes.

I asked, "Have you got the note?"

She said, "Yes," and produced it from her tablet.

I took the note and read it out loud: "Quit fooling around with me, Jackie and Dakota."

"Well," I said, "Lester shouldn't have been passing notes, but perhaps he was just trying to be nice instead of tattling to the teacher when the girls disturbed him."

Lester vigorously nodded his head, and no one commented further. The logic was pretty obvious for all to see. To be certain though, I said he could stand up and apologize, as well as Jackie and Dakota, but that his seat would stay where it was. I don't know if I did the right thing, as it's hard being prosecutor, judge, and jury.

Oh, I had a misquote in my last letter. We didn't go to a young folks gathering last night, it was a family deal, which turned out to be just as much fun.

Thursday…

Lonnie and Luella's grandchildren have been here all week. Luella is enjoying herself to the fullest, and I'm getting a taste of what happens when the grandchildren are around. The quality of care definitely goes downhill. Lonnie looked glum at the kitchen table all week, which I think keeps his food service from completely falling off the cliff. Mine is still okay, so don't worry. I don't need much anyway.

I did get my shins kicked under the table by swinging feet until I learned to keep them out of the way.

The calendar in my room was just turned over to the month of April. Ah…the last one to turn before I see your face again. Yippee! Christmas seems like another world away, so long ago and so distant.

This week has been hectic at school, with the rush on to complete the books and the children's minds on little else but getting out of those four walls. I take deep breaths, and I vow that we will make it somehow.

I caught Dawn cheating today again. Last week she tried cheating on her spelling words, so this time I talked with her and asked if she didn't know it was wrong to cheat. She claimed, amidst great sobs, that she had never heard of such a thing. I pitied her, as she seemed half scared out of her wits when I called her up to my desk during recess time.

I sent a note home with her sister Dakota, explaining things to her mom. Hopefully another talk at home about the evils of cheating will do the trick. The school year is almost over, so I didn't take any drastic steps. I told her we'd have to take further steps if this should happen again. Hopefully a blowup is preventable, as I will try my hardest to avoid it.

Tonight is a volleyball game in the gym, and then Sunday the young folks singing. The very last one I will attend before I leave for home. A very sweet thought indeed.

I've written another poem for you. I hope you like it.

See you in the
near future,
Eugene

Of You

Thinking, musing, longing,
Hoping, sighing, wishing,
Pondering on how sweet you are,
Wishing you were not so far
Away from me, our miles apart,
Still bring you closer to my heart.
Sorrow mines my heart away,
With pain from day to day.
Leaving all that space to fill,
Emptiness that never will
Be full and life complete,
Until our hearts again will meet.

APRIL

My dearest, dearest Eugene,

Thank you for the wonderful Easter card. It's so beautiful, and the words inside just wonderful. I also received a letter from you. My lucky day indeed, I think.

I thought this was going to be another boring day, but it has turned out quite differently. Mom and Dad are on a trip to northern Indiana for communion church. They went to fill the carload, and we're doing the chores by ourselves. We're done now with the morning work and casting about for something to do for the rest of the day since it's Good Friday.

Lo and behold, I decided I was going to have some of the girls over. I hitched the horse to the buggy and was off to spread the invitations, rushing back home to get ready. Your sisters came, plus Kathy, Martha, Lora, Susie, Julia, Diane, and, of course, Sarah. We had the most glorious time making pizza and taffy this afternoon. Then everyone's brothers arrived for the evening. Sarah is the star of the show these days, charming everyone's socks off. I can't believe one of the boys hasn't asked her home yet. She is everything I wish to be.

We ended up singing songs for thirty minutes after the pizza was finished and eaten. Taffy pulling came after that. You should have been here. It was absolutely hilarious pulling the gooey stuff around with our hands. Your sisters outdid themselves trying to get the biggest pieces. You have a great family, and they seem to like me.

It was such a fun day, and I still can't believe I pulled it off. Maybe being the oldest in the family has something to do with my fear that it would all be a flop. But it wasn't at all. It left me with such a good feeling that everyone enjoyed themselves.

Joseph Burkholder asked me Sunday after the hymn singing when your school lets out. I said, "The last week of April!" grinning and punching my fist into my hand a couple of times.

He laughed at that.

Then Sarah said, "Yeah, when he comes home she's going to smile her ears off."

There was another burst of laugher after that.

Sarah added, "She'll smile so much her teeth will get brown from sunburn!"

I'm glad that you and those gals are getting along better. Don't get upset if they still have their grumpy days.

I squealed with delight when you said you'd be home by the end of April, and that it will only be four more Sundays.

Mom said, "See, I told you it'd be here before you know it."

Don didn't want to attend the singing Sunday night, so I drove myself. Darrell went with Harvey's young folks, even though it made things crowded for them. I guess I thought it would look more appropriate. Plus, I didn't want to make you jealous again.

I was so lonely for you all evening that I didn't feel like smiling to anyone. The girls seated on both sides of me were busy talking after the hymn singing, so I decided to leave early. Plus the steadies had all marched out, making me feel even more unhappy.

One of your brothers and Adam helped me hitch the horse to the buggy, which was nice of them. They even checked the harness and tightened it. Somehow it had slipped back. I think Don had warned me that it slips back, but I had forgotten.

I told them, "Don mentioned not to drive fast lest the harness slip back."

Adam said matter-of-factly, "You're not supposed to drive fast period."

I laughed but it was a long, lonely drive home. I think the next time Don can't go, I will take Darrell along for company. Don't worry, I'm not serious…just lonely. Rest assured that he means nothing romantic to me.

The only excitement on the way home was the horse acting up. He likes to pull hard on the lines when it's cold, and even Don has a rough time hanging on. If Dad knew how he acts, he probably wouldn't allow me to drive alone, but I think it's fun.

I love you,
Naomi

Hi, dearest Naomi,

I opened your Easter card and read the letter. It's so good to hear from you.

Tell Betsy and Rosanna to stop pestering you.

The news around here is that Amanda quit the boy she was dating. I guess he was a little too pushy from the get-go, asking her on their first date whether she would be willing to move to Arkansas. I would have a hard time imagining any of Saul's girls moving anywhere. I guess true love could provide the motivation, but this apparently wasn't of that kind.

Janie is the oldest of Saul's girls, and she has never dated that I know of. She's quite strong in her opinions against marriage. We've had frequent arguments, with Janie warning me that I'm getting into deep trouble by marrying you, that marriage is nothing but problems one had best avoid. I don't know where she gets those ideas, as her family is very loving.

Anyway, I disagree, and Janie can just feel however she wants to. This sentiment might be rubbing off on Amanda though, who is close to her. I guess I should have warned the boy from Arkansas that he needs to marry the oldest sister first, like Jacob of old, before he gets to the second sister. Hah! Now Janie will kill me for sure if she hears about this remark.

Last Sunday I was at Saul's place after church with two other boys, and we all got on this subject. One of the boys thought Amanda shouldn't have been so quick to drop the boy from Arkansas, and this set Janie off. She went into a long list of all the negatives of marriage. Bossy husbands, men eating food with their mouths open, extra laundry, children on the way, babies crying in the night, and keeping a husband's bed warm.

Luella and Lonnie were there, so I think the last remark was directed toward Lonnie's well-known need around here for cold night bed warming.

Anyway, Luella snorted and stuck up for Lonnie. "It's worth it," she said, "keeping a good husband warm. And you just don't know what you're missing."

"I wouldn't want his cold toenails warming up on my legs," Janie shot back, and they were at it again.

Lonnie laughed through the whole thing and didn't seem offended at all.

This afternoon Lonnie and Luella are taking their grandchildren home, and I'm going along for the ride. Not that I particularly wish to see more of the grandchildren, but it will help pass the time.

There is shopping planned for afterward. Mainly for Luella, as I don't need anything. But if there is a bookstore in the mall, I will certainly visit it. I might even spend some hard-earned dollars if I can find a book that looks interesting enough.

I wonder what you're doing at home. You probably have a get-together of some sort, and dinner, and a young folks gathering, but I will not torment myself with such thoughts any further.

Saturday...

It's 9:30 on a Saturday morning, and I'm done filling out your birthday card. I'm afraid I won't have much to give you for your birthday. A wonderful girl like you deserves more than my few purchases. I wish I were home to celebrate with you properly with homemade ice cream and pecan pie. I would even eat small portions myself just to mark the occasion.

Yesterday we left around 2:00 for the trip back with the grandchildren. We stopped at the bank so I could get money orders for income tax payments. Now that duty is off my mind. The forms were mailed this morning.

After dropping off the grandchildren, we ended up at the mall. You wouldn't believe how many shopping malls they have around here. I purchased a new pair of Sunday shoes, which took a while to find, but they had what I wanted and the price was good.

Lonnie and Luella are planning on attending the Apostolic church tomorrow for something different to do. I learned a new superstition from Luella yesterday. She claims that whoever turns over the calendar in any given room is boss of that room for the month. I laughed at her, so she quickly ran to the calendar in the living room, which hadn't been turned over yet, and turned it.

So to even things out, I checked their bedroom, and that calendar wasn't turned yet, so I turned it. This is really ridiculous. I think it's high time I find worthwhile things to do back home.

Well, I had better finish this extended letter. I wait impatiently to see you again. Whoa, here's a poem yet. I hope you don't tire of them.

I love you,
Eugene

Jerry and Tina Eicher

A Ballad

Like a bud that doesn't know
Into what it's yet to grow,
So you are, my dear, so unaware
Of all the wonders you will bear.
Of all the happiness you'll bring,
How you will set my heart to sing.
How wonderful your love does seem.
More than the world I deem.
None like you ever touched my life,
Or made me feel it worth the strife.
This world has been a better place
Since your love has left a taste.
And still the more I see of you,
The deeper grows the thought I knew.
That there is none that's half as sweet,
A dearer one will I never meet,
And as I see these things in you,
I know that it is ever true,
That you have yet to touch your store
For deep within you lies yet more.

My dearest Eugene,

I finished the book you gave me, *For Better or for Best*, reading it through in two evenings. A wonderful book and interesting. Now, if I can only put what I learned into action.

I'm wide awake for how late it is. Tomorrow is communion church at Richard's. I'm not exactly looking forward to sitting so long, as my back has been bothering me, but as long as I don't bend over too far, I'm okay. My neck is stiff from pulling that taffy last night, but that was my own fault. It was fun though and well worth the pain afterward. I hope I won't have to crane to see the minister tomorrow.

I really need to get to bed, so my love to you and take care. The closer the time comes to your arrival home, the happier I am and the more I long for you to be here.

I miss you,
Naomi

My dearest Naomi,

I finished reading your letter I received today. It was a very cheery one, which was nice. You don't know how wonderful you are.

Now wait a minute. Why are you driving that wild horse of yours? I don't think you should drive him under any conditions, even if you like excitement and adventure. I want you in one piece when I arrive home. So really now—take care.

The weather is currently rotten around here. It decided to put forth a little sunshine this morning, but soon it changed its mind. Now it's pouring rain.

I'll get your birthday present out tomorrow. It's not too much of a gift, so don't get your expectations up. I prefer for the package to arrive late rather than early, but it's hard to judge with this mail system we have.

Just think, you'll be twenty and of age next year. Isn't that something? You're all grown up, and I'm not there to celebrate. I would cry some tears, but that's not going to help things.

On Thursday and Friday we're having achievement tests at school. The lower grades go first on Thursday, followed by the upper grades on Friday. It's an all-day affair for both days, with only the students who are taking the test present that day. These are the same tests the public school children take. They have to be properly timed. Two of the school board members' wives will be present both days to monitor things. I guess in the minds of the authorities, we teachers are tempted to fudge the results.

With Thursday and Friday taken up, I have less time on my schedule than I thought. So I guess I'll need to double up for several days to speed things along. It's important that we finish all the books and keep good grades for all. I think we can, and everyone should pass with flying colors.

Luella allowed me to read the letter and card she's sending you. I told her it wasn't necessary, but she insisted. She said this would make her feel better. Tomorrow night is the big night with the annual "end of the year" school board meeting. Teachers don't go. They elect a new board, and I suppose talk about what teachers to hire next year. I've already been told they plan to offer me another year if I want to accept. I told them I can't.

Some of the boys want to go sparrow hunting again tonight. I imagine I'll go along, even if the last few outings were flops. I think the sparrows have sent out scouts to monitor our movements each night.

I've informed the schoolchildren that if anyone wants to get sick they are to take the next two days to do so and not wait until Thursday or Friday. They thought that was funny, but I was serious.

I will be seeing you this very month! I can hardly get my mind around the fact. These four months since Christmas have been like centuries passing with the speed of glaciers. Lonnie laughed at me coming home from town the other Saturday. He said four months was nothing. But that's what he thinks.

May the end come swiftly!

I long for you,

Eugene

Good morning, dearest Eugene,

This finds me quite sleepy. I haven't been going to bed especially early. Then last night Richard and Joan had the young folks over to clean up the place. I really enjoyed the evening. It certainly was something different for a change. We were all supposed to wear boots and old clothing because they have lots of mud.

We girls worked together as a group, and the boys had their own jobs. Every time the girls finished a job, we'd ask Richard, "What's next?"

Finally he said, "Not again!" and we all laughed.

I was picking up rotten boards in one place, and as I turned to take them to the trash I went right down into a hole. It was a fence-post hole full of water. My boot filled up with water and my lower dress and apron got all wet. I pulled the leg out, and the girls standing around me were wide-eyed trying not to laugh. Thinking I should say something, I blurted out, "I'm wet!"

They thought that was funny. I guess it was, but not at the moment as I headed off to dry out by the burn pile.

Tonight is the sewing, and I think volleyball is planned afterward. That makes two things for this week, but probably nothing for the rest of the month. Yuck! You're lucky to have something going so often.

Well, I'd better get back to work.

Lots and lots of love,
Naomi

My dearest Naomi,

So the day after tomorrow is your birthday! I hope you can do something you enjoy. You deserve a treat. But likely you'll be babysitting, if I know you.

We had a big flip-flop in the school plans. Instead of achievement tests on Thursday, there will be a regular day of school. Anthony and Larry's uncle was killed last night. Their father called me this morning, and I notified the school board chairman right away. The board had a conference call and decided to change plans. That still leaves the upper grades on for Friday.

Since the upper graders had planned to be off on Thursday, there was plenty of grumbling today about having to be there. So I enjoyed a day of school with irate and emotional girls huffing and gruffing around the schoolhouse.

Tomorrow night there is a youth singing planned instead of the regular Bible study. They do this the first week of the month so the ones who don't come to Bible study can attend. In case you wonder why they don't come, some of the parents object to Stan's Bible studies even though he is a minister now.

Have a happy birthday, Sweetheart. A very happy birthday indeed.

I love you,
Eugene

My dearest Eugene,

What a dreary day. I awoke to thunder and rain, but it's supposed to be nice later, according to Dad's weather forecasting. I hope so. I can't remember when we last had a really beautiful day. Oh well, this is spring arriving, I'm sure.

Thank you very, very, much for the beautiful motto, the pin with the words: "Someone Loves You," and the lovely poem in the letter. I do so love that little pin. It's so cute. I wore it this evening at the supper table, and Dad got this amused smile of his. Thank you so much.

I'm glad you didn't get me too much because I'm afraid I won't be able to get you that much on your birthday. Mainly because of the shortage of money around here. I don't think the farm is doing that well, and now my babysitting wages after the wedding will come my way instead of going to Mom and Dad. I know it has to be that way, but I feel sorry for them.

The schoolchildren received their report cards a few days ago, and Larry had two F's again! Can you believe that? One was in geography and the other in reading. He was given a hard time for it, which he should have been. Wait until I get a hold of him. His ears will be red indeed. There's no sense in one of my relatives doing that poorly in school. The boy is smart if he would apply himself.

We went past the cabinet shop on the state road yesterday, and the Waglers had put out "Happy Birthday, Naomi" on their sign. The gesture sent warm circles around my heart. Now if you were here, the day would have been perfect even with the rain.

Janie had better not talk you out of marriage or I will have something to say to her. She is the limit. What's wrong with the girl? Perhaps she hasn't met the right person yet? Someone like you—but don't be getting any ideas. You are not available anymore.

Oh, Darrel Hooley has given up on his Amish joining idea. I'm not sure what all the reasons are, since I heard them secondhand, but he's not staying at Harvey's any longer. I think that's sad, and I'm sure you also do, even with your pretend fits of jealousy. It's hard to join the Amish if you weren't raised in the faith.

The time is getting closer! Yippee...

I love you,
Naomi

Hi, dearest Naomi,

I do love you, although you might not love me after you get done turning this page upside down and then right side up each time you read a new line. Sorry. I'm bored, but even if I'm mean, I can still be sweet.

I received a letter from Darrell Hooley today saying he has changed his plans on joining the Amish. That's a shame, if you ask me. The man had such high hopes that this was the answer to his spiritual needs. Well, I guess we all change our minds, and he has decided to return to the *Englisha* way.

Apparently his job at the hospital has a lot to do with his decision. He has extensive medical training and is loath to try another profession at his age. Bishop Enos thought they could make it work, but there were some of the ministers who had questions. When Darrell found that out, it pushed him over the edge, he said.

I'm sorry I won't get to meet him, but perhaps he'll still be around somewhere when I get back. He sounds like an interesting person—as long as you're not driving him to the hymn singings. By the way, did the buggy wheels ever fall off? I was hoping they would at least wobble a little, but fat chance on that.

There's not much going on around here. The upper graders had their achievement tests, and now the long weekend is upon me. But I will not complain. The time for leaving draws nigh.

I still love you.

Eugene

My dearest Eugene,

Mom and Dad went along to the singing tonight at Harvey's place, which was good because our single buggy is on the blink and we drove the surrey. I would have felt like an old maid pulling in with that thing, even with Don driving. We stayed for ice cream afterward—on special invitation, of course.

I heard today that Adam and Brenda have moved their wedding date, but that our date in June should still be okay. I asked Ruth tonight to be table waiter with Jason, and she was thrilled so that should be taken care of.

Sarah teased me this afternoon, wanting to make sure I really wanted to get married. She informed me I was going to miss the young folks terribly. Which might be true, but I will have you, and that is so much better. The girl teases a lot, but I love being around her. She can make me laugh quicker than any of the other girls, and there is never a dull moment around her.

Sometimes I can hardly believe or understand why I should be so blessed with someone as wonderful as you. You light up my life.

Missing you,
Naomi

Dearest Naomi,

Much to my disappointment, I haven't received your next letter yet. Well, this way I can look forward to the occasion tomorrow.

More food supplements arrived today from the doctor in Missouri. That's the last shipment from his prescribed treatment. I should now be on my way to permanent good health. At least that's what he says. And I do feel good, so why not believe him? The diet has been excellent for me, and I have no complaints—even with all the horrible food I have to eat.

Saturday is my planned trip to Chicago because the last date was cancelled. This time, hopefully, nothing will come up, but you never know. Preacher Stan has been telling me for some time he wants me over for supper, and last night he said this Saturday would be a great weekend for it.

"I'm going to Chicago with Richard," I told him.

"Oh, no," he groaned. "Then maybe we can plan for next Saturday."

I accepted gladly, so the rest of my Saturdays here are taken care of.

There is a funeral here in the community on Thursday, and I figured I would lose another school day, as they usually cancel for such events. The school board consulted amongst themselves and thought otherwise since none of the students are close relatives. So we will have the lower graders' achievement tests that day.

Remember the arithmetic race from way back? It has finally concluded, and Dawn took first place. Instead of simply handing out the prizes, I told the children there would be a treasure hunt before school closes. I'm trying to liven up these last few days for one and all. They will find the prizes at the end of the hunt.

Tuesday evening…

Here I am again, home from school and all cleaned up for the evening with no place to go. What a bummer that is. I forgot to ask in my last letter what you did for your birthday.

I'm working the poor students half to death at school, trying to get done with the schedule. The fast ones are keeping up, but the slower ones are sweating. Somewhere I miscalculated the timing, and now I'm rushing to complete the books. Hopefully the students will survive.

My goal is to have little work planned for the last week so we can practice the "last day of school" program. They don't have "last day of school" festivities here as I'm used to, with games all day, but only the evening program, where the whole community is invited.

Did you used to hate vocabulary in school? I know I did, and there seems to be a large number of the students here who also do. Perhaps the disease is catching? But hooray! This week will be the last of that, with the final test next week.

I'm also trying to finish social studies this week. The first-grade reading class is almost completed. They are coming to the section of their books where all the fairy tales are. That gets them laughing and enjoying themselves. It doesn't help anyone else though when they start cutting up and making faces at each other. And I mean right during schooltime while sitting at their desks.

Each day brings me closer to seeing you again. Let that day come quickly.

Stay sweet,

Eugene

My dearest Eugene,

What an evening! Betsy, Rosanna, both moms, your sisters, and I all piled into Gene's van to shop for furniture. Your mom had seen some advertised in the local paper. At the first place they had a table with four chairs, all in good condition. The table has a Formica top that looks like real, light-colored wood. The chairs are overstuffed and dark brown. They are made with soft vinyl and rollers, and they swivel. I am very pleased with them. The cost was only $100 for the whole lot, so I made the purchase. I hope you like them. I really hate to make household purchases without you here. We can store these in Mom and Dad's basement until we need them. Yippee. Won't that be wonderful?

The next place had a bedroom suite, which I wasn't interested in but your mom was. Plus, I have no place to store the set even if I had liked it. They wanted $150 for the bed, dresser, and chest of drawers. I don't think anyone really liked the color, but your mom said at this price she can't be choosy. She offered the man $125 and he accepted. When she pulled out her checkbook, he waved his hand and said, "No checks, please." So that cut the deal off at the roots.

On the way home we stopped at the Dairy Queen for dipped cones. Your sister Mary didn't get one because she's trying your diet. We had all started eating ours, and Gene was driving when I handed him the box with the last two cones in it. He started battling with the box, trying to get his cone out. Your mom said he'd better be careful. "You worry too much," Gene replied. About that time one of the cones went splat on the floor, and your mom let out a screech: "There it goes!" We all roared. Gene wasn't so sure of himself when he tried to take the second one out.

We butchered a cow yesterday with just the immediate family helping. Well, Ada did come up a little in the evening. We were all exhausted by the time the work was done. I drank two big cups of coffee to keep going and was suddenly buzzing with energy around ten o'clock. Why it waited so long to kick in, I have no idea. Anyway, our freezer is now full of hamburger, and Mom and I will be canning all day tomorrow. I think Ada might come over to help for a few hours, but she has her own family to take care of.

By the way, Mom told me, "If you're twenty now, you have to act it." Yuck. That's no fun.

I love you,

Naomi

My dearest Naomi,

If this weather keeps up, I declare I'll be floating home in a boat.

School continues wrapping up. I have finished checking the students' social studies workbooks tonight, so that's done. I think I'm almost as thrilled as the students are. There are still tests for next week, but nothing serious is on the horizon.

Tomorrow is the achievement tests for the lower graders, which I hope goes well. I told the students yesterday that if they wanted to get sick, tomorrow would be the day, not Thursday. Sharon and Laverne weren't here today, so perhaps they took my advice.

I drew up the pictures for the arithmetic treasure hunt. The prizes had been purchased some time back, and hopefully they aren't stale. A large bag of candy for the first-place winner, Dawn, and smaller sweets for the second- and third-place winners. For someone who doesn't eat sugar, I should have purchased healthier foods, but I had a feeling it wouldn't be appreciated. And I don't want to leave too many bad memories behind.

Thursday…

Your belated Saturday letter arrived today, having been passed somewhere in-between here and there by your Monday letter. At least they didn't come on the same day. Soon we will have a more reliable form of communication.

You don't have to worry about Janie affecting my views of marriage. I am quite safe from her diatribes. And if I weren't, your charms would surely wear me down. It's wonderful to be loved by you.

I want our love to continue that way and to grow if possible. Isn't that what love is supposed to do?

Take care of yourself,

Eugene

My beloved Naomi,

My, I am being treated like a king. Three letters have arrived right in a row!

So you are buying furniture. Wow, you are serious about getting married. It still seems a dream to me, one that could slip away into the clouds on the horizon. It would have been fun being there for the purchase. Still, I have no doubt you made a good choice. I will love the chairs.

It seems as if the last few weeks of school are the best days. Everyone, including the teacher, seems more lighthearted, more prone to breaking into a smile, as if the burden of the year is almost over with. I guess it is! There are only two more weeks to go. We are almost there.

Tonight all the school board members and I are gathering to check the achievement tests. Hopefully everyone did well. It would be embarrassing if a bunch of the students failed.

Tomorrow will find me, bright and early, on the way to Chicago with Richard. I wish the date would have come sooner because now all the happy stuff is crammed into the last few weeks. We also have plans to see the *Passion Play* while in Chicago. I will write you all about the trip when I get back.

Love you,
Eugene

Hello, my handsome prince,

I woke up to a gorgeous day, and I hope your day is also beautiful as you take off for the day trip into Chicago. It would have been wonderful to be with you.

Mom and I went to a patio sale yesterday. Not that I was really looking for anything, but Mom wanted dishes for herself. She found some, and I wandered off to this cute little card place that carried wedding invitations. Of course, I had to look things over. They had about ten books filled with different invitations a person could order. I saw the exact ones several of the wedding couples in our community have used, so this is where they must be coming from. I will wait to order though. There is still plenty of time, and you will soon be home to help me decide.

Being a teacher sure sounds interesting and hectic sometimes. I can understand how it might wear you out mentally.

Well, I now have ninety-five letters and sixteen cards from you. All of which I treasure very much.

I'm sitting here thinking how wonderful you are and wondering how to put it into words. I can hardly believe our separation will soon be over. I want dark thoughts of our parting to be washed away by thoughts of a glorious spring, followed by years spent together after we're married.

Has the doctor told you for sure you have to stay off of sugar forever or is that your own idea?

Did you know our school picnic is also on the thirtieth? Perhaps you can make it. How I do look forward to seeing you again.

I love you,
Naomi

Dearest Naomi,

Here I am again on a Sunday afternoon. The Chicago trip went great. I saw so many things, I can't even begin to list them all. The enclosed postcard shows a picture of the Museum of Science and Industry building, which contained everything imaginable. A whole room was used to show how computers are made and how they work. There was a mini farm, which contained nothing new for me. There was a "whispering gallery," where you could go all the way across the room and hear another person whispering from far away. That was pretty neat. This must be done by bouncing the sound waves across the room.

They had mirrors set up that showed a picture of yourself standing there, and then in the next mirror, and then in the next…until you couldn't see yourself anymore way off in the distance.

There was a coal mine we could have toured, but the line was too long so we didn't wait.

They showed a short film of people doing live acts in a circus from years ago in a room with a mini setup of the show.

One of the last things we saw were life-sized models of babies developing—about thirty of them spanning the entire time of the pregnancy. Richard thought this had to do with the Pro-life Movement, although he couldn't find any signs saying so.

There was a planetarium where we walked out onto a platform. It was as if we were in a spaceship and able to view the stars around us. It gave me shivers of delight. It was as if I were in the very middle of the heavens with great splashes of stars all around me.

We also watched a film on a large sky dome. It was quite something. The seats lean back, and things rush toward the viewer from all sides as if they were alive. I think I jumped more than once, especially when a train came rushing out of a tunnel and roared over my head.

Richard wanted to take tours of the taller buildings, but we ran out of time. You would have enjoyed the trip, and perhaps someday we can see it all—just the two of us. Wouldn't that be great?

Monday…

The new moon is hanging in the night sky, and it brings back memories of you and me and our times together.

Brandon called me Dad in school today by mistake. He laughed heartily afterward and said, "Excuse me." I thought it was funny too. I liked the sound of it though.

Our quartet isn't going anywhere—as I expected. We sang one song in public, "There's a Golden Tomorrow." Thankfully nobody passed out.

The ideas for the "last day of school" program are coming together well. I plan to have all the upper graders write compositions on assigned topics. I'll ask Lonnie and Luella to read them in front of the crowd. That ought to be fun. The children are in an uproar, knowing their work will be read in front of everyone. I thought this would push them to greater heights of writing.

We will sing three songs, listen to tongue-twisters read by the students, and then there are awards and diplomas to pass out. I'm aiming for a light and informal atmosphere in contrast to the Christmas program.

For a little extra touch, I'm making up a "Certificate of Award" for Lonnie and Luella, which will be presented in recognition of their good care of the teacher. I'll have all the school board members sign it. I'll sign it too. I hope to keep it a surprise, but you never know with Luella.

We're getting the studies out of the way, one by one. Today was seventh- and eighth-grade English. Soon it will be over for the year. What a school year it has been. Probably one of the best years of my life so far, not withstanding all the pain from the loneliness. How is it that joy and sorrow walk so closely together?

We were done with supper tonight when the deacon and his wife drove in the lane. They were downstairs talking with Lonnie and Luella about something for a long time. At least I don't have to worry about it being about me.

The last two days have been splendid weather-wise, with blue skies and gentle winds from the south. I think spring has come to aid my journey home. In order to celebrate the weather, I gave the children an extra free period after the last recess today. I stood inside, watching them running around and playing softball. They have become dear to me, creeping into my heart when I wasn't looking. I wonder what the years ahead hold for them and for me.

A lot of the children are working ahead in their books, putting on one last, grand push. I'm afraid they will get done and then sit around bored to death. Well, they have been warned.

Jerry and Tina Eicher

Soon I will be home and driving you home from the hymn singings. I wonder if my horse can still run in the night, but I suppose my brothers haven't left her idly wandering the hayfield. She's too good a horse for that. And you are much too good a girl for me.

With much love,

Eugene

My dearest Eugene,

Good morning. I'm still half asleep since we didn't get home till late from the singing, and then we sat up talking.

The sad news around here right now is that James Yoder has officially left the church. Someone saw him in town the other day with his beard shaved, his hair combed to the side, and wearing a dark-blue suit. Word has it he's determined to buy a van, but everything seems to go against him. He has his driver's license now and can drive other people's cars.

Three of his boys are refusing to go along to the *Englisha* church, but I think the rest of the family has gone with him. The strange thing is that the new church he's going to told him the doctrine he holds on the election of the saints isn't correct. I guess he took correction from them when he wouldn't listen to our ministers. It's a strange and sad world when things like this happen.

When we were done talking, I went upstairs to get much-needed sleep, but what did I do? I started thinking about your homecoming. I got so excited that sleep fled far away. It must have been an hour later before I finally dropped off.

I think I'm still walking on air, gliding around from room to room. Mom says I have a dreamy look, but the real problem is that I'm half asleep. Somehow the two states of affairs go together very well.

I love you!
Naomi

My beloved Naomi,

Each day brings me closer to seeing you again.

You will likely get this letter on Monday. By then there will no longer be a weekend between us, but only one straight week. I can hardly believe it. If you can't think of me without losing sleep, perhaps you had better stop until I arrive. I can't have you all sleepy when we need to talk for hours.

I'm very surprised that James Yoder has turned out the way he has. I've always liked the guy. I guess you never can tell when someone will go bad, and it's hard to believe Millie is also excommunicated. She always said she wouldn't go with him.

We had a ruckus in the house this evening. Actually, it started last night when the drain in my tub upstairs finally stopped up. I mean completely, so I suggested at the breakfast table that my dad always used some sort of drain opener for such emergencies. Tonight I came home to find Luella almost in tears. Lonnie had purchased drain opener and poured it down the drain. It proceeded to foam back up, eating into the enamel on the tub. It must have been powerful stuff. Lonnie got it out before it ate a hole in the tub, but now the bottom is rough, and Luella hates rough tub bottoms.

The drain is now unplugged. We ran a wire down through the trap, and punched the gunk to open the pipe. Water now rushes down. So much for magic drain opener.

Most of Saul's family came to visit school this forenoon. It made me a little nervous, but I survived. They had nice things to say afterward, which I hope were sincere. I can't imagine Janie not letting her tongue fly if she didn't like something I did.

There is a redbird singing outside the house, and I've cracked open my window to hear him better. He swells out his chest and sings his loudest. I think he wants to sing to me a pretty farewell song and wish me well on the trip home.

The weather has been awesome, which stirs my blood with desire to be out of the schoolhouse and somewhere outdoors. I hope things stay nice until Tuesday, when the treasure hunt is planned.

I walked home in my shirt sleeves last night, a very first for this year. It felt so good, so refreshing, so liberating from the cold of winter. Now for the hot sun on the skin, feeling the kisses of summer breezes, seeing the light in your eyes, and this old boy will be happy indeed.

I love you,

Eugene

My beloved Naomi,

I received your card today, and it was wonderful. You make beautiful things. It surprised me though, as I wasn't expecting a card this late in my stay here. Thanks. I just sat there looking at it, thinking that soon I will see you again. It can't be that long now. Surely we will be able to speak to each other after four months. I've had fears, I must admit, that there will be icebreaking necessary. And I might get a little nervous, but it will be okay. Don't worry about it. We'll still be the same people we always were. If we survived our first date, we can survive my homecoming.

I've been looking forward to this for so long it's hard to believe that the time has finally arrived. But somehow it has, and the end is almost in sight.

With all my heart,

Eugene

Hello, prince of my heart,

This finds me rather in a rush, as usual. I want to clean my room and water my parched plants before 11:30, as I have to stay the rest of the day with John Bach.

Last night I babysat for our neighbors' grandchildren across the road. I didn't arrive home until 11:00. There was a gathering for the young folks at Paul Miller's place, but I missed it, which is okay. Sarah can fill me in on Sunday if anything exciting happened. She knows the date coming up next week, and I'm sure she'll tell me there was no news that will compare with that occasion.

There was the usual volleyball game on Wednesday night. The weather was cold, so the game wasn't really much fun. I think your homecoming is casting a long shadow over everything else. I do wish you would hurry.

Your Chicago trip sure sounded interesting. Made me a bit envious.

Enos and Nancy's wedding is this week. I wish you could be here for that, as I will be left high and dry again for the hymn singing. I hope you don't mind if some boy takes me to the supper table. It would be out of pity, I can assure you. Hopefully there will be enough girls to go around. I will inform the matchmakers to place me at the bottom of the list, and I'm sure they'll understand. *Yah,* fat chance!

We want you here, along with Lonnie and Luella, for supper on the Saturday night you arrive, so please pass on the invitation.

Monday morning…

I'm in a rush again, trying to get this very last letter off to you. I will send it on its way with a kiss for you. It's hard to believe you'll be here soon. Please tell Lonnie to drive carefully.

There is wash to do, and my fingers will freeze with the cold weather outside. Yesterday we were at Harvey's house for church, and a bunch of us young folks stayed for the afternoon. It wasn't a very spectacular day in my opinion, as I was bored and restless.

The reason for this being the last letter is that I don't want you receiving any after you have left Iowa. That would be terrible. I also don't think there will be any news that needs to be shared before I see you again. Yippee. After that we can talk and not write for a long, long time.

I didn't mind the writing until these last few weeks. It's been rush, rush, and when I write I like to take my time. Well, it's rush, rush again.

Lots and lots of love,
Naomi

My beloved Naomi,

I hope this letter finds you well and still grounded to the earth because I want to see you when I get home.

Tonight I have the treasure hunt for the children, and it looks as if the weather will stay nice until at least tomorrow. Maybe it will stay nice until Friday, the last day of school.

The *Passion Play* in Chicago on Sunday afternoon was awesome. I have never seen anything like it in my life. Crowds of actors played out the life of Christ, starting from the birth of John the Baptist and ending with Jesus' ascension into heaven. The whole thing lasted more than four hours. There was never a dull moment. It all looked so real.

I now have something going every night until I leave, except for Wednesday. There's the final supper with the school board members, the ball game, the school program, and then seeing you on Saturday. I have enclosed two of the best essays the children wrote. Lonnie and Luella will be reading all of the essays on Friday night. There is also a goodbye poem. One of the school board members' wives wrote it, I'm sure, but they are keeping it a secret. And I've written a poem for the children to be read too.

Anyway, I'm in a daze of delight, if that's possible. My head is as light as the breeze blowing down the road. I walked home from school tonight drinking it all in. This will soon be the last walk home for the school year, and this will also be my last letter, so I'm taking a deep breath and writing really slowly. Who would have thought this day would arrive? But is not all well that ends well?

> With much love
> as always,
> Eugene

Velma, 7th grade

The Best Things I Like About School

There are so many things I like and enjoy about school that it's really hard for me to pick out which ones to write about.

First thing, it's always fun arriving early in the morning and talking to all my friends before the bell rings. Of course, it's very exciting right at the start of a new year when you get nice new books to work in. It's such a difference from when at the end of the year they get to looking pretty tattered and worn.

I like the story hour every morning when the teacher reads stories to us. And the time we spend in singing and learning new songs.

I like most of the studies that we have, but there are some I would rather leave behind. It isn't long till recess time, and they are always fun. I enjoy playing lots of games, especially when teacher helps us. And, of course, it's always fun to learn new ones people come up with.

On art day, it is always interesting to try drawing and doing different things that the teacher has us do. When it's dinnertime, we have almost an hour to play. After dinner, it's again fun to listen to the afternoon story hour, when the teacher reads to us.

I always enjoy the little surprises teacher comes up with now and then, like going on field trips, touring some kind of factory, or maybe a free period.

It's always fun when the Christmas program comes around, and we learn new poems and songs. After that comes Christmas vacation and a break from all the studies. And once the program is here, you know the year is half over with.

After all my school years are past, I'm sure I will think back on all the good times I've had and realize how lucky I was to be able to go to a private school out in the country where there is peace.

Jared, 7th grade...

The Worst Thing About School

Teacher told me to write my feelings on the worst

things about school. Now that is a hard decision to make, isn't it? Should it be the studies, or the kind of grades I sometimes get, or the rules, or the girls, or writing stories?

At one time or another, all these things seemed to be the worst. But now I think the worst thing about school is being chained to this desk and not caring to work. I watch all those John Deere and International tractors and combines come out in the spring or in the fall. It seems as though everyone is free and can enjoy it but me.

I will show you an arithmetic problem I do not like.

"Miss Day wanted to buy a coat at a sale that was reduced from $25.00 to $20.00. How would you find the percent the coat was reduced?"

Another I don't like is, "Mary's father had been paying $576.00 a year on a house he rented. This year the rent was reduced to $420.00 per month. How would you find the percent of decrease in the yearly rent?"

Now I don't have to worry about this for another four months and six days. Hurray!

Poems for the children

Of all these children, I'll try to tell
The things they do, so good and well.

Brandon is a boy that gets things done,
When he's working at school or on the run.

If you want to see a boy who digs in and tries,
Then you should meet Mark with a sparkle in his eyes.

Laverne's a sweet boy, though he often needs Doc,
To Iowa City, his family races the clock.

Anthony is quick as a spider in a shoe.
For the size that he has, amazing things he can do.

Dawn is cheery, each morning, each day,
Just like most little girls that I know anyway.

Brandon is handsome and a sound head has he.
Who would dare guess what that combination will be?

When the problem is difficult, Larry ponders hard,
But what a smile on his face, when he finds the right card.

Like a robin that preens its feathers just so,
That would be Lacie, the girl that I know.

Not many things out of Lester you'll hear,
Unless some exciting event draws near.

Sharon takes off to Florida each fall,
For the sun and the beach, she leaves us all.

Dakota is quiet as the cloud that glides,
And you never would know the spunk she hides.

If you're reading a book, and it can't be found,
I'd advise you check if Dora was around.

She's another who's gone, to Florida they fly.
Lydia's off for the South, and I still wonder why.

He's a boy who tries, his cheeks all grim.
Did you say Dennis? Yes, that would be him.

Jackie's the fun of the party and of any giggling bunch.
I'd have her over any day for popcorn and punch.

Velma might be the kindest heart you have seen,
Oft she holds her brother's hand against a world so mean.

Jared jumps to his feet when Bible lessons come around.
The rest of the time, his thermostat's down.

Crystal completes her duties, so well and so fast,
It's little wonder she's at the head of the class.

Dena's a young lady, beyond her years she's old.
She dreams and wonders what her world will hold.

And about the teacher, I'd better not tell,
What you already know is sufficient and well.

Eugene Is Going Home

Teacher Eugene, he is leaving,
It's hard to watch him go.
We know his school year has been lonely,
His days and weeks went slow.

But now no more will he be with us,
His teaching desk swept bare.
The games and classes that he gave them,
His students will no longer share.

The school year will be over,
The children leaving down the road.
As a teacher they so loved him,
He lifted many heavy loads.

They ask him for forgiveness
Where they fussed and failed their part.
But he still showed them love and kindness,
Even with his heavy heart.

We would not dare to keep him,
While others reach and yearn,
And with faces longing, waiting.
Expecting his soon blessed return.

We know a special one is watching,
Making room at heart and side,
Welcoming with long anticipation,
The day when she can be his bride.

May God give you strength and courage
For whatever dreams you have planned.
May life by always kind and gentle,
And give you only goodness from its hand.

We say goodbye to teacher Eugene,
Knowing miles between us now will lie.
We take comfort that again we'll see you.
Sometime, some year, beyond their goodbye.

Jerry and Tina Eicher

EPILOGUE

The soft morning sun beat on the barn roof, currents of cool morning air moving up through the rows of packed benches. Luella clasped her hands. Eugene would be married soon if the Bishop's face was any indication. The sound of his voice had been rising and falling for over an hour in the steady rhythm of Pennsylvania Dutch.

Luella leaned forward as the bishop stretched his hand toward the seated couple, speaking even softer now, his gray beard tight against his chest. Eugene rose and Naomi followed suit. Luella held her breath. How could this moment be more beautiful? For so long she had imagined it in her mind. A real Amish wedding—and she was getting to experience it.

The bishop was saying something as he studied Eugene's face. The official nodded at Eugene's quiet "*Yah.*" The bishop turned to Naomi, and Luella leaned forward again. The bride's "*Yah*" came even quieter, carried back along the sides of the barn in the near silence. How could 400 people, with plenty of children seated by their parents, be so quiet? It must be the Amish way of raising their children in obedience to the faith and respect for the church services. Luella brushed her hand over her eyes.

The bishop was joining the couple's hands, and Luella caught Lonnie's eyes over in the men's section. A peaceful smile filled his face. He was enjoying the moment as much as she was.

Glancing back toward the front, Luella saw the bishop releasing the couples' hands, and Eugene and Naomi sat down again. How quaint this all was, but still very appropriate. No announcement to the world of their married status. It just *was* and would be until they died.

Thank You, God, for allowing me to be here, Luella thought.

A man shouted a song number from the back of the barn. Another man led out and the audience joined in the singing, bursting into joyous sound.

After their wedding...

Eugene and Naomi Mast settled into their home community in Indiana for several years. Two boys were born: James and Andy. They were followed by two daughters: Marie and Susie. Andy is married now—the only one of the children so far.

It's been close to thirty years now since that eventful nine months of separation when Eugene followed his dream to teach in Iowa. Eugene and Naomi often look back with joy at the years of blessing God has given them in their marriage. God's faithfulness has always been with them, and they're confident He'll be faithful in the future.

About Jerry and Tina Eicher...

Jerry Eicher's bestselling Amish fiction (more than 400,000 in combined sales) includes The Adams County Trilogy, the Hannah's Heart Series, and the Little Valley Series.

After a traditional Amish childhood, Jerry taught for two terms in Amish and Mennonite schools in Ohio and Illinois. Since then he's been involved in church renewal, preaching, and teaching Bible studies.

Tina Eicher was born and married in the Amish faith. She and her husband, Jerry, are the parents of four children and live in Virginia. Tina homeschooled all of her children for portions of their school years. Tina and Jerry are also the authors of *The Amish Family Cookbook.*

Visit Jerry's website!
http://www.eicherjerry.com/

A CHECKLIST OF JERRY EICHER'S BOOKS WITH HARVEST HOUSE PUBLISHERS

THE ADAMS COUNTY TRILOGY
Rebecca's Promise
Rebecca's Return
Rebecca's Choice

HANNAH'S HEART SERIES
A Dream for Hannah
A Hope for Hannah
A Baby for Hannah

LITTLE VALLEY SERIES
A Wedding Quilt for Ella
Ella's Wish
Ella Finds Love Again

FIELDS OF HOME SERIES
Missing Your Smile
Following Your Heart
Where Love Grows

STANDALONE NOVELS
My Dearest Naomi
Susanna's Christmas Wish

NON-FICTION
The Amish Family Cookbook
(coming September 2012)

My Amish Childhood
(coming January 2013)

For a taste of Amish cooking, try this!

The Homestyle Amish Kitchen Cookbook: Plainly Delicious Recipes from the Simple Life

BY GEORGIA VAROZZA

Just about everyone is fascinated by the Amish—their simple, family-centered lifestyle, colorful quilts, and hearty, homemade meals. Straight from the heart of Amish country, this celebration of hearth and home will delight you with the pleasures of the family table as you take a peek at the Amish way of life—a life of self-reliance and peace of mind that many of us long for.

You'll appreciate the tasty, easy-to-prepare recipes that include Scrapple, Graham Nuts Cereal, Potato Rivvel Soup, Amish Dressing, and Snitz Pie. At the same time, you'll learn a bit about the Amish, savor interesting tidbits in the "Amish Kitchen Wisdom" sections, and find out just how much food it takes to feed the large number of folks attending preaching services, barn raisings, weddings, and work *frolicks*.

The Homestyle Amish Kitchen Cookbook is filled with good, old-fashioned family meal ideas to help bring the simple life home.